Betrayal
A Fiction Novel

Copyright © 2008 by C.D. Nolan

All rights reserved. No part of this book may be used or reproduced by any means, graphic, electronic, or mechanical, including photocopying, recording, taping or by any information storage retrieval system without the written permission of the publisher except in the case of brief quotations embodied in critical articles and reviews.

This is a work of fiction. All of the characters, names, incidents, organizations, and dialogue in this novel are either the products of the author's imagination or are used fictitiously.

iUniverse books may be ordered through booksellers or by contacting:

iUniverse
1663 Liberty Drive
Bloomington, IN 47403
www.iuniverse.com
1-800-Authors (1-800-288-4677)

Because of the dynamic nature of the Internet, any Web addresses or links contained in this book may have changed since publication and may no longer be valid. The views expressed in this work are solely those of the author and do not necessarily reflect the views of the publisher, and the publisher hereby disclaims any responsibility for them.

ISBN: 978-0-595-52601-7 (pbk)
ISBN: 978-0-595-51663-6(cloth)
ISBN: 978-0-595-62655-7 (ebk)

Printed in the United States of America

US Copyright number is: TXu-1-583-724 Effective date of registration. August 13, 2008.

Canadian Copyright info: "Betrayal" June 4, 2008 158987

iUniverse rev. date: 11/20/2008

"BETRAYAL"

A Fiction Novel

BY

C. D. Nolan

iUniverse, Inc.
New York Bloomington

Dedicated to all those lucky people who found true and everlasting love,

And were smart enough to grab onto it, and live

With Joy and Happiness.

It only takes a minute to get a crush on someone,

An hour to like someone,

And a day to fall in love with someone,

But…it takes a lifetime to forget them.

Unknown

As time goes by you learn that if you don't ever take a risk, then you will truly be risking everything.
This book proves if you take great risks you get great rewards.

C . D . Nolan

CHAPTER 1

The rain was pouring down on Caity Anderson's windshield as she pulled into her condo parking spot. Putting the car in park, she sat there lights on and wipers on high. She sat just staring out of her front windshield looking forward at the large fur trees that flanked the parking lot in front of her car.

She'd cried all the way home and sitting there finally in park, she suddenly burst into tears. Slowly reaching for her facial tissue box on the front seat, Caity leaned forward and rested her head on the steering wheel. As she sat there, rocking her head gently, she cried as if she would never be able to stop.

Reaching over and grabbing yet another large clump of tissue, and pressing it gently on her tired and weary eyes, Caity allowed herself to slowly lean back against her head rest. While her mind drifted to the sequence of events that had just happened less than an hour ago, she sat there numbly listening to the rain tapping loudly on the roof of the car.

Her eyes were transfixed on the rain drenched windshield, while she sat there thinking back to the few minutes that had suddenly changed her life forever. She wasn't really sure if it was all some weird nightmare that she'd just envisioned, or had she really lived through those unbelievable moments at Jack's house?

Just a short while ago, Jack and her had been finishing their dinner, sitting on his couch and just talking about things. It had been a rare weekend when they had spent the entirety of it at Jack's home acting like high school sweet hearts. His girls had gone away with his ex-wife for the weekend, and their absence had allowed them the freedom to just be themselves. Sitting there remembering the last two days made Caity shiver with reality.

The two days had actually been the most normal of all the times she'd ever spent with him and at one point she felt like she'd have to pinch herself to see if it was real. Just like so many times before she got there on Friday night and stayed till Sunday. This time it had been very different. Somehow, Jack had been out of character. He was committed, relaxed, and acting normal. Not an ounce of tension in his body. Jack had been smiling and loving the entire weekend. He'd even spent a great deal of time talking about plans for their future and the things that they should and would do together. Places they would go, and best of all he said that he thought it was time his two girls finally met Caity.

Caity stared out at the rain still coming down hard on the windshield, and remembered back to how she'd been sucked into all of Jack's dreams and promises. He had said so many wonderful things and all the while she'd forgotten the number one rule her Dad had always taught her." Judge a man, not by what he says, but by what he does and how he treats you". Dad would always say; and tonight it echoed in Caity's ears, over and over and over again! If Caity was to judge Jack by his actions the last hour of the weekend, she was a fool who'd been totally betrayed by the one person she thought of as the love of her life. Betrayed to the point where she felt like all the blood had been drained from her now limp and chilled body.

She continued to gaze forward, watching the water drenched windshield as if it was a television screen replaying her life. One minute Jack and her were giggling and tickling each other on the couch in his family room; and the next minute while he was leaning over to kiss her on the nose while sliding down to cuddle her, the phone rang and their world was thrown off its axis.

It was Jane, his ex wife. Caity could tell by the way Jack's body had suddenly become tense and ridged. He was instantly filled with anxiety and instant anger. His eyes became suddenly dark and the smile was gone from his face. He suddenly looked old and hard. From what Caity could gather from the conversation, Jane's car was overheating and it was now Jack's problem because his girls were traveling with her.

He would have to drop everything and go out to the east end of town and pick them up and help her.

Caity remembered how the phone call went on way too long. The next thing she knew, he hung up the phone by slamming it down and started storming around the room. He was acting all weird and adolescent, and he was stamping his feet hard into the floor. He was so angry that he'd actually forgotten she was even there.

Caity remembered how stunned she'd been watching the series of events. She'd heard all kinds of stories from him of the kinds of things Jane did to torment him, so nothing surprised her anymore. Jane knew how to continue to get away with all the annoying stuff as long as Jack let her; and it didn't look like he was going to put a stop to it any time soon.

Caity remembered having her eyes transfixed on him as he stormed around the house in a rage, and then suddenly without notice as she stood up, he turned fast on his heals. He'd grabbed her by her shoulders and with a cold hard deadly stair, and at the top of his lungs; yelled, "GO HOME!"

His dark brown eyes were unrecognizable and hard focused right on Caity's mouth as if he was going to kiss her. He'd already looked right through her and she'd been so shocked she couldn't even move. She held her breath and stayed completely ridged.

Caity hadn't even known him at that moment. She remembered standing stiff in fear and shock and thinking that if she could just reach him for a moment and calm him down, she could help him deal with whatever had him off on this tangent. Without really thinking much about it, Caity whispered, "kiss me," looking right into his dark hard eyes. Closing hers as if to wait for his lips to touch her lips she was expecting a caress and a softened moment. Instead, he tightened his hands that were still gripped around her shoulders and shook her. As she suddenly flipped her eyes open, she looked right at him only to see him yell at her, "No. I don't want to!"

With that, he spun her around, and started pushing her to the front door. As he passed her bag on the way there, he grabbed it and shoved it in her arms. As he opened the front door and pushed her out, he was yelling at the top of his lungs. Caity was sure that half the neighborhood would hear him but it was what he said and not how he said it, that hurt so bad. He was yelling that he couldn't do this. That he couldn't take a chance again. That he couldn't risk his heart and life and money not one more time; and that God was going to punish him yet again. With that he'd pushed her out the door and slammed it behind her.

Caity honestly didn't know how long she stood there in front of his door. Stunned, shaken, shocked and full of disbelief. Suddenly, when she was leaning against the front door trying to get her wits about her, Jack suddenly opened it. Madder than he'd been just a few short moments ago. He caught her from falling, he pushed her up, spun her around again to look right at her and told her to go home or he'd call the police and have her removed. With that he pulled the door slamming it behind him, and headed off to his garage. Seconds later he and drove off; leaving a trail of rubber and smoke.

She remembered looking right at Jack at that moment, and not recognizing him. Not knowing who he was and where was the other Jack she had just spent the most romantic weekend of her life with.

Standing there trying to decide what to do, Jack pulled back into his driveway, almost taking the garage door out as he came to a sudden stop. He walked out in a huff, grabbed Caity by the elbow, and escorted her to her car. Opened the door and got her to sit inside. "Go home, it's over." was all he said. And with that he'd walked back to his car, got in and for the second time peeled out of his driveway and drove off to meet Jane and the girls.

She hadn't remembered one second of the drive home or how she even got to her parking spot. As she sat there in the rain, gathering her thoughts and emotions, Caity realized this would be the last time Jack pulled something like this. Although tonight was the most dramatic and drastic event between them, she couldn't continue to be his punching bag for his emotions; no matter how much she was in love with him. Tonight it was clear that he didn't have one loving emotion in his body for her, or anyone.

Caity had never in her life felt more naked, and betrayed. How she was going to get out of her car, and go up to her condo with out completely losing it? She had absolutely no idea!

Turning the engine off and grabbing her purse, she got out leaving her umbrella behind. She was drenched before she'd even locked the doors, and she walked slowly in the cold spring time down pour, hoping to have it wash away her pain.

CHAPTER 2

The clock down the hall was just registering two am, as the rain drizzled on the condo's picture windows in both the living room and Caity's office. It had been yet another long draining night filled with heart break and disappointment and Caity had left a trail of tissue all over. There were trails from the kitchen to the patio, all over the living room; from the seats of the chocolate colored couch, to all the way down the hallway and back to her desk and around her chair. It was like it was snowing in Caity's condo, but instead of snowflakes there were mounds of bunched up tear drenched tissue everywhere.

Caity had cried non stop since she'd entered the apartment just past midnight, and now with deep sadness and a fist that gripped her heart almost to the point where breathing was difficult, she'd finally settled at her desk. She'd been staring at the computer screen through misty water filled eyes, remembering how many times she'd come home in just this fashion. How many times had she felt like her heart had been ripped right out of her chest? It had been bad in the past, but never like this!

How many times had Jack and her had a romantic evening or weekend and at the end of it all, just like tonight; he'd suddenly tell her that he couldn't do this or something to that effect. How many times had she fallen for him telling her how much he loved her, let him romance her heart till it skipped and he'd kissed her till her knees were weak. How many times had he told her that he loved her like he had never loved anyone before, held her; promised her a world of tomorrows, and then dumped her yet again?

Caity sat at her desk, heaving tears and shaking her head. Every few minutes she was pulling at five or six tissues at a time to absorb all her tears. She sat choking as she sighed and cried. Holding her head in the palms of her hands whiles resting her elbows on her desk. She was coughing and slightly choking on her tears. How could she have been such an absolute fool again? Why did he always have this pull of bringing her back into his life and then no sooner did she fall for it, he'd be dumping her again? As she sat there shaking her head from side to side in the palms of her hands; she felt confused, hurt, vulnerable and very emotionally naked. Caity sat there trembling and feeling traumatized by what had happened.

There was tissues strewn all over the floor, the desk and the shelves as she'd randomly threw them around in anger and frustration while cursing Jack and his two personalities. How could one man be two very extremely different people? How was it even possible? Which one was the real Jack, or where both personalities really him? At this point Caity didn't care. She wanted to know but was too beaten to think about it anymore. She'd have to stop making excuses for him and start taking control of her life. It was time!

She had a glass of wine sitting beside her for courage, but more so to calm her down. She hadn't taken a sip in order to keep her mind clear, hoping to make the right choices when it came to what to do next.

As she looked up the rain was beating on the window pane with the same force as her tears streamed from her heart. She sat there thinking how ironic the whole moment was. The evening completely reflected what she was going through and the dark dampness outside was fitting for the mood she was in.

She looked down from the window and straight at the computer screen. She didn't know how long she'd been sitting there but it had been long enough to write two different emails to Jack. The thing was, she didn't know which one she should send him, or for that matter if she should even send one at all. She wondered if he'd even read it or if it would even make a difference this time. Caity had already read and re-read the two emails twice, and was very undecided as to which one she should send? What was it that she needed to say? More over, what was it that she needed? What had to be said? How could she end it all when she loved him so deeply? How could she love someone this much and this true and yet have them treat her so badly? How could life be so very cruel after showing her how amazing it could be when you were in the arms of someone you truly loved? How could he say he loved her and yet hurt her so intensely over and over again? She really believed that she needed Jack and the love she was sure they shared; but in her heart she knew nothing was ever going to change.

Caity was confused, scared, hurt and frustrated but most of all she felt a deep sense of betrayal. Jack had been the one person she had entrusted her whole heart's happiness to. She had given Jack the deepest and truest part of herself. Worse yet, when he had coldly watched her fall apart in front of him, and didn't even drive her home to make sure she got there safely in her condition! When she left his house and headed home, she heaved in tears all the way while weaving all over the road. Looking back she couldn't believe that she'd gotten home safely without getting into a major accident.

Caity's thoughts were filled with so much confusion and anger that she needed to re-read the two emails she wrote and make a decision as to which one she should send. She knew she had to send one, but which one and did it really even matter which one she sent? No matter what, she had to make the decision and close the book on this nightmare before it did her in.

Caity shook her head thinking how sad it was that she always had to resort to an email every time Jack went off in this nutty direction. It was only way she could reach him knowing full well that he wouldn't answer his phone and talk to her. She knew he wouldn't call her, return a call, or even take a call from her until he'd want to see her again. One thing was for sure, Caity was done with playing that game ever again! It was time. But which email should she send? Having a real problem trying to decide, she wiped her eyes and decided to read them both for the last time.

Looking through blurry eyes, she pulled up the first email in her drafts, and made the font bigger so it was easier to read while letting out another heavy sigh. She'd written it and had spewed out all her thoughts and feelings and although her gut said it was probably way too long; she knew she needed to say everything that was on the screen. She stared at it for a few seconds realizing the full magnitude that was attached to sending it. She reached over for the glass of chardonnay that she'd poured hours ago, and took a few sips for courage. It warmed her inside like a brief hug. The warm liquid gave her the gentle calmness she needed to read the emails for the last time. Taking a few more sips. She paused and took a deep breath while slowly starting to read from her heart.

She knew the first email was a complete dumping of emotions. It said everything she felt inside but read like she was a rambling fool. Sadly it was exactly how she felt. Slowly and calmly she started to read it, gazing at the computer screen and half seeing Jack's face as it was tonight when he'd told her to "GET OUT." Pushing away her painful emotions, she focused on the computer screen and read the draft of the first email. It read:

Jack,

I'm sending you this last email wishing I could send it by real mail or say it in person, but knowing that's impossible so email will have to do.

I have come to realize that looking back over the past two years I see a lot of sadness while the special times we have shared are imprinted in my memory forever. How can we be so wonderful together and the minute we are apart it is like a bomb went off? The closeness we once shared where we would talk for hours has died because you never let us just have normal lives together. Brick by brick you managed to build a wall so that our openness and trust got buried in arguments. Because I never had such a deep sincere closeness like this with anyone before, it was like a drug that I couldn't get enough of.

Every time you came back, I thought it was going to be different this time. But every time that it never changed, made it harder and harder for me to be my trusting, loving, myself. It's hard to be really happy when the man you love suddenly doesn't include you in life's most important moments! Holidays, especially Christmas, you made me feel like I was suddenly a stranger! What were you thinking? I'm at such a loss to understand it. I really believe that there has to be someone else. This all can't be just because of the church and religion. Can it? How can it be?

In the beginning, I believed we were the luckiest people in the world to have found each other. I wanted to share your whole world and my whole world with you. Instead, I've spent days and weeks wondering what's happening with you! When is the next time you're going to call? Or will you? I don't want to sit around anymore wondering if you are going to call.

I've wasted way too much of my time pacing and hurting in my heart. I can't continue like this anymore!

I can't understand anything anymore. If you truly love me like you say you do then you have to do one of two things right now. Either chose to commit to me now, or never ever, ever, ever come back! Never! And I mean never! Pretend I am dead, because when someone is dead you can never have them back no matter how badly you want them or how deeply you love them. When they are dead they are lost forever!

You say I am a test of your faith. Wrong! I know I was a gift to you and you were a gift to me sent by God. Maybe you are no longer capable of living and loving. Maybe you have used religion as your safety net to hide behind your fear of being hurt again. So tell me, has it really worked for you? Maybe one day you'll realize that religion should never be used to hide from life. Jack, there are millions of truly dedicated religious Catholics who continue to live normal lives through divorce and other of life's difficulties.

In life there are only two choices, you choose to do something, or you choose not to. There is no such thing as I can't. "Can't" is just an excuse for not dealing with life. There is no such thing as "Can't." There is only..... "I will" or "I won't."

I really can't live in this cloud of chaos and wonder any more! Ever time you say you won't come back; you always do and end up hurting me to my very core all over again. I have decided that I need some kind of deadline to finalize it for me so if I don't hear from you before you leave for your business trip, I'll know that you never loved me! That the wonderful guy I fell in love with, who said he loved me with all his heart, was just a prisoner locked inside you. If that's the case you are condemned to a prison that you've chosen to build and maintain.

I'm actually terrified of sending this email and terrified of not sending it. The reality is that judging from all your crazy behavior, I know exactly what to expect! While my heart is praying that you'll allow yourself to follow your heart, logic tells me that you are incapable of it. That your ex-wife will control your life forever and if I let you, you'll continue to destroy mine!

Your life could be so different if you took the chance! But maybe it already is. Maybe you have already taken the chance with someone else that I don't know about and you're just using me. I really don't know what to believe anymore! If there isn't anyone else, well too bad! What am I supposed to think with the way you've been acting? I know that the world can be filled with adventure, joy and love but you have to take risks to find it.

I know that taking a risk on something or someone you want and believe in is always a million times better than never changing things at all. Living with a lot of "what if this" and "what if that" and of course the ever nagging "If I had only" will haunt you to your grave. I am so very tired of wondering where you are and what you are doing, and with whom? I finally feel it's time for me to take charge of my life and let go forever.

I promise you the one thing I will NEVER forget and hold close to my heart forever, is the cold hard way you treated me tonight! Your cold, hard words, "GO HOME, IT'S OVER!" will haunt me to my grave! Caity :

Caity shivered as she finished reading the first email. There were so many other things she wanted to put in there but realized sending one page or ten pages probably wouldn't make much of a difference. She sat there and opened the second email in her draft file. Feeling so very tired and drained she sipped the last few drops of wine. It felt like a warm hug as it trickled down and gave her the energy she needed to look up at the screen and read the second one.

Jack,

Only a truly sad man can use God, Religion and the Church as his justification for treating someone so horrifically. I now truly believe that you have done as you said, exactly as you chose to do, that you were doing exactly what you wanted to do!

And that is all so very ugly that I will gladly walk in the opposite direction and pray that my path does not cross with another person who pretends to love and claims to love but only does so for his own selfishness and personal gain.

Words mean nothing without the actions to back them up and I should have paid close attention to your behavior and not your words! I am now grateful for clearly seeing you as you are, and not who you have pretended to be. To claim to love someone as deeply as you have claimed and then treat them as dreadfully as you have done, can never and will never be understood, or for that matter thought of again.

Go in peace and pray that you can be forgiven but know that you can no longer have credibility through your words, and that the actions you have taken to achieve your goal, have betrayed your heart, and the soul of another. Peace be with you. Caity

She sent the second one…………..

CHAPTER 3

Caity Anderson sat their in a pool of used tissue, red eyed crying and choking in between heaving sobs of tears. She sent the email knowing that the last horrible conversation they'd had, would have to be for the last time she'd endure anything like that! She really couldn't take this abuse and heartache anymore! The truth was that she really didn't understand any of it.

Her friends often described it as a drug that Caity was addicted to, and in a way it was. She was passionate about how she felt when Jack and her were together. Just like drugs, every time they broke up, the coming down part was more horrible and way harder. How many times had she had these conversations with Jack in the last year? Too many! More than once would have been too much, but in reality it was more like fifteen or maybe even twenty times. Why did they keep doing this to each other? Was it a tormented love? Or was he the greatest actor that ever lived on the face of the planet?

Caity didn't know what to believe anymore. In the past she believed everything out of his mouth and today he had little or truly no credibility left. Why did Jack get such pleasure in hurting her to the very core of her existence? Why did he love to make her cry and then come back and apologize? Was he really sorry? Was it always really the religion-church thing like he said or was it something even worse? Would she ever really find out the truth? One thing was for sure, this time Caity was going to find out even if she had to hire a detective for her own piece of mind.

Caity knew that even her friends didn't know what to think. Some said the religion-church thing was believable, others said it was all just a lie so he could have her and obviously another woman. What drove Caity nuts was not knowing the truth. Was Jack this obsessed Catholic religious freak who let a priest and cult like guilt control his life? Or was it worse? Was his obsession about money? He was always worried about money. God knows he paid his ex-wife a ton of it to get rid of her and that still ate at him like a cancer.

The fact that his ex-wife cheated on him twice, was probably that the reason he was so screwed up! He had given the woman a second chance because his babies were small. What were they at the time? Just about eighteen months and three and a half, she thought. She thought how horribly sad for the children, never mind what it had obviously done to Jack. Caity sat there doing the math and trying to make sense of the last ten years, but none of it made any sense. She couldn't understand a woman who had cheated while still being pregnant. How could his wife have had an affair while carrying Jack's child?

Caity loved Jack so much that she wished things had been different and that his children were in fact theirs. Jack had said as much the first time they were making love. She remembered him cupping her face in his hands and looking lovingly into her eyes and telling her that they would make beautiful babies. That he wished his children were theirs, and that he wanted to have a baby with her. Jack was so messed up that Caity knew he wasn't ready for another child, and that he couldn't handle the two he had. She remembered how disappointed he was that night when she told him that although she really wanted to have her own, she physically couldn't.

She thought back to the wonderful first weekend that they had spent together. Maybe the real reason Jack was the way he was with her was because she wasn't able to have children. Maybe it was because of his Catholic religion and the control it held over him. He held the belief that in order to go on in another relationship, he would have to produce a child. Caity was confused and hurt and knew she would never really know the answer to that too! How sad! No wonder he was so messed up! Look how messed up he made Caity with all his different excuses and stories. She didn't know what the truth was any more. For all she knew, there was another woman who was walking parallel in her shoes and living her life with Jack as well. Maybe it would be easier if Caity could believe that.

The one thing Caity did know is that Jack didn't trust anyone, but she never thought that she would be made to pay for all his ex-wife's failures. God, she was so confused she didn't even know what she thought anymore, and for that matter, how she felt about it. The only thing Caity knew was that her heart hurt so bad she felt as if she was suffocating, unable to catch her breath and that if she couldn't get a grip on herself she'd have to get some help.

Looking over at the clock and sitting there with her eyes swollen almost shut, the clock said four. In a few hours the alarm would go off and she'd have to call in sick, again. No one could see her like this. She was a mess from the inside out and needed time to figure everything out.

Caity liked sitting in the dark, it helped her think. She thought back to the beginning which was almost two years to the day when this whole mess started. If she had never gotten that new address book, if she had never called him; if only! Caity wished desperately that she could turn back the clock, but knew in her heart that nothing would be any different because it was destiny. Why? She didn't know, but destiny, she was sure of it! If she had never gone through this she would never have found out what really being in love with someone felt like. At forty, Caity had discovered for the first time in her life, what everyone around her had always been talking about. She'd finally discovered what real love felt like. That feeling you get in your heart when that person enters a room, or when they hold you in their arms, or just hearing their voice on the phone. All of those amazing feelings she had never known; and would now have to spend the rest of her life without.

How very sad life was; she thought, just sitting there wondering if she put a cold cloth on her face if the pain would go away. Probably not, it never did! Jack always hurt her to the very soul of her existence, reaching a place in her heart that no one else could. Sadly she knew he had changed her. She was getting as good at hurting him as he was at hurting her; and she hated that the most about the whole thing. He would hurt her like he did tonight and she would lash out saying things just to hurt him, not meaning half of them. She did it just so he could feel her pain. How did they get here from where they started? She didn't know, except that he kept telling her it had to do with the Catholic thing. The priest and the guilt. The fact that he wasn't supposed to have a life anymore, because he was supposed to remain celibate. He was supposed to remain without love for the rest of his life because he had chosen poorly when marrying.

Caity closed her eyes, tiredness finally rushing over her. She washed away in to a world of clouded dreams, remembering everything, traveling through time with her dreams taking her back to where it all started. To a time when her heart was happy and carefree and when life looked like an adventure just waiting for her to jump in to. Life was supposed to be joyful and Caity sighed as she fell deep into the past in her dreams. Thinking back, she remembered seeing Jack's number, calling him and the rest was fate. That call led to many nights sitting on the phone talking about all kinds of things. Months of conversations, and waiting for the phone to ring. Remembering how many times she was nervous when she'd call him, wondering if he would even make the time for her. She was never sure if he would, or if he would say he had too many things to do. She never knew how he'd react, so she often waited for him to call her.

Months of this weird dating continued until one day suddenly Caity realized she was in love with Jack. Totally in love where she thought of him first thing in the morning and last thing at night. Dreaming about the past, deep in a troubled pattern, Caity began to cry heavily in her sleep. She was crying so hard that when the phone rang she was disoriented, and stunned. It was Jack, or was it Jack calling her in her dreams.

Actually it was her alarm clock ringing; and Caity didn't hear it in her deeply unconscious state of remembering. She was dreaming of Jack, their romance, and how it all began.

CHAPTER 4

Clouded in her dreams, in a deep sleep she thought back to two years ago. It was January first 2002, what a wonderful day Caity thought. It was sunny and the snow covered neighborhood looked like a picture postcard just waiting to be framed. Caity lived for the sunshine and today was a day she could just sit at her little table in her sunroom and soak it up. It had been a wonderful Christmas full of family, being the eldest of two girls wasn't always the easiest, but it had its good times too! Caity was always happy from the inside out. Her friends described her as being full of life and her big blue eyes were known to envelop you and just eat you up with their sweet inviting smile. People said that eyes were the windows to the soul and if that were true Caity's were true of heart were always sincere and much too honest!

    Sitting down at her table she pulled out the last of her Christmas presents, the great new little leather address book her Mom had bought her for her purse. Mom was always remembering the little things. Caity was giggling to herself as she remembered how much tape her old address book had. Actually it was probably all tape now since she'd had it for some twenty years. Thinking it was time to redo it and retire the old thing. Sitting at her table she sat looking at the old book, filled with memories of friends and different times. She had turned forty earlier this year, and the twenty years of memories were just sitting in this little old address book.

It wasn't long before Caity reached "F" in her old address book and there it was. The name "Fraser." Jack and Jane Fraser and their two daughters Chloe almost seven and Nicky almost five. Of course Jack and Jane were now legally separated living in different houses. Looking back Caity had always wondered what Jack had seen in Jane. She'd been one of those players; she'd picked him up at some wedding, slept with him the first night, and convinced him that she was deeply in love. Of course at the time, Jack hadn't known that Jane was living with someone, which to Caity showed his lack of character. All of Jack's friends knew, and by the time Jack started to develop serious doubts about Jane and whether or not she loved him, the wedding had been only weeks away.

Caity remembered hearing stories of how he took off twice during those two weeks, desperately trying to talk himself out of not panicking. What Jack had really wanted was to cancel the wedding all together. Of course he didn't, instead he attended a clouded event full of his doubt and his sweating forehead of fear. Jack had been desperate to get married and have children. He was devoutly Catholic and knew that his dreams for tomorrow had all been based on that day. A day without true love, true happiness and worst of all true commitment on Jane's part. It hadn't been till years later that Jack discovered that Jane's married lover, her boss, had of all things had attended their wedding.

Caity shuddered remembering all the gory details. Jane needed a groom, Jack needed a wife. What a perfect fit. Caity remembered the sad details Jack had shared in all those long telephone calls where they shared their depths of their souls. It turned out that Jane's millionaire boss and lover needed her to appear to be happy in order to get his wife off their trail. In return for settling down, Jane got an awesome promotion, a private bank account amongst a long list of other unbelievable things. The original plan was that once her boss got his life together and most of his money hidden, they would both file for divorces. Hmmm.... and what was that expression? Live happily ever after. All Caity could think about was how mentally ill they both had been! The world was full of nut cases and those two had taken the cake!

Thinking back, to Caity the whole story seemed unreal and completely nuts. After all; Jack was apparently a very devout Catholic, who despite his religious claims, had committed sins against his beliefs by sleeping around with his fiancée out of wedlock for a whole year before the wedding. There was Jane, raised as a Catholic but the farthest thing from being pure, life could imagine. Truly, when Jack told the story, he said his ex-wife deserved an academy award for the performances she gave in and out bed for the whole year before they got married. She'd pretended to be deeply in love and couldn't wait to spend the rest of her life with him, or so he thought. When his gut feelings were ringing off the hook for weeks before the wedding, he wanted so badly to walk out, but he didn't. He talked himself into believing that if Jane loved him that much he could make himself grow to truly love her and they could build an amazing life together. For Jack, that life had to be filled with children and growing old together and what better choice than a woman that was totally in love with you.

The greatest sadness of all for Caity, out of this whole story, was that she believed in his heart Jack was sincere and only really wanted what everyone wants. That special kind of happiness that you can only share with one true love. Unfortunately his fear of aging and not achieving his goal was what lay the ground work for his slow and painful destruction.

And it did destroy him! No one but Caity really knew the extent of that damage, and she had only discovered it through lengthy, conversations during which she listened to all of Jack's pain and frustration. Most of all she heard just how scared of living he really was.

Jack possessed unhealthy amounts of fear. Fear of tomorrow, fear of being lied to, fear of being taken to the financial cleaners again, and worst of all, the fear of finally finding true love and having to admit it to himself.

The very worst part of the whole sad story was that once Jack discovered the whole truth of Jane's sordid story, he became part of what Caity referred to as the "Catholic Cult".

Tossing and turning in her sleep while deeply dreaming of the past, Caity was consumed with her troubles.

Even hours after she first started dreaming, tears were still sliding down her soft reddened cheeks, as she kept remembering all of her stories while making wishes that the present could be so very different than it was. As she turned over and buried her face deep into her soft fluffy pillows, Caity fell deep into a dreamless dark sleep.

CHAPTER 5

Weeks later, with almost little or no sleep, Caity sat leaning forward, elbows pressed into her knees and her face buried in her hands. She sighed deeply. She was so drained. Pausing and looking upward through her hands she could see Maggy's concerned face. Maggy, was a tall, extremely friendly faced woman, with long night black hair, with curls that trailed down to the middle of her back. She could have been a model, but instead she was Caity's "stress counselor" and lately, her best friend. Caity was in to see Maggy four times a week now and it didn't seem like anything was getting better.

If anything, Caity knew that her whole story was just as confusing to Maggy as it was to her. Crumpled tissues between her fingers from the hour of spilling her guts and crying, was how every session ended.

Today seemed to be different. It was as if all these weeks, Maggy had been putting together pieces of a complicated puzzle and today she seemed to have put them together to create a really clear picture. There was a deep, sullen silence and every crackle in the room that surrounded each breath Caity made. Maggy cleared her throat, grabbed Caity's two hands, making Caity look right up at her, dead on; straight into her deep thinking eyes and said, "You know Caity; I think I have a plan."

Caity could hear her heart racing and thumping in her ears, so loudly, that she stopped breathing for a few seconds, and then heard herself say in a whispering faint voice; "What plan?" Maggy looked at her and said, "Before I tell you, I'll go make a call to see if it's possible. Then I'll tell you about it." Maggy stood up to leave the room, on her way out, she looked back at Caity and gave a reassuring thumbs up as she closed the door behind her.

Sighing deeply, Caity leaned way back against the headrest of her oversized chair, looking up at the ceiling as if hoping to find answers written there. What in the world could Maggy possibly come up with that would take her out of the dark fast spins of confusion? What did Maggy see with all these link-less puzzle pieces that she couldn't? Hopefully she'd soon find out. Lord knows she couldn't take this much longer. Two full years was more than anyone should have had to bear. Worst of all, it wasn't the two wasted years, but that Caity was plunged into Heaven and Hell over and over and over again until she could predict how high the highs would get, and how low she'd crash. Caity didn't understand anything and today, Caity sat here looking desperately for answers, so that she could put her mind and heart to rest and somehow finally find the strength to walk away from the love of her life. She was hoping to find some type of happiness, and the peace she needed, and release herself from all the sorrow that had become so much a part of her life.

Suddenly Caity was startled by the door handle snapping closed. She was so deep in thought that she hadn't even heard Maggy walk back into the room.

Maggy was standing over Caity, watching her. How sad she looked in the sunshine that was beaming through her large picture windows of her office. It seemed to highlight the dark circles under Caity's eyes. Normally, Maggy was sure that Caity never looked older that thirty but today, Maggy thought she looked more like a deeply aging widow that was grieving a lost spouse. Certainly much older than her forty years! Caity was a producer of T.V. commercials and from what Maggy heard they were some of the liveliest award winning pieces out there. How could someone whose work could be so vibrant and full of laughter and energy, hide the real life pain from her co-workers and family? Maggy didn't know how Caity did it, just that she did.

Maybe it was impacting her life more that Caity knew, and all Maggy could think of was that she hoped that her plan would work. Even Maggy needed to know what the truth was! The story was all too confusing, and Maggy's curiosity was killing her.

Was Jack a cheater? Or, even worse, was he a lying manipulative guy that was just using Caity just as of his pawns? Was Jack some deeply religious person whose mind and life was controlled by those who ran his church? Or even worse, was there some unknown even sicker reason he had used Caity and hurt her so badly?

If Maggy was to bet using all her experience as a counselor, she'd go with the first reason. Let's face it; in her job she'd seen that story all too many times. How many women and men, had been emotionally destroyed by some moral-less individual that somehow managed to get away with all this stuff. This time though, Maggy allowed herself to get emotionally involved in the story and this time it was just as important to her to find out, as it was to Caity. It was different because even after all of the info Caity had provided her with it didn't give Maggy enough insight to be able to come up with any answers. That was why Maggy had just called her brother.

Maggy looked at Caity, sitting there in a dizzy state of confusion. Maybe her brother, the best private detective she knew; could finally get them the much needed answers they were looking for. He was the all time skeptic of people's lives, and religion, and always said to trust no one but yourself. Maggy guessed that he had witnessed too much in his forty-six years to have a normal life or for that matter a relationship. After all, her brother spent most of his time finding proof to destroy relationships, personal and otherwise; while in an ironic twist of siblings, Maggy spent most of her time trying to heal them. Go figure! How could the two of them, who were raised in the same house, be so opposite in their professions? She knew she'd never understand her brother, but today she was grateful he was there for her.

Maggy was so deep in thought, that she hadn't realized Caity was talking to her.

"What"? She said as she looked over. "I said, you look like you're off on another planet." Caity smiling as she spoke, that false put on smile that Maggy was always saddened by. "I am," Maggy said, " I think I may have an interesting solution to help you find, well; hope you find at least a few answers so that if you don't ever get over loving Jack; you may be able to at least leave him behind and get on with your life. How about it? Are you game?" Caity let out another deep heavy breath, and although she was not saying a word she was glued to every word Maggy said, as she excitedly nodded her acceptance.

With that, Maggy started to fill Caity in on the plan. "My brother Stewart, or Stew as everyone calls him, is a private detective. He owes me a few favors and has agreed to look into this for us. That is, if we give him enough info he can look into it." Maggy paused, watching Caity's eyes appear to temporarily pop out of her face. So what do you think? Do you want to really know the truth about Jack?" Speechless with gratitude and hoping to finally find a light at the end of the tunnel, Caity just nodded with approval.

Maggy went on, "Stew says that people always say they want to know the truth until they find out what the truth is, and then they're usually sorry they ever found out. I personally think that in this case you need to know, good or bad. Caity, for you, knowledge is freedom! I really think you should meet with him." Maggy let out a very deep sigh. She sat there looking right at Caity but couldn't read just what she was thinking. For the first time she saw a light in her eyes that she hadn't ever seen there since the first day she'd met her. Weeks and weeks ago. Again, Maggy repeated herself. "So, what do you think? Maggy was waiting for some kind of response and after closing her eyes, and then opening them up again as if she had said a little prayer; Caity paused; speechless as usual. Her look was just the same as a little girl's standing in the Barbie Isle at Toys"R"Us. This was a dream come true. A private detective! If he could even get her a few answers and some proof as to what the truth was, Caity would have piece of mind and hopefully find her spirit again. It was her spirit that she missed the most!

Suddenly, letting out a squeal sound Caity looked right back at Maggy and said, "Wow, when can I meet him? Will he have time today? Can you come with me? Is he good at finding these things out? How long do you think it will take?" Caity was rambling at full speed and Maggy couldn't keep up.

"Stop, slow down Caity" Maggy said, "O.K. Yes you can meet him today, actually tonight at your house if your schedule is O.K. with that?" Maggy was sure it would be when Caity jumped in and said. "Yes, that's perfect, I'll give you the address and directions." Caity heard herself speaking but she felt like she was watching the events take place from somewhere out of her body. She felt like she was floating on some type of weird drug effect and didn't know if she could catch herself and get both feet back to earth. As Caity wrote out her address for Maggy and the brief description of the directions which included twists and turns to her little condo on the South side, Caity grew suddenly and deeply sad again.

She was thinking of Jack and that strangely in the two years they had spent together he had never once been to her place. He had said it had to do with his religious guilt thing. Caity and anyone she ever told about it thought had seemed very strange and truly suspicious and they all felt it was because of the great lies.

Caity was always sure there was another woman, because it felt that way, but she could never prove it. She so badly needed to know! After all, Jack never went anywhere in public with her. It seemed they always got together at his place on the weekends when he didn't have the girls. In fact, now that Caity was thinking about it, she didn't really know who Jack spent his time with when he wasn't with her. She had always gone on his word that he had been with the, but the truth was she didn't know very much about a lot of his time. Now hopefully she'd find out.

Totally upset all over again, Caity had completely lost her moment of jubilation deeply entranced by dark sad thoughts. So much so that Maggy had to grab her arm and give her a shake to bring her back to reality. Shivering as if freezing cold, Caity shook herself and apologized. She told Maggy she couldn't wait till they got to her place tonight, and that the day would take forever to pass before she would meet Stew. As Caity walked out of Maggy's office, closing the door behind her, she felt like yet another chapter of this weird story was ending. Fearfully she knew, that another was about to begin.

Would she have the strength to handle the truth? What if it was another woman after all? That would mean that Caity had spent and wasted two whole years believing in the church and the Catholic religion excuses which was why she was in this mess to begin with. What if it really was all one sick lie?

Caity didn't know what was worse, but the reality was, she was about to find out. Ready or Not!

Chapter 6

Stew sat there nervously tapping his pointer finger on his knee cap. Thinking back to earlier in the evening, when he had been taken aback by Maggy's new friend. He was shocked at how when he'd first met Miss Caity Anderson that he'd suddenly felt like he was sixteen and back in high school all over again. Looking back Stew was rarely, if ever nervous; but taking one look at Caity when he'd first walked into her apartment made him go weak at the knees. He hadn't bargained for the fact that this apparent nut case which Maggy was trying to help, would turn out to be one hot knock out.

From head to toe, Caity Anderson was gorgeous! She was at least five nine in those heels, with shoulder length golden blonde wavy hair that caressed the sides of an almost perfect complexion. When she walked she carried her sleek slender body with the perfection of a runway model. Her clothes accented just the right womanly curves that were attached to a picture perfect set of long slender legs a man dreams about having wrapped tightly around him. When he looked right at her face Stew had been captivated by the deepest blue eyes he had ever seen. He'd been completely mesmerized. Stewart Banks had thought himself to be some cool and controlled womanizer but this woman had stopped him dead in his tracks. He remembered a million thoughts running through his mind in the few split seconds of intros all the while thinking that Miss Caity Anderson had an incredibly inviting and sexy smile that exposed a mouth a man could get lost in.

He'd been unexpectedly taken aback by what an absolutely captivating visual package his latest client turned out to be. Letting out a deep sigh he thought back to how sad it was that Maggy had described her as the "old fashioned" marrying type! The thing that had upset Stew the most was his body's sudden physical reaction to her. Even now as he sat here waiting for the two women all he could think about was, "What a package!"

As he threw his head back on the head rest of the chair, Stew was wrestling with his inner emotions. He hadn't been prepared for the fact that he could be affected by a woman in this way. It had been so long since he'd had any emotion at all that it left him shaken. Sighing wasn't something Stew found himself doing very often but tonight it seemed like it had become his whole existence. He sat there obsessing at how in the world could a woman who looked like that be "the marrying kind" while obsessing at different ways he could think of to get her straight into his bed. Shaking himself, he knew he had to get a grip on his new found self awareness and make sure that Maggy didn't pick up on it. All he knew for now, while he worked on her case he'd fight his physical reactions with cold showers until things developed more naturally.

One thing was for sure, Stew knew that Caity Anderson was definitely the kind of woman that a man dreams of having on his arm for all others to envy, and admire. As for anything else, he'd have to wait and see but he knew that he couldn't wait to find out!

Still entranced in his thoughts Stew was thinking that either Caity was some kind of nut all wrapped up in this great God given package, or she'd been suckered by what has to be the greatest con-man and asshole on the planet! This so called guy had pulled a real job on her and Stew was suddenly angry and very protective. Suddenly he wanted to take this guy out back and pound the crap out of him. If what Maggy had told him on the phone today was true, then not only did this Jack guy deserve a good beating, but Stew was hoping the truth would nail him hard.

Caity had told him in great detail what had happened between Jack and her the last two years. It had been so stressful for her that suddenly as if someone had pressed a button, the minute she was finished speaking she started making these loud whistling sounds and went into a full fledge asthma attack. It was obvious that the stress was the cause, and after a half hour they'd brought her here to get oxygen. Staring up at the ceiling Stew started wondering when it was that they had painted the ceiling last....obviously from the way it looked it may even be the original paint. The rust stains, cracks and obvious water leakage spots ....indicated that it must have been years. Pausing for a moment...Stew reflected back......Boy, it had been a long night and sitting here on this ugly yellow vinyl couch in the emergency waiting room at Toronto Hospital was getting to be all too uncomfortable after the night he'd had so far.

Stew realized that he hadn't seen either Maggy or Caity for at least an hour. Well he thought, he'd better stop sitting here and daydreaming, might as well use this time to write down the facts and start thinking where he'd start with this case.

Some how he'd have to wipe out the physical picture that kept running through his head and start putting some of the bizarre pieces together so that when they finally left the hospital he could get right on the case.

He knew he was a good detective. He'd spent years perfecting his craft and making quite the living at it. Actually, it had made him wealthier than he had ever dreamed of and although he'd ended up in his profession because it had been his passion, Stew had in fact become one of the few elite in his field.

Still sitting on the ugly yellow vinyl couch in the emergency waiting room, he decided it was time he put his detective hat on and stop thinking like a man. It was time for him to focus and put a list together, so that he could plan out his strategy. This was going to be like any other case he'd worked on and he'd have to pull himself back in gear and concentrate. He'd have to let himself enjoy the perks later, once he'd solved and closed the case.

Adjusting himself in the seat to get more comfortable, he leaned forward resting his elbows on his knees and his chin in the palms of his hands.

Hummmm, let's see.....he thought, lightly scratching his head with his left hand while totally entranced in his thoughts. Knowing that the best route was always to go through the list and start at the beginning, and that he was only as good as the information he could collect, Stew pulled out his small leather note pad and started to list everything in chronological order.

His notes were a mess as usual but Caity's story hadn't helped either. It was all over the map and now Stew needed to make sense of it, if he was going to get this wrapped up with in as little of his time invested as possible. After all, this was a favor. He wasn't even getting paid this time. It's not like he needed the money since he'd made so much he could have retired by now, but he knew he'd be bored without the excitement of his job. Stew loved what he did, he loved catching people lying and he loved watching them pay for their sins. It was a high he'd never gotten anywhere else in life and he'd always go out and get another case right after he finished one. Luckily Maggy caught him just before he started looking for his next assignment.

O.K. now where was he...oh ya......the list. He wrote it down in the order he could remember.

1- *Caity had known Jack for over 2 years*
2- *She'd attended his wedding 10-12 years ago*
3 - *Somehow mutual friends were the reason they'd crossed paths a few years ago and from that somehow got together*
4 - *The weird part of the story was that they had both been interested in each other some seventeen years ago at some party before Jack had met his ex-wife.*
5 – *In the very beginning of their relationship they went away for a week together,...so much for the religious excuse!!!*

Stew stared at the paper with his notes which read like one of those cheesy soap operas. Even though he hadn't written down all of the facts he almost couldn't believe what Caity had already told him. With his mind wandering he wondered what it would be like to be lucky enough to spend a whole week with a woman like Caity. Stew's heart started beating like it was in his throat. How was it possible that at his age he finally met a woman to have this affect on him? By all accounts, Caity Anderson was either nuts and inventing this story, or knee deep into something that would leave her so wounded forever. The next guy would be beaten to a pulp and spit out with the old "No Trust" bullshit he'd seen so many times. Shaking his head, Stew refocused on his list. He would need it later when he'd be working on the case of Mr. Jack Fraser, the so called crazy guy. Shaking his head in disbelief, Stew was sure that Jack was just another lying bastard who probably had more than one women falling for his bullshit.

Now where was he? Oh ya...

6 - *All the weird stuff started happening their first week, the day after they first went to church together. Jack found out that Caity wasn't Catholic and belonged to the United Church and according to Caity, Jack not only went pale at the table but began to act a little nuts. He started inventing weird excuses to his whereabouts, he insisted he loved her and wanted her in his life. All the while did everything possible to shut her out.*

7 – *When they got home Jack told her that this relationship was serious for him, that he was committed to her. It couldn't be more serious for him. Caity felt the same way and began to relax about the whole religion thing but things really began to spin out of control*

8 - *Some of the weird things that Caity talked about were that he always picked fights with her right before holidays...Christmas, New Years, every holiday. Jack had never spent a holiday with Caity in the two years they were together. .(How weird was that? Stew thought). The worst part was Caity always felt there was another woman and Jack always swore there wasn't and that he always said he was just spending it with his family and his girls. Caity said that he always felt so sick during these times, she always ended it with him but he somehow always talked her into getting back together with him.*

9 – *Oh ya, Stew thought. She was never allowed to call the house when the girls were home and she was never allowed to just drop in.*

Stew paused again, how could Caity fall for his sick bullshit? This guy was quite the number! He was obviously a top of the line actor and manipulator, and Caity was just the typical female that always falls for that kind of crap! As a guy, even he though it made him sick at times while working on a case, Stew was never surprised at the kind of crap that guys dished out just to get laid. O.K. So he was tainted, skeptical and a firm believer that most men had an angle and used it; while he also believed that most women always fell for it. Sadly in his job, Stew had been proven right on too many occasions not to be affected by what he'd always discovered when working on cases.

Well, as bad as it was, Stew figured he'd have this case and this bastard's game all wrapped up in a few hours. At worst, a few days, if that! He'd tail him, grab some great pictures with whatever woman he was with, prove to Caity this guy was a total jerk and then he'd work on her for himself. What could he say; Stew was just a guy with motives. Smiling, he felt pretty smug. This would be a great week after all! Stew sat there thinking that he'd been alone way too long! For the first time in years he'd actually met an honest woman. If Caity was anything, Stew knew she was honest and that was the sexiest thing about her. Why not get a girl like Caity for himself. He knew Jack didn't deserve her and from what she spoke about wanting in a relationship, was someone to grow old with. She was a BABE!

Hmmm what a package and it was just within his reach. Stew wasn't sure he liked the thoughts going through his mind about growing old with someone. That seemed too far off, but it sure could be good for a few years. O.K, he was getting ahead of himself. What he really needed to do was focus. What a week! What a week indeed. Hmmmm, he kept sighing to himself.

Stew was thinking fast. He'd trash this guy, get the girl and finally not owe his sister any more favors, although truthfully she never asked for much and he never really minded. He adored his sister; she had a way of driving him nuts, with some of her crazy patients!

Stretching out on the vinyl sofa Stew looked up from his daydreaming to find Maggy standing over him, shadowing out the light and for some reason her facial expression bugged him. Maggy was shaking her head, hands on her hips and a facial scowl a mile long.

"What?" Stew asked in a defensive tone. "What?" she repeated. "Stewart Banks, I know you better than you know and let me tell you, if you don't think I see you're up to something. It's written all over your face!" Maggy let out a deep sigh, "You've got that sinister grin you always get just before you're up to no good!" " Relax Maggy, I was just thinking how easy this case is going to be and how I'll have it wrapped up in a few days at worst, that's all. Promise!!"

"Stew, that better be all! I told you how much Caity has been through, and the fact that we're sitting in an emergency waiting room has got to tell you to behave yourself; right? Caity doesn't need you complicating her life any more right now, especially since I'm sure it will be tough enough on her after she finds out the truth. Whatever that ends up being."

Stew stood up and wrapped one long arm around Maggy's shoulders and whispered in her ear. "Come on Maggy, you and I both know that I'm going to find that the guy is a repeat cheater and a player. Even your gut has to be telling you that, and that's why you called me to begin with. I'll just make sure I'm careful how I give her the news and I'll promise that you can be there when I do. O.K?" Stew looked around to make sure no one had approached them without them knowing, and then continued to whisper. "This guy sounds like a typical leach, and a bull-shitter, with a great con story that takes advantage of sweet trusting women. We both know that Caity needs to know this and get on with her life, however long that takes!"

Maggy turned and looked at Stew dead on. Whispering back, and looking right at Stew's face and said "I don't know Stew, after all the things I've heard I don't think it's that simple. My gut feeling says that there is something really bad happening here!" Stew shrugged, he used both of his strong arms and grabbed Maggy's shoulders and looked down at her small five foot five frame and smiled. "Maggy, you're getting too melodramatic! I think you got to stop watching those soap operas of yours and start thinking straight! You're just too emotionally involved this time". Throwing his head back and coming back looking straight on at Maggy, Stew let out a gasp of air and said. "Maggy, I promise you one thing. In a few days we'll have the answers and we'll know the truth, now, where is Caity and how is she doing, anyway?"

Just as he finished his statement the doors to the rooms opened and Caity walked through looking a lot better than she had when they brought her in a few hours ago. She looked a whole lot calmer too. The doctor must have given her something for her nerves and she looked almost at peace walking up to them. Stew wrapped one arm around Maggy and the other around Caity and said, "Shall we go, ladies?" Caity just nodded, and Maggy silently analyzed her friend through her old fashioned worried eyes.

"Well beautiful" Stew said in Caity's ear. "It's time we get you home so you can get your beauty rest. The world will look a whole lot better tomorrow, trust me!" Stew whisked Maggy and Caity out of emergency at the same speed he had rushed them in. He couldn't wait to drop them off and start tailing his latest project. Even in emergency Caity was gorgeous! Her long blonde curly hair, those luscious peachy pink lips, and the bluest eyes Stew had ever seen. Not to mention she had a body right out of Glamour magazine, and better yet, she was available. Stew was a driven and motivated man now. He was more than ready to get this show on the road and get his chance with Caity.

It took Stew less than an hour to drop off Caity and then Maggy at their perspective houses and to get back to his place to pick up his cameras and equipment. He'd grab a coffee at his favorite all night shop and be off to park outside the guy's house. His prey was waiting and Stew was filled with that old adrenaline rush he lived for.

An hour later, Stew came out of his front door, slamming it behind him. He was carrying his bags full of equipment. Suddenly he could feel weird shivers up and down his spine. He quickly looked around and uncharacteristically chose to ignore them.

Chapter 7

Jack sat in the dark shivering as he leant forward on his steering wheel. This old winter beater car of his had seen better days but it had certainly come in handy last year. He'd used it night after night, whenever he got a chance to sit outside Caity's apartment and just wait. Tonight was a shock though, all this time he'd been trying to prove to himself that she was like all the other women he had known in his life. Cheaters!! Cheaters who said they loved you and before you knew it they were playing you like a fool. Till now in his heart and head he always believed that Caity was really different, and that she was faithful but tonight he was shattered. Tonight he sat shivering with butterflies in his stomach. Boy, he hadn't had those since he'd caught Jane cheating on him years ago. She'd been pregnant with Nicky and just starting to show, he'd nearly went out of his mind back then. Tonight he was shivering so bad that he couldn't wait to turn on the engine and heat himself up. He'd have to wait, because those damn headlights always came on when the engine was running. He'd asked his mechanic if he could disconnect them, but after a long song and dance it turned out to be way too complicated.

Jack's coffee was barely warm, so it certainly wasn't helping any with his bodily chills. He sat there thinking that he was grateful that at least it was spring and not the middle of winter. It was only a few weeks to Easter. All he could think about was thank God he'd picked that fight with Caity so he wouldn't have to have her around for the holiday.

He'd wait a few weeks after that and start things up again, at least until his birthday in June when he'd break up all over again. He put both his hands on his forehead, rubbing his face up and down thinking that all this was sounding really nuts. Not to mention that he'd spent most of his night tonight just sitting outside some guy's house trying to figure out who he was an how long had Caity been seeing him? Or was she? Was he Caity's boss? Was she just like Jane and having a work affair? Who was he? Jack didn't know because he'd never met anyone in Caity's life and it was suddenly driving him crazy.

The guy was something right out of one of those stupid men's magazines. Really tall; he was at least six two or six three. Sandy blond perfectly layered hair, and an expensive chocolate brown bomber jacket which couldn't hide his obvious work out shoulders. God, this was driving Jack up the wall. His heart was racing and he was beginning to think he was on the verge of a heart attack. Picturing that guy with Caity made his heart beat heavily in his ears. Shit this hurt like hell! Jack hated this guy from the minute he first saw him park his car at Caity's. He'd seen him walking around her apartment and it had sent Jack right through the roof. Caity wasn't one to keep her living room blinds closed so he was often able to see most of what went on inside her second storey corner apartment.

He couldn't figure out who the other woman was. Who was she and what did she have to do with Caity and this guy? He had seen enough pictures to know that they weren't relatives, but not enough pictures to know who they were. That dark haired woman had already been in Caity's apartment when Jack arrived to his favorite spot on the hill over looking Caity's place. Just as he'd parked the car he'd noticed this guy parking and going in. What had shocked him was seeing him appear in Caity's place in front of the living room window. Worst was that he was standing there as if he owned the place! Jack's blood went cold through his veins as he thought about it.

Jack could have kicked himself now though because he had somehow fallen asleep during the evening sitting there watching them and he'd had no idea when they left, or how long they were gone. For that matter where they had gone? All Jack knew was they'd made enough noise when they came back to wake him just in time to see the guy drop Caity off at the front door and drive off with that black haired woman. Thank God Caity went up alone! Jack couldn't take much more today. Maybe, just maybe; that was a couple that Caity knew, but somehow Jack didn't believe that.

As soon as Caity went in Jack started his car and tailed Stew and Maggy. First he'd driven to the women's house and judging by the fact there were no physical actions between them, made him think they couldn't be a couple. The guy had dropped her off and peeled out of there in a hurry, and he'd followed them because he needed know if he was heading back to Caity's. The irony of the whole thing was that he suddenly realized that all three of them only lived only about fifteen minutes from his house, so that tailing them in the future was going to be easy.

Caity lived in North West Mississauga a suburb of Toronto, while Jack lived in the ritzier wealthier part in the south end of Mississauga in an older more established area. The dark haired woman lived almost smack dab in the middle part which Jack referred to as the working class homes, but worst of all was this Mr. Magazine lived in what Jack was envious of. That new development part, half way between Caity and him, just east of Erin Mills. This guy lived in one of those millionaire jobs. The houses Jack always dreamed about owning one day. It had a three car garage in a separate building at the side of the house. An eight foot brick and iron fence surrounded the property while electronic wrought iron gates were remotely controlled by an obviously lavish security system.

The house was huge, three stories on a ravine lot and obviously very private. In fact Jack was worried that a patrol car would be checking him out any time now if he hovered too long. He watched him go in, park his car and switch his electric driveway fencing closed. He suddenly moaned because his butterflies were feeling more like an ulcer these days. Taking a deep breath and letting out a heavy sigh he leaned forward just guy about to start his car. Just as he thought that the guy was obviously staying home, he looked up to see that the guy was coming back out of his house. Staring right at him, Jack saw that he had changed into way more casual clothes but still something you'd expect to find on a male model type. Worst of all he was carrying a duffle bag. Jack stopped breathing. Suddenly he could hear his heart pounding in his ears. Oh for God sake, this guy was going back to Caity's for sure!

"Shit!" he loudly whispered under his breath. He knew it! Caity was just like all the others and he'd know for sure tonight. Jack wanted to burst into tears. He knew men were supposed to be tough but he was in love with her. A love like he'd never known before, a total love where he constantly day dreamed about growing old with her, finding a way to have a baby with her. All of those feelings you heard about but never knew could exist. Why hadn't he ever told her? Why had he been such an idiot? He'd thought he could control his time with Caity forever. He knew how much she loved him, and since she always forgave him of everything he did, he never felt like he'd really lose her until now!

In one big swoop, in just a second of time, Jack could feel all of his dreams shattering and suffocating him right here in his car. Jack watched as Mr. Magazine walked over to the middle garage. He'd seen his Cherry Red hardtop BMW M3 earlier and was curious what kind of car he would have behind door number two.

Jack sat forward not believing his eyes. What? You got to be kidding? An old brown Ford Taurus, no way. It looked like a cop car of all things. It had no hub caps, large spots of rust on the sides, and a piece of fender missing. This guy couldn't be a cop, not in this neighborhood. The thing was pretty close to a scrap car. This was so weird; he just couldn't wait to see what was next. Maybe this guy was one of those car freaks and he didn't trust parking his beamer at Caity's overnight. Jack knew if he'd stay any longer he'd be noticed. Besides he could beat this guy to Caity's place and watch him arrive from his favorite spot on the hill.

Jack started his car and headed off before this guy could notice him. He couldn't wait to get warmed up and then finally confront Caity with all this. Placing his heat on high he adjusted all the vents on his old Volkswagen. He could see the headlights of the Taurus turn on just as he was pulling out. Jack didn't know what the rest of the evening would bring but he felt his life was over as he drove the short distance to Caity's place.

Chapter 8

Stew started Maggy's old beater and it purred. He'd been working on it for weeks for her. Why she didn't get rid of this piece of junk was beyond him. He'd even offered to buy her a car, but Maggy was too practical and not a taker. Stew had a selfish reason for wanting to buy her one, he always worried she'd get killed in this old thing. Well at least she let him work on it whenever he was worried. The thing that bugged him was that she was always trying to pay him for the car parts and worst yet she'd even tried a few times to pay him for his labor.

He never let her get away with that stuff and he always took his sweet time fixing it so at least Maggy could enjoy driving his car for a few weeks. He always lent her the Cherry Red Dodge Ram Pick up. She always joked that she had better buy a big ole cowboy hat to drive it and he'd always meant to buy her one. As siblings they were a team, got along dandy and always had a few laughs, but boy were they ever different. Maggy was the optimist, she believed in people, the future, dreams and romance. Stew on the other hand believed in himself and the fact that few people if any had morals and values. He knew romance was something for women's magazines and those books they bought with the mushy pictures on them. Maggy often read those and he's found a few left behind in his truck at times. Unreal! He remembered reading a few pages out of curiosity and laughing out loud at how hokey all that shit was.

Maggy always got frustrated when he teased her about it, and he loved to get her going. Funny thing was, tonight after meeting Caity, all he could think about was romance. Boy, he had it bad! Better get this case wrapped up and Caity in his bed before he'd lose it. She would be just the distraction he needed at this point in his life. Nothing like a little Suzy homemaker that had a really hot body to get his groin working on its own. It was going to be a long night if he kept those thoughts up and forced himself to get going and work at finding out about this nut case.

Stew drove down his street thinking how weird life was getting and how in such a short time he'd gone from professional detective to personally involved. He couldn't remember if he'd ever felt like this on a case, but realistically he knew he hadn't. Better not let Maggy know what his motives were because she'd make his life a living hell over it. If anything, Stew couldn't miss how protective she was over Caity. As he watched her, he realized that Maggy had been acting more like a Mom then a councilor tonight and he wondered if she would be able to help Caity once all the truth came out. Oh well, he'd know soon enough.

Stew was so entrenched in his thoughts he realized he was just a few blocks from Jack's house. He'd have to drive by a few times and find a place to sit and hide. As he drove by on his first pass he noticed that there were no lights on in the windows. Guess he was still out. Good thing, it was always easier to see what was going on and get pictures when people were coming and going instead of having to sneak up to windows and stuff.

Caity had given Stew a good picture of the place, the see through sheer curtains in every window, the best way to see in was in the back of the house. Problem was that this neighborhood would have cops going by on a regular basis and Stew didn't want to look like a burglar. He had quite a few friends on the force but all it would take is one nutty neighbor and his cover would be blown.

Ah yes, there it was, the nook across from Jack's house. It was kind of an end of a street that didn't fit. A house wouldn't have fit there and it wasn't big enough for a mini seat park, so the city had paved it. Caity and other of Jack's neighbors had often parked there. What a jerk; Stew thought. Jack had actually made Caity park across the street at times so that no one would see her car on the driveway. What a Jerk! Worse yet, Stew couldn't understand how Caity could love him enough to do that. He'd have to ask her more about questions so he could at least put things into perspective. Boy, talk about one sick soap opera, and Stew didn't even have all the details yet!

Stew jumped out of the car and laid an old black blanket across the front. It was dark in this nook and with the blanket blocking any shimmer from the chrome he would go totally unnoticed in the darkness. Now he just had to sit and wait.

In the meantime Jack was headed back home. Obviously Mr. Magazine had another woman he was with tonight. As he drove, Jack's mind wondered to Caity. She'd been such a happy joyful person when they had first started seeing each other. Because of his Catholic obsession with his status, Jack never referred to her as his girlfriend or used the term dating. He preferred to call Caity his "special friend" so to speak, a term he knew she hated. Caity would always say to him that she quote, "Never slept with her friends." To her it was always an insult when Jack talked that way and he knew it hurt her.

Actually thinking about it tonight he didn't know why he always set out to hurt her, and then feel awful about it. He just assumed it was his way of keeping the distance between them. While he drove haphazardly drenched in his thoughts, he remembered back to a night a few weeks ago where he had once again been an absolute bastard. He'd made love to her and dumped her again all in the same night, once again because of the rush of emotion and guilt that always came over him. Caity had been heaving with tears streaming down her face. The heartache imbedded in her face. How could he keep doing this? God he loved her. He wanted her in his life so badly he didn't understand what made him act like such an idiot all the time. It hurt him to the core and always tore him up inside so he didn't understand why he couldn't get past all these ghosts in his head. If he was going to be honest with himself he'd have to admit he was acting like a mad man.

Caity was a magnet for him. He could never control himself when she was around. When he was with her the world felt right. She made his heart beat and he couldn't get over how right it felt. That was why he'd spent so much time fighting with her and avoiding her. When Caity was around, Jack couldn't think, he'd lose himself in her smell, her hair, her soft skin, the way she moaned in his arms and the way she clung to him with such passion every time. She couldn't be faking that; no woman could fake it that good! He knew now that Jane had faked all their times together, comparing the two was impossible because they were exact opposites.

Caity was everything he had ever dreamed of, everything he had ever wanted; he loved her more than he ever thought possible. He was always amazed at how he finally discovered what love really felt like, and it terrified him. He was absolutely and completely terrified to take a chance again. What if he got royally screwed again? He had to admit that he had never known feelings like this before. Never felt his heart beat like the way Caity made it beat. He never felt as alive as when he was with her. She went right to the core of his heart and he ached when he wasn't with her. Seeing that guy in her apartment tonight felt like he would die a million deaths and then some. What a relief to know he didn't come back! Maybe he was with that dark haired chick after all. What a relief for tonight, if not forever. Jack was weaving all over the road as if he was drunk and didn't even notice. He was consumed by his thoughts and he certainly wasn't paying attention to the road like he should.

Remembering back to the last night he'd seen Caity, she'd been screaming at him with tears streaming down her eyes. Telling him that he wasn't religious but instead that he was obviously part of some sick cult. That normal people didn't act this way.

Jack suddenly hit the brakes and his wheels locked as the car started sliding through the intersection. He was so deep in thought he had missed the light turn red. Luckily the guy coming from the other direction saw him coming and had slowed down enough that he didn't hit him. Jack went right through the intersection and slowing down he pulled over to the side and came to a full stop. His heart was in his throat for the tenth time tonight. Shit, he almost killed himself. He leaned forward and put his head on the steering wheel in order to calm himself, but his knuckles were clenched to the wheel and he suddenly burst into uncontrollable tears. They flowed down his face and through his shadowed unshaven face, and he could feel them drip down onto his shirt. He felt like he'd never be able to get a grip on himself tonight and all he could think about was burying his face in Caity's chest and having her warm arms around him.

He had no friends to call to pick him up and rescue him tonight. He'd made sure when he and Jane split that he cut himself off from everyone he'd ever spent time with. He'd focused on his work and with his kids, until Caity changed all that. Sitting here deeply wishing he could be rescued, he tried desperately to pull himself together so he could at least get home. His knuckles gripped the wheel hard because he was frustrated with himself. This was quite the life he had carved out for himself, and he had himself to blame for everything. He sat there for what seemed an eternity before he had the energy to get it into gear.

Shaking himself he took his foot off the brake and slowly drove in the direction of home. He was only a few blocks away but it felt like miles until he pulled into the safety of his driveway. Sitting there, turning the engine off, Jack's body began to shake as if he was in some type of shock. He wasn't able to shake the events of the night and he sat there just staring at the garage door. Not really thinking of anything, just staring off into space as if some miracle would appear on the door and release him of this hell.

Slowly he moved around getting his things together; his briefcase and stuff from his busy day. If anything, Jack knew one thing, he'd better call his shrink and make an appointment to see him as soon as possible, before he lost complete perspective. That is if he hadn't already. He was so consumed in his thoughts, that he never noticed the blob of darkness in the lane way that was usually lit with the neighbors' lawn lights. Stew had managed to disconnect them when he had arrived earlier, and Jack had been so consumed by his problems that it never caught his attention.

As Stew sat impatiently in his car with his camera's zoom lens focused directly on the back of Jack's head, he wondered what was taking so long. What in the hell was this guy waiting for? He wasn't on his cell phone finishing a call; it seemed like he was just sitting there as if transfixed on some dot on the garage door. Sitting there frustrated, Stew made a mental note to contact Caity and get her to give him all of Jack's info tomorrow, especially cell phone numbers and his home phone.

That way, next time he could always block out his number and call Jack's cell if this happened again. Doing that usually made people react and move faster, at least he probably would have gotten out of the car by now. Stew wished he had remembered to ask Caity today which would have prevented him from sitting here and losing patience just watching what appeared to be nothing.

    Stew ended up waiting another fifteen long minutes before Jack finally got out of the car. As Stew taped Jack on his video camera walking into his house, he wondered if it would give him any information that would help. Strangely enough, Stew always taped people because it usually ended up showing things that he missed with his eyes. He often played tapes over and over again until he got answers to things he was looking for. Often the naked eye missed important details and his tapes always paid off. Looking at Jack, Stew figured from the way the man was walking that he must be drunk. He was hunched over and staggering from side to side and with the zoom lens zeroed in closer on Jack and he appeared to be shaking as if he had Parkinson's or something. Stew knew that there was a lot of info he needed if he was going to get this case under wraps quickly, so the first thing he'd better do is talk to Caity in the morning and get some tough questions answered.

    Stew sat in front of the house long enough to watch the motions of lights going on and off until what must be the master bedroom at the side of the house, the lights went out for good. It was well past 5 AM when Stew finally threw himself on his own bed. Fully dressed and feet dangling off the side of his bed. Stew passed out cold, dreaming of a million things, but mostly Caity.

Chapter 9

The sun was streaming through the windows, shining on Caity's pillow and right into her sleeping eyes. It was Saturday morning and one of the few days that Caity's alarm didn't wake her. She could feel the warmth of the sun on her face and she was dreaming of the ocean and the beach. She could feel the ocean breeze and smell the salt air. Suddenly she could feel Jack's arms around her, lying in the sun and kissing her with the sound of the waves in her ears. Jack was kissing her passionately. Kissing her face with little kisses that went from one ear around her fore head and down and around to her other ear and down to her neck. He was telling her how much he loved her, he was holding her close, and he smelt wonderful. Caity had his cologne memorized in her mind, her nose and her heart. She could smell him, feel him and he felt so good. She snuggled tighter to the pillow she was cuddling and in her deep sleep Caity was happy. Her heart skipped beats and danced in her chest. Jack was smiling and still kissing her when she heard the bells. What were bells doing on the beach? It was like a strange ringing sound, kind of like a cell phone.

Did she bring her cell to the beach? Where was it? She was reaching around in the sand when she realized Jack was gone. Where had he gone to? Jack? Jack? Where are you? She yelled out. Suddenly Caity was screaming out Jack's name. She'd been calling out to him to come back. She felt a chill and a cold shiver and suddenly Caity was waking out of her deep sleep. Suddenly Caity felt like she had been dropped into a cold shower.

Sitting up in her bed, with the warm sunlight streaming down on her through the window, she was still shivering. Suddenly she was so deeply sad realizing that it had all been a dream and that she wasn't on some beautiful beach with Jack. That Jack really wasn't telling her that he loved her, and that the kisses were all in a dream of remembrance of an evening they had spent together months ago. Everything with Jack was months and weeks, not days. Everything was a web of questions with no answers, clouds of doubts and fears and never the peaceful moments that she experienced in her dreams. Maybe Jack had only been a dream, someone that played a role and didn't really exist. Caity wished she would stop dreaming of him because she hated waking up drained. She always hated the let down she always felt when she realized it was all just some weird fantasy.

Pulling herself together, she threw herself back on her pillows and wondered if Stew had found out anything last night. Probably not, I mean who gets that lucky first night out? Really? Certainly not her! Caity knew that she would have to be patient. Where Jack was concerned there were definitely a lot of secrets and weird things that happened with no explanations. Caity was sure there was another woman and she desperately needed to know the truth so she could get on with her life. Caity's heart was breaking. It hurt wondering what the other woman was like. How could he do this especially since his wife had cheated on him? How could he do this to someone else when he hated when it was done to him?

Caity let out a kind of screech in order to catch herself. She obviously needed to stop thinking about Jack. She let out a deep sigh and buried her head in her pillows. Damn, the phone was ringing again. It's obviously what woke her from her great dream. She reached over and looked at the call display, unknown number, unknown name. Great, it better not be Jack because she couldn't handle his games right now. Maybe she should let it go to the answering machine. Oh well, she knew it would drive her nuts to know who it was, so she picked it up. "Hello" she said in an irritated voice. "Well, it sounds like you didn't sleep much, grumpy today? Stew said. "Who is this? Caity asked feeling like the voice was familiar but she just couldn't place it.

"Women, oh how soon they forget you! They make you sit out in the dark for hours freezing in your car following their boyfriend around and the first sight of morning light and you're history." Stew said in a laughing and teasing voice. He was feeling cheery and it resonated in his voice. Caity paused. "Oh Stew; I'm sorry, I didn't recognize your voice. Sorry, and I was sound asleep when the phone rang."

Caity and Stew talked on the phone for over half an hour before they decided on a place to meet, which ended up being for lunch instead of coffee. Stew admitted to being a hamburger junkie and so he picked one of his little mom and pop greasy spoons that made the best hamburgers and fries in the city. Caity had to admit she'd been craving junk food for months but stuck to weight watchers as much as possible. She was always trying to lose that extra ten pounds that hung on her hips these days. Seemed like after you hit forty your hips seemed to drop and expand somehow. It seemed like fun to break her dull drum diet and meet Stew at what was sure to be a great food place.

The Fire Pit as it was called was all a bustle as Caity walked in. Looking around to see if Stew had gotten there first, she was relieved when she saw him. Pausing for a second, Caity was surprised at how attractive he really was. Stew had a smile on his face grinning from ear to ear like a little boy in front of a toy shop and he looked like he had just showered and was a little damp. As she got closer to him in the line Caity could smell his cologne. Polo; oh but it smelt so much better on Stew than in the bottle. Strange she thought, Jack wore Polo too! Not many men did these days but to Caity it seemed like both men had the same smell and it was like a rush of emotion swept over her the closer she got. They had to wait in line and put their orders in and while they waited they chatted about the weather, the restaurant, and nothing that had any real meaning. Stew ordered the Hungry Man Size and all the fixings. He tried to talk Caity into it but she knew that was way too much food for her so she ordered their normal special with fries and went to find a table while Stew paid. He had insisted on it; which really impressed Caity.

Funny, Caity realized that Jack had never treated her to anything, except one awful meal at some chicken place. That night he was supposed to be eating out with her to put a plan together to make things easier to spend time together and all Caity could remember of the meal was that he was mean, insulting and nasty. He had even picked on her for not finishing her meal and that he had paid for it with his hard-earned money. That dinner lasted only an hour instead of the evening they had planned to spend together and after Jack had dropped her off at her house Caity once again had felt cheated and beaten.

"Penny for your thoughts" Stew said as he sat down. He was carrying a tray of what seemed to be a mountain of the greasiest and best smelling food Caity had ever seen or smelt. "Unfortunately, something just triggered a brief memory of a time I spent with Jack and it over took me for a moment. Sorry!" Caity held back the water in her eyes as she spoke and Stew just pretended not to notice.

"Well, those memories will fade with time, I promise. They'll get easier to forget and before you know it you'll wonder what you ever saw in the guy. Right?" Stew was persistent in trying to get an agreement from Caity but all he got was a resistant nod of the head.

They sat there in their corner booth looking out on the street, not saying much the next half-hour as they chomped into their food and drinks. They kept up a semi casual conversation about a lot of nothings. Stew talked about his favorite things, his boat that he loved to take out when he was off, and the fact that summer was his favorite time of year. Caity talked about feelings. She was feeling lost, and very down; but mostly sad like she was at a continuous funeral or something. The thing that she didn't understand most was why Jack had such a hold on her heart. No man had ever affected her life like that and she knew no man in the future ever would. Stew knew that women were cut from a different cloth than guys; he'd learnt that growing up with his very emotional and feeling sister. Guys shut down their emotions, and ignored them. Women on the other had had to talk about them, analyze them, re-talk about them, figure them out, adjust them and reanalyze them again. To Stew is seemed like women had boundless energy when it came to feelings and expressions and although he spent a great deal of time around emotional women in his business, he still hadn't quite understood what all the fuss was about.

Sitting there munching on the last of his monster hamburger, he looked up to see a blob of mayonnaise stuck to the tip of Caity's nose. She had been giggling at some joke he had made and hadn't noticed that her nose dipped into her bun, and now on the very tip of it was a soft dabble of the white stuff. Stew knew that Caity was one of those women that had no clue of how adorable or gorgeous they were.

The type that was so hard on themselves they never realized the real impact they had on guys. Like right now for instance, he was sitting there fascinated with that dabble of mayonnaise and all he wanted to do was lean forward and lick it off. God that would be exciting, and then lean in a little more and just taste what her lips tasted of. Burger of course, but something more inviting; passion. Caity wore passion like most wear an old T-shirt. She didn't even realize how sexy she was sitting there in her pile of mess, burger drippings all over, fries scattered in her mounds of ketchup and licking each finger every time it had something foreign stuck to it.

"Are you O.K. Stew? You seemed to be lost in some deep thoughts." Caity's voice brought Stew back to reality and he had to think quick or she'd probably bolt from him like a scared rabbit. "Ya, Ya I'm fine. I was just thinking that we should go have a coffee up the street after lunch. I just realized it's way too noisy in here to talk in depth about all the things I need to cover. I sure needed this boost of junk food; so how's your burger?" Stew was trying to buy a little time to try figure out how to get the mayonnaise off Caity's nose when before he realized what he was doing, he reached over with his napkin and wiped it off almost as a parent would do with their child. Caity sat back and giggled. "Was I wearing my lunch?" Stew smiled, nodded back and all he could come up with was, "Yap."

They sat at the Fire Pit for over an hour, lunch had been fun. At Stew's suggestion they left Caity's car at the Pit and drove for coffee in his car. Caity felt the seats just hug her as she got in. She'd seen these BMW's on the road before but had never sat in one. Now this was a sports car! Hmm and he even drove standard. It was something that always impressed Caity, when a guy drove a standard shift car. It seemed like a silly little thing but she always saw it as very masculine. Strangely enough, that's all Caity had ever driven. Every car she had ever owned was a standard and to her it was more interesting to drive than some automatic boring thing. She snuggled closely into the glove leather seats and looked sideways over at Stew. Caity sat there just thinking, she was fascinated how sweet he was for a private detective. She had always pictured those guys to be somewhat like Kojak or Columbo or something.

Realizing she was staring she quickly turned her head to look out the window, but everything about Stew was in her mind, right down to that great smell. His cologne filled Caity's mind with memories that she cherished, and a new little something extra. Caity realized that Stew was the first guy that had actually caught her attention enough for her to stop thinking about Jack, since she'd first fallen in love with him. She'd actually stopped thinking about Jack through lunch and that fact was huge! Normally Jack was in her heart and mind twenty-four hours a day, but today, Stew was fun to be with. He'd made her laugh and best of all he treated her as if she was special. Thinking back, Jack was never really fun to be with or hardly ever make her laugh, except on their very first weekend together. Other than the fact that Jack had treated her poorly, the truth was that he had never ever treated her well either. Everything with Jack had always been strained and difficult as if Caity was the devil and Jack was trying to win against him.

Caity was brought back to the real world as she felt Stew pull the car into a parking spot at the coffeehouse. She should have known, he'd pick Starbucks! To Caity, Starbucks was a status thing that people with a certain income always went to because it was the thing to do. Actually, she'd never had a coffee there that she didn't have to water down, but she wouldn't tell him that. She'd just order like she did with her other friends that frequented the place.

Starbucks was unusually deserted for a Saturday afternoon, especially since the bookstore always brought the crowds in. Caity liked it that way, it was probably the first time she'd come here and been able to sit in the big old teddy bear chairs by the window. While they sat having their coffee, she gave Stew a lot of information that she thought might help. Jack's telephone numbers, including Jane's, his brothers, father, and a few people she knew of at his work. She told him the name of Jack's Psychologist and which Catholic parish he belonged to. Caity realized when she was speaking that in reality she really didn't know a lot about Jack. That besides the times they had spent together, she didn't know where he went on weekends when he had the kids, where he spent most of his time when he didn't, and the things he liked to do and all kinds of things like that. In fact, Caity felt a huge knot build up in her stomach while she was filling Stew in on what she knew, because it made her realize just how little she knew about him.

The knot grew tighter with every passing minute until it tightened in her lungs. Caity was breathing really poorly when Stew interrupted her and told her she sounded like she needed to take her asthma medicine. She did, and although it cleared up the breathing right a way, it did nothing for the sick feeling she had inside her. Maybe she was in love with a fake person. Maybe Jack was someone who really didn't exist, a person he had created for just for Caity and him. All she could think about was that she just needed to know some things about Jack including what the truth was as to why he couldn't spend normal times with her.

Caity desperately held back the tears when she told Stew about how important it was to find out if there was indeed another woman. Stew leaned forward and was holding her hand to comfort her. He knew that her heart was breaking with every fear she expressed. Caity felt weird. Here she was sitting with a total stranger and it was a better afternoon and more comfortable than the last five or six times she had been with Jack. Suddenly she felt like she'd been the worlds greatest idiot the last two years and all she wanted now was to find out the truth and confront Jack with it. To be able to set her self free of the memories. What if all the church and guilt stuff was true? Or what was it about the other woman that was better than Caity?, Or worse yet, why did Jack need Caity and another woman?

Stew stopped Caity and all her ramblings and told her he would do his best to find out as soon as possible. He asked if she knew where Jack would be today, and since it was a kids' weekend Caity only knew one thing. Wherever Jack was, he'd be with his girls. Or at least that's what he always said he'd be doing.

Stew drove Caity back to her car just past three thirty. He had to admit it may have been a fact finding mission, but he couldn't remember when he'd had a better time just being with someone. No use thinking about it, after all the things they talked about today it was clear that Caity wouldn't be good for anyone else for a long time. He was looking in his rear view mirror as he pulled away. She got into her little economy car, a metallic beige Hyundai. All Stew could think about was how a woman that beautiful and that intelligent could have been taken by this arrogant idiot. This guy was obviously a player and a complete jerk. Oh, Stew's blood just boiled every time he thought of it. Right, well no use dwelling on it, if he hurried he could plant himself in church just in time for Saturday evening mass. He'd look up the address on his cell phone internet and get moving. He wanted to get a good seat in the back, so he could observe and maybe use his mini camera to take a few shots. After all, he never knew what he'd come across so it was best the he was always prepared.

An hour later, Stew was outside St. Anne's Roman Catholic Parish, just five minutes from Jack's house and according to the internet about the same distance from Jane's. Interesting, let's see, what was the term Caity used, ah yes, a divorce that just keeps on going like a marriage. Stew didn't know what she meant exactly but he figured it had to do with the close proximity of the living arrangements.

Stew walked in, blessed himself appropriately with the holy water and found a peaceful spot in the centre of the very last row near the exit. Boy, he hadn't been to church since his mom made him go in high school. He couldn't remember what he'd done just that she wanted to save his soul, sure hope it helped because he hadn't been back since. Strangely enough, Stew was pretty spiritual, just not the type to talk about it, or for that matter go to church. Even Maggy thought he was a devout atheist, but what people thought didn't count. It's what was in your heart that mattered.

At just fifteen minutes to five, people started heading in for the five o'clock mass. Typical types, Stew could picture that half of them were good for one hour a week and the rest of the week you could count on them being hypocrites. That's why he had always hated church. The false niceness, kind of like Christmas, and then get them out of church and you couldn't trust them with your dog. Stew stopped day dreaming when he saw Jack walk in. He was dressed in jeans of all things. He had the two little girls with him. Stew checked his notes for their names and jotted down a description of each. What surprised Stew the most was that they were with some woman. That couldn't be Jane, could it? Was this guy nuts?! Wife cheats on you twice, once after you take her back, you get a separation and you somehow forget the divorce. But worst yet, then you go to church with her every week, and sit with her and the kids and pretend you are one big happy family. I don't think so! That would be absolutely nuts!! This must be the other woman that Caity was worried about. Obviously, Jack hung on to her because she was Catholic and Caity wasn't. Oh brother, what a loser! Well, this coming to church thing may have paid off. He might just have this case solved tonight. Only problem was, Stew wanted more time with Caity so that was going to be a real downer. Maybe he wouldn't tell her for a week or so and still meet her and stuff. Sitting there, totally captivated by his four subjects, he realized that he'd have to play it by ear.

The mass was well under way when Stew realized he was so busy watching these four that he was forgetting to get up and down and kneel in the parts he was supposed to. He snapped a couple of shots with his mini cam, Jack on one side the two girls in the middle and the woman on the other side of the girls. How cozy. All Stew could think about was that if this wasn't another woman and it was Jack's ex-wife, how sick for the two girls. I mean really. To pretend to have a normal church life after all they've been through, who would believe it? Stew couldn't wait for mass to be over and to follow them out. Hopefully he'd get a lot of info tonight that he could use. He didn't have any other cases to work on, and Maggy had called him twice today and left messages hoping for some kind of news. In the depths of his thoughts he could hear Father O'Malley wrapping things up. As he suddenly slipped outside and got into his car so he could be unnoticed and ready for the chase at least. Life was going to get interesting. Just as he turned on the engine, and he saw Jack the girls walk out of the church with that woman. Putting the car in gear, Stew decided it was time get to work.

Stew sat there in amazement as Jack got into his car with the girls and this woman got into another car parked just next to them. He called his contact at the cop shop, ran the plates and wasn't shocked to find out they belonged to Jane Fraser, Jack's ex-wife. His buddy even emailed a copy of her license with picture. Sure enough the guy was one sick puppy.

He put his car in gear and followed Jack and the girls back to Jack's house, watched them get out, go in and waited about an hour while he heard them in the back yard playing. As he realized nothing interesting was happening he decided to head to Jane's house for a few hours and check things out. He'd come back later and see if the situation changed. Either way, he probably would have better luck with this guy on a weekend when he didn't have the girls.

Chapter 10

Three days went by and it was already Wednesday morning. Stew's phone was ringing. God it was seven in the morning, who in the world would be calling him at this time. He'd gone to bed at three last night after staking out a number of locations. This case was getting so interesting that Stew was hooked; he was like an info addict and was becoming worse than Caity with wanting to know the truth about this whole sordid story.

Reaching over he grabbed the phone and found out it was Maggy. Stew couldn't believe it, that damn Taurus wasn't going to start for her again this morning. Shaking his head in disgust he couldn't believe it, especially since he'd just finished doing a tone of work on the damn thing. Rolling out of bed he promised to pick her up in half an hour and get her to work on time.

Driving over to Maggy's, Stew decided he would take her to buy a new car tonight. He'd promise not to spend too much money, but this time he wouldn't take no for an answer. Maybe something like that little compact that Caity had. He was sure he could convince her this time. He'd use the excuse of her safety and the fact that she was the only sister he had. He certainly could afford it, and it would make him feel better to know that the boys and her would be safe driving around in a new car.

Maggy was waiting on her front stoop and was so happy to see Stew pull up. She was over booked today, swamped with a group meeting in the morning and appointments back to back in the afternoon. All she could think of was that she needed to get to work really early so she could prep for her day. Thankfully she could always count on her brother. "Thanks a million Stewy," she said as she got in. Making herself comfy in the front seat, Maggy adjusted everything including the temperature. She loved being pampered and with this morning's frustration she needed this. "So, can I ask how you are doing on Caity's case?" Pausing and looking over trying to read Stew's facial expression. But there was nothing there to read, which was normal. Stew knew how to hide what he was really thinking, a skill he developed in his job. He was so different now than when he was a young boy.

Stew stopped as the light turned red and looked straight on at Maggy. "You know Sis; this is one of the toughest cases I've had in a long time." He threw his eyes in the air and continued. "Did you know that this Jack guy goes to church more than just Saturdays, he went Sunday night after he dropped the girls at his ex-wife's house, and then he went again Tuesday night! Not only that, he's there for hours. What in the hell is this guy doing, becoming a priest or something?" Stew asked Maggy as if he actually believed she had the answers.

Maggy paused, thinking about what he'd said as the car continued toward her work. She looked at Stew and said, "I'm sorry Stew, I really believed that this was an open an shut thing, that in one or two days you would prove he's just some player and cheater and then Caity could let go of this image she has of him. This wonderful loving mixed up, screwed up guy image that can only be in some far-fetched movie. I mean, let's face it Stew, what man is so religious that he is willing to give up sex for life and claim he has to remain celibate. For God's sake even Priests these days are having sex everywhere". Stew was shocked hearing his sister talk that way. Of all people, Maggy had always been the religious one in the family, so it shocked him to hear her slander the priests that way.

"Maggy, I'm actually shocked," Stew said with a deep sigh. "What's happened to you? You used to be so religious, how can you even talk that way?" Stew needed to know. For some unknown reason this was suddenly so important to him that he pulled the car over to a side street and stopped. He put the car in park and leaned sideways waiting for her answer. "Well, the truth is I haven't been to Church in eight months. I was volunteering and worked with quite a few of the families of the abused boys and once I went through all that I just couldn't bring myself to go back. You know Stew, I've changed. I have my relationship with God now, directly. Not through some man that calls himself a priest and uses that trust to hurt innocent children". Maggy was teary, "Stew you wouldn't believe how awful everything I found out was." She blew her nose and sat there hurting from the inside. This was the first time she ever told anyone about this. She kept it bottled up inside her and it ate at her daily. At the time she questioned her whole existence and the roots on which she was raised. Maggy was hurting inside so deeply that Stew finally understood why she was so adamant at helping Caity. By helping her friend, Maggy was trying to actually heal her own wounds.

Stew sat there holding his sister while she cried into his shoulder. They must have sat there for half and hour before they finished talking about a few of the key things. He had somehow even managed to convince her to let him buy her a car tonight. The things he learned when he least expected to. Here Stew thought Maggy was so held together, that she had everything in her life under control. Now he knew that her image was just a façade, and the pillar of strength that he knew as his sister was just as vulnerable as the rest of them. He was just seven years older than her but today he felt more of a father figure than an older brother. Their parents had died over ten years ago in a freak snow storm on the highway. From that day onward they had clung to each other emotionally. Sadly Stew just realized that over the past few years with life being so busy, he hadn't been there for his sister like he should have been.

Maggy looked up from his shoulder and asked to use his cell phone. Still leaning on his shoulder she called in sick, which was something that even shocked her co-workers. Maggy always went to work even if she was sick as a dog or when the weather really should have stopped her.

Listening, Stew heard her have a colleague take over her group session in the morning and had one of the secretaries cancel all her afternoon sessions including one with Caity. She hung up with the office then called Caity directly, leaving her a message after one of her staff said she was tied up in the T.V. studio in production and couldn't be disturbed till after ten. Maggy leaned back into her side of the car and asked Stew if he felt like having breakfast somewhere; her treat.

After deciding on Appleby's one of Maggy's all time favorites, he put the car in drive and headed down to Mavis Road.

They drove in very deep silence, listening to the car engine the whole way. Neither of them spoke but were entranced deep in their thoughts of the brief conversation they had already had that morning. Once they were at a nice little booth off to one side of the busy restaurant, their coffees in front of them and their hearty breakfast ordered, Stew decided it was time to talk about things. All he had to do was start her off and away she went. Maggy told him horrid details of the cases she had worked on the last few months. She went on about the great lengths the church took to hide it all the awful details by trying to pay off the families. It was right out of the typical reports you heard about on the evening news. Most of all, he heard how it affected his sister, deep inside her heart. She questioned her faith, the trust she had, her core beliefs; everything!

She was embarrassed about the fact that she had been such a blind follower for so long not believing half of the stories that she had heard until she had actually had to work with the boys and their families. Maggy told Stew how these few were just the tip of the iceberg, and after researching a lot on her own, she found the numbers staggering. Not to mention the long term affects that were unbelievable. One of the families that she worked with actually confessed that the father had been abused by a priest when he was young and that when it had happened to his son he nearly went out of his mind. He'd actually gone to his parish and beaten the pulp out of the priest and had been charged with assault. The Catholic Church actually dropped the charges hoping to bury the case like they had with all the others. Maggy went on and said it wasn't natural for men to remain celibate and that was proof enough for her. She'd become nervous about her own parish priest so she couldn't even attend church anymore. She was especially worried about her own two boys whom she had grilled until she was sure that nothing had ever happened to them. By the time Maggy finished talking; her eggs were half eaten and Stew was on a second helping that he had ordered.

Maggy sat there just staring at Stew now who had the most shocked look on his face. It was almost as if all this was suddenly just too much for him. So that's why when Caity approached Maggy about this "Catholic Cult" theory and betrayal; Maggy got so caught up in it. For Maggy it was personal somehow. That's why she contacted Stew that day. She was searching for a peace that Stew knew she would probably never find after all of this.

"Wow, and I don't know what to say Maggy, except, how come you never told me about all this shit till now?" Stew rubbed his two hands through his hair feeling so totally taken aback and so overwhelmed. "Well, in some ways I couldn't talk about it for the longest time, and then I thought who in the world would believe me if I gave them all these details. The truth is part of me just wanted to tune it all out and pretend it was all gone." She let out a deep sigh, stuffing cold egg and toast into her mouth as if trying to find relief through her breakfast. "So, now you know why Caity's case caught me in the gut. I don't know what the tie in to the church is, if any; but my gut feeling tells me there is way more here than guilt and another woman. I just haven't been able to put all the pieces together."

Stew was finishing his fifth cup of coffee, some of the best he had in a while. He wanted to say something meaningful to Maggy, but he knew he'd have to take it all in for a while and think about it before he could say anything about it.

"How about going car shopping after you're finished those eggs? The dealership is just down the street and I really need to do this for both you and me. What do you say? Do you wanna take some new fangled machine out for a spin?" Maggy nodded at Stew's wonderful generosity and she knew the two of them needed to talk about something other than the gruesome realities of life right now. Besides, she had finally realized this morning when the Taurus didn't start that she should have taken Stew up on his new car offer months ago. She was risking her life and the lives of her two boys in that wreck and she'd finally succumbed to admitting it while kicking the old beater with her best pair of high heels. What a relief it would be to drive a new car! No worries at least for a few years. Maggy knew she'd insist on the cheapest model with no extras because all she cared about was a reliable new car with good breaks and an engine. She wouldn't even care about the color. Stew could have the honors and she knew it would make him feel good if she asked him to pick it.

It didn't take them long to decide which one. Maggy loved Caity's little Hyundai Elantra. It was a roomy little thing with split back seats, air conditioning, a radio, and CD player for the boys. What else could a girl want? They were sitting looking at car colors when Stew looked over and asked her what her preference would be. Although Maggy absolutely loved red and she'd once had a red car, she'd gotten practical, that metallic beige that Caity had never showed the dirt and the girl said she hardly ever washed the thing. Besides, Maggy liked the way the car looked in that color, it gave it a little class for a mid size car. Stew loved the red also but with his cars he knew they were high maintenance for keeping clean, so he agreed with Maggy's color choice. Although Maggy thought she was getting the stripped down model, Stew ordered the one with all the extras including the hatch back. It would come in handy when carrying all the boys sports equipment and for Maggy's penchant of hitting garage sales on Saturdays.

Within a few minutes Stew had also managed to pay a bit extra to have the car prepped and ready for six that night, a surprise for Maggy. He knew she needed one, and he felt great about all this. It made him feel like Santa Clause and he couldn't stop. The last thing he did was call his insurance and pre-pay three years of insurance for her. Now he could breathe. He had felt a little disconnected from his sister the last year and today he felt like they were right back where they aught to be. Maggy might be slightly mad at him for splurging but he knew she'd be relieved at the lack of worries.

Maggy had been on the phone with Caity while Stew had set up all this extra stuff. Luckily, Maggy's cell phone conveniently only had a signal on the other side of the dealership. Thank God they'd had a lot to talk about because it bought him just the amount of time he had needed.

Wandering over to where Stew was sitting with the sales man, Maggy plopped down in the adjacent chair and tapping her brother on his shoulder looked right at the guy and said, "Isn't he just the world's best brother?" Maggy leaned on Stew's shoulder just as the sales man answered with a "You bet miss! The car will be ready at six as ordered so when you get back just come see me to sign the final papers and you'll be driving off with your new wheels within a half hour of that." Grinning from ear to ear, and having made quite the commission for having everything done so quickly he was off to finish the paperwork and leave these two alone to talk, so Stew could tell her about the insurance and the upgrades.

"Wow!" was all Maggy could hear herself say and then she was totally speechless. Watery tears of gratefulness built up in her eyes until she caught her breath again. "What say we get out of here and have a few laughs before six?" Stew said as he prodded her elbow to stand up the rest of her body. Maggy never said a word, she just followed him out to his car got in and sat down in total appreciation of her brother. Even though he had the money to burn, he didn't have to do this today, and her heart was filled with gratitude and joy that she hadn't felt in a very long time.

Next Stew took her to Canadian Tire, a store that specialized in everything for cars and home and he knew it would have the little extra's she was hoping for. He insisted on buying her a few fun things for her new car. He knew Maggy had a penchant for fun things so he got her extra cup holders for the boys. He also got her those Disney character covers for all four head rests, neat Disney rubber mats for the front and back to protect the new car's carpets, a trunk organizer and a compass for her dash. He got her a cell phone holder and some other silly things that she had picked out in jest. All in all it was a fun hour and brought them to the time where they should really grab another bite to eat. Since food was always super important to Stew, he dragged her to yet another of his favorite jaunts. The "Chicken Hut" as Stew called it. Their specialty was roasted chicken and ribs with mounds of fries. Stew never ate healthy until he was home, and on the road he had developed a lot of favorite food stops. Of course the fact that he worked out almost daily helped with his eating habits and Maggy joked about how lucky he was not to gain weight eating all of this stuff.

In no time at all six o'clock rolled around, Maggy got her new car and was beaming as she drove off in the direction of home and picking up the boys at their respective friends homes. She was like a new woman when he left her, and all in all Stew had to admit that this was one of the best days he could remember in years. Suddenly he was enjoying the money he had worked so hard to accumulate. It had never brought him happiness like this before and he reveled in the moment.

As he drove home to shower and decide what he would do with Caity's case tonight, if anything; Stew was glad he hadn't told Maggy about certain things he had discovered so far. It would have been too upsetting and in fact it may have ruined their great day. To Stew, this was one of his best ever!

He'd take a long hot shower, give himself the night off and start again in the morning. Right now he just seemed to really need a touch of absolutely normal life. Home, bath and a good TV show. Maybe he'd even rent a movie on the way home. And if that wasn't normal he didn't know what was.

Pulling into his driveway after the iron gates opened, Stew got that familiar shiver down his spine again. It figured; someone was watching him; he was sure of it, But from where? Oh Boy, this was getting complicated because as he looked around Stew saw Jack across the street, sitting in his car, just watching him. Knowing full well the best action to take was to ignore him for now. Stew slowly walked into his house and closed the front door behind him.

Seconds later, from a side window, he watched him drive off and let out a sigh of total relief. Stew knew he wasn't ready for this angle, and he hated someone doing to him what he did to others. Stew was angry at himself. Somehow he hadn't been careful enough when staking him out one of the past nights. Obviously this jerk followed him home and was now trying to figure out who he was, if he didn't know already. Bummers! He couldn't believe it. This was the first time he had ever had this happen and he was so frustrated he kept rubbing his hands through his scalp as if that would make it all better.

Well, like those old movies said. "Damn the torpedoes, full speed ahead." Somehow he'd have to turn this around to his advantage. But how! Well he'd leave it for tonight. He was suddenly too aggravated. Feeling way too tired; all he needed was a hot shower and bed. He'd think better in the morning on a good night's sleep.

Half hour later, Stew lay in bed, refreshed from the steam and the soap. Sleep evaded him like the plague and all he could do was lie there and think of Caity. He pictured her giggling like she did when she thought she was funny. He could see her with tears in her eyes when she talked to him about Jack. But worst of all, Stew saw something he recognized in her that reflected himself. It was a deep kind of loneliness that comes from a longing of sharing your life with someone and never succeeding, and that; Stew couldn't get out of his mind. It was four in the morning before he finally passed out, and just three hours from when the alarm would go off. Stew would be aggravated and sleep deprived again tomorrow, something he had only since discovered since he had met Caity. Something had to give and give soon!

The rhythm of Stew's snoring filled the air while in his dreams he dreamed of only one thing, and one thing alone. Caity!

Chapter 11

It was Saturday morning just after ten and Caity was sitting at her dining room table wondering what was happening out there as she gazed out the big picture window. It had been just over two weeks since Stew got involved in the case and almost as long since she'd seen or heard from him. She'd seen Maggy four times a week and talked to her on the phone almost every night. They had become great friends now and her bond with Maggy was no longer patient client but a kind of kindred spirits thing with two people needing each other for completely different reasons. Maggy kept telling her to be patient, that Stew needed time and would never tell them anything until he was sure it was the whole truth. Caity grew increasingly impatient as the days wore on, and it was taking a toll on her spirit, and health. Work was harder with every passing day because it was tougher and tougher to concentrate and worst of all it seemed impossible to be really creative. It had gotten to the point where even her boss had noticed now and gave her most of next week off even though it was a short week, with Easter Monday just two days away.

Caity sighed such a deep sigh it echoed throughout her apartment. Easter Sunday was tomorrow. She let out another deep sigh and shook her head. Just how many holidays had Jack already ruined for her anyway. She was doodling on the Saturday paper, counting tomorrow would be, oh my God! Twelve if you counted birthdays, but worse yet, counting other occasions, Caity got up to twenty and decided she didn't want to really know anyway. The fact was that if she was really honest with herself she would have to admit that Jack really wasn't a blessing in her life at all. He was more like the worst thing that ever happened to her. Sighing for the tenth time in as many minutes, Caity came to the full realization that the truth was, she had really been cursed when Jack came into her life. He'd given her only tidbits of time where everything was wonderful and the rest of it was all a rollercoaster from hell. Except on a rollercoaster you know when the ride is going to end, with Jack it was a never ending plethora of horror.

The phone rang and Caity pounced on it without looking who it was but for some absolutely crazy reason, wishing it was Jack. It wasn't, of course it wouldn't be. How could it? They hadn't talked since they had that whopper fight just before Maggy introduced her to Stew, and Caity knew that Jack never made up until after the holiday was over. That way, he could continue to keep her a secret from his family, the girls, his ex-wife and of all things Caity wondered about his sick sister –in –law. According to Jack, she was always chasing him even though she was divorced from his sleaze-bag brother. Throwing her head back and letting out yet another heavy sigh, Caity forced herself to focus on the conversation that was happening on the phone. While her Mom had spent a great deal of time telling her all the latest about the family, Caity had been off in another world of thought.

Thank-God her Mom hadn't noticed yet, but she'd have to focus if she was going to catch up and get right in there. After a half hour of "uh-huhs" and a lot of "your kidding," Caity hung up the phone and got dressed. She'd promised to spend the day shopping with Mom and have dinner at her parents, and Caity had to admit she felt like she'd been rescued from herself. She and her Mom were kind of like best friends with an age gap, and her family was always a great relief from reality. Grateful that her mother had managed to keep Caity's secret about what was happening with Jack so that it wouldn't be an evening of reminders, with family members thoughtlessly asking about it. Whipping out the door, Caity had a slight spring in her step hoping that with the holiday almost over, she might find out what she needed to know by next week or the end of it at least.

Meanwhile, Stew spent most of Saturday cleaning up the mess of information he'd been gathering. He had to admit he was good at what he did. He'd managed to be-friend the receptionist at Jack's work and head on in there when Jack would be out of the office for two days. He'd bought her a fabulous lunch and ended up meeting quite a few of Jack's colleagues and his secretary. The minute they'd heard that Stew was a dear old friend of Jack's, planning a surprise for his birthday, they obliged him with lots of info on Jack and a ton of insights. Of course, they got to know Stew as Fred, and Fred needed everything to be kept secret till the big surprise bash. Stew tried to find out if Jack was dating someone from work and surprisingly enough, he wasn't just dating one of the girls but had actually gone out on first dates with quite a few of them.

What a jerk, Stew thought of Caity and how hard this would hit her. Apparently it had all been going on the last few years while he had Caity going on the church celibacy thing. They had all been one date only, never getting to see him again. He always took them to rather posh restaurants and parties, and yet Jack had told Caity that he wasn't allowed to date. He used the excuse that his religion wouldn't let him get on with his life. Worse yet, Jack had never taken Caity out anywhere at all and the sad truth was they always got together at his house on a Saturday night. Jack would make her dinner and the rest was history. Sadder still, Stew thought was the fact that he had talked about Caity to all of these women. He had described her as the girl he needed to end up with. That Caity was the right type of girl for him. Unfortunately, it appeared to be that Jack was attracted to the type that Stew fondly described as "bitches." They were the type that controlled you. The type that you had to do everything for; everything their way, buy them a ton of stuff and take them to expensive places. The exact opposite to what Stew knew Caity was.

Strangely enough, Jack ex-wife fit the bill perfectly; it's only a wonder as to why it didn't work out. Stew found out that Jack had left a trail of women behind him that were just like Jane. Each woman he had dated was exactly the same. Greedy for what Jack would buy them and where he would take them, they were definitely not worth wiping your feet on let alone that they were all were totally unfaithful to him. He appeared to always be totally drawn to that type of woman. This was where it was strange. Caity was the exact opposite to anything Jack had ever dated. It probably scared the life out of him to the point that he had decided to cheat on her before she would do it to him; just like the others had in the past. Stew figured Jack had guilt, this time because he knew Caity wasn't like that, nor would she ever be. Jack had repeatedly lied to Caity about there being no one else, and in Stew's mind, he was just a complete and total idiot.

Looking at his watch, Stew couldn't believe that he'd spent the entire day going through all his notes and evidence. He hadn't been able to find out if Jack had slept with any of these so called dates, but he knew Caity would see it as cheating anyway. Actually, strangely enough, Stew himself thought of all of it as cheating anyway. Although he had been quite the ladies' man over the years. Stew had principles and morals, and he'd only ever dated one at a time. He always felt that it wasn't fair to anyone, especially if you were sleeping with them. Stew sighed, the worst part about all this was that Jack had known the way Caity saw things and still went out of his way to do all this and hurt her. Stew's blood was boiling. He wished he could just walk up to this ass hole and pound the crap out of him.

Throwing himself on his big brown "huggy" sofa, Stew threw his head back, plopped his long legs up onto the matching ottoman and flung his arms over his head and onto the back of his neck to think. How in the world was he going to tell Caity everything he'd found out so far? The worst thing was that the women weren't the worst of what Stew found out.

He closed his eyes enjoying the comfort of his sofa. This couch was one of the best purchases he had ever made, and when ever he came into the den, Stew always appreciated his big old fluffy teddy bear couch. It was the kind with the big high back with built in puffy pillows, "huggy" big fluffy arms and the silkiest pillows on the seat anyone could ever find. The best part was that he'd ordered this model in a soft velvety suede material that made you feel cuddled every time you sat in it. Stew laughed to himself softly, he was thinking of how Maggy absolutely hated this thing. She'd sit down and simultaneously always fall back and fidget and try to fight it and sit up straight in the darn thing. Maggy always complained that the couch was suffocating her, so he'd gone out and purchased other harder single chairs in the same material just so when she visited she could sit and relax when they came in here to chat.

Stew hated what was ahead for next week. He'd tell Maggy what he found out first and use her expertise to find the right wording to tell Caity. Relaxed and in a mindless consumed manner, Stew forgot all about Emma being there, until she'd had just about enough of his ignoring her. Emma had been with Stew since she was a baby. She'd been two months old when he adopted her and was all the family Stew had thought he had needed. Emma had a graceful softness about her that made very little noise when she roamed around the house until she was actually right into your face. She stood over Stew front paws on the sofa and back paws stretching over the floor. Emma was a six year old Bouvier des Flandres. It was the type of dog that was from Belgium or someplace like that where they managed cattle of all things. Stew giggled at the thought. He remembered how the breeder thought Emma was perfect for him because he came across like such a hard headed bull.

A big black wooly dog with the softest dark eyes Stew had ever seen. She had the best disposition for patience and acted like a puppy when it came to needing attention. Emma loved Stew's cologne and made no bones in hiding it. Every time she'd hear him snuggle into this couch it was like her cue to come up to him and place her nose in his neck and make her presence known. Stew loved the attention so much that he'd stayed with the same cologne since he'd picked her up that day. Something about Polo that made this dog love him. Maybe it was just familiar stuff, but from what he was told by women, Polo smelt amazing on him and the dog certainly agreed.

While he was lost in his play with Emma, acknowledging her entrance, rubbing her back and patting her head, Stew found himself relaxing for the first time all day. Emma had a way of making his life less complicated. Dogs were simple creatures. All they needed was love, affection, and lots of food a day. Emma of course, had the added luxury of a built in doggy door for when she needed to dispense with the days giving's. Stew was laughing out loud as he and Emma played on the couch. She threw herself lengthwise on the couch beside him throwing herself on her back, smacking him in the shoulder with one of her back paws as her cue for him to rub her belly. Dogs made life uncomplicated; they brought you back to the basics and out of the doldrums. While Stew was half paying attention to her, Emma whacked him in the shoulder again until he finally gave her all his attention and wrestled. It was just after eight as the two of them were in their peak wrestling mode when the doorbell rang and Emma jumped off the couch and bolted for the cherry wood front door, barking her deep throaty bark all the way to the door.

Once she got there, as trained, she sat straight up and went silent but only inches from where the lock met the door frame. A low and constant growl slowly emanated from her throat as it always did until Stew found out if it was friend or foe. In Emma's case, she wanted to know if it was the postman, for whom she had a serious and passionate dislike. Looking through the peaky hole, Stew was stunned to see none other than Father O'Malley himself.

He had to take a deep breath and put his thoughts together. He knelt down and looked at Emma. Some days she was his very best friend, confidant and best of all his counselor; and today was going to be no exception! He cupped her large black furry head in the palms of his hands, and looking deep into her big round dark eyes while he pressed his warm nose on her very cold black one, Stew took a deep breath, paused and said, "Emmm, I think it's gonna be a really long night girl. Sometimes I think I wish I was just a big ole dog". With that, Stew opened the door and greeted their unexpected guest.

Almost at the exact same moment just ten minutes down the road from Stew's place, Caity was also getting up to answer her door. As she walked toward the condo door she figured it was her neighbor from down the hall since no one buzzed her to get into the building. Debbie was a great neighbor, lots of fun and usually looking to sit and have a glass of wine on a night that she didn't have a date. As she peered through the peaky hole on the door, Caity's heart leapt through her throat. She actually had to take a second look because she couldn't believe her eyes. It couldn't be. It was; Jack! How was that possible?! Jack swore he could never come to her house because he said that if he came to her house the priest wouldn't give him forgiveness, because he actually came looking for it. He'd always said if she went to his house and they slept together apparently the Catholic priest would give him forgiveness when he went to confession.

As that whipped through her mind, Caity had a weird thought of how sick that actually was, and playing it through her mind just now it seemed a million times worse than when Jack actually first said it standing in front of his sink in the kitchen. There was a second knock at her door bringing Caity back to reality. As she opened it she could hear her heart pounding in her ears and the blood rush right to her face. There was a hint of excitement that she hadn't felt before. Did this mean that things would be different from now on and that they would have a normal relationship? As a million thoughts raced through her mind, she opened the door for Jack, not saying a word, but scared at what he would say and scared he wouldn't come in. In reality, Jack never understood the fear that constantly plagued her whenever it came to them. Jack paused, leaned forward and hugged her so hard she thought her ribs would break. As he hugged her, Jack pushed her forward, slipping her past the door so it could swing closed.

At that second while he locked the door behind him, he slipped his lips on hers and his tongue down her throat rendering her breathless. It took Caity quite a while to catch her breath and organize her thoughts as her knees went week with Jack's kisses. She threw her head back looking deep into his eyes and said, "What's happening Jack? Are you hear to tell me you can live a normal life now, and that you want to spend Easter Sunday with me and your family tomorrow?" "Well?" Jack threw his head back and then to look forward looking deeply into Caity's eyes.

"You are all I could think, I can't sleep or eat without you anymore! Caity, I know I can do it this time. Love me. Hold me. Tell me you still love me and need me". Jack took a deep breath and paused waiting for Caity to say something. " So? What are you thinking?" He asked as he pulled her closer rubbing her back in appreciation noticing that she was not wearing a bra under this great T-shirt. Caity looked up at him with tears welling in her eyes, the last two years had seemed to be in hell and she couldn't believe that things would finally be normal. Jack kissed away all of the doubts she may have had. He wasn't giving her any chance to think or reject him.

He'd brought wine and cheese and they sat cuddling on her couch while Jack told her how much he loved her. Without another thought, Caity and Jack ended up in bed just hours after he arrived. Cuddling afterward, Caity had her head resting on Jack's chest as he snored in his sleep as usual. Looking over at the clock it was one thirty in the morning and she suddenly was terrified of what tomorrow would hold. Knowing full well of all the times Jack had said he loved her, and then the day later broke up with her. Caity's heart beat in fear to the rhythm of his snoring. She said a little prayer asking God to finally let her have her happiness and fell asleep.

Less than fifteen minutes later, Jack woke her from a dead sleep dressing in a mad panic. She looked up at him and asked him where he was going. Caity couldn't believe it. He looked panicked and in a hurry and in just seconds he'd ruined the evening. "Where are you going? Why aren't you staying" she pressed him with her panicking words. "Caity, I can't do this. I just needed to be held tonight and knew you would take me back. I mean really, how did you expect me to have you over with my girls, my father who hates anyone that isn't Catholic, my brother and his ex-wife and my friends. How did you think that would even be possible? You knew that we were just two people in need tonight, like we have always been. Caity don't look at me like that. I can't stand it. I've told you before, I don't like hurting anyone and now you are trying to make me feel guilty." With that statement Jack headed for Caity's front door at a speed Caity could barely keep up with. Her tears were flowing so hard that she could barely see him leave.

Jack slammed the front door behind him and when she opened it she could see him half run-walking down the hall. Caity yelled after him not caring if she woke up the whole condominium, but Jack never looked back at her, not even as he waited for the elevator. He got on and never looked back as Caity heaved in pain and tears while she felt her lungs start to suffocate. She went back into her apartment, locked the door behind her and slid down along the door to the floor and face down on the cold ceramic tile. Caity heaved and cried and started choking in a massive asthma attack. She didn't care as she choked and made no effort to get up to get her medicine. She wanted to die and thought this asthma attack had come at just the right time.

Suddenly hearing the knock on the door behind her, she caught her breath, stood up in a panic assuming it was Jack coming back to apologize. She was now turning blue from her asthma and barely got the door open, only to find Debbie standing there in total concern.

Seconds later, Debbie pushed passed her and was dialing 911; Caity was blue and almost not breathing at all. Debbie realized she'd have to wait till the hospital to find out what had happened here, but somehow she knew deep down that it had to have something to do with Jack. The bastard did it again! Debbie wished she had some big male friends she could hire to beat the living crap out of that guy. As she went through her thoughts, she realized that Caity was really blue and now not breathing at all while she heard the emergency crew come racing down the hallway with equipment in hand. God, Debbie knew it was going to be a close call and a long night, and didn't know who to call, but knew this was serious.

Once they got the oxygen attached to Caity, and they hooked her up while on the phone with the hospital, the ambulance crew was told not to move her until she stabilized. It didn't look like she would but Debbie was praying, and in tears, fearful her next calls would be to Caity's family to inform them of the loss.

Forty five minutes later; after a lot of drugs, oxygen and intervenes, and a heated blanket that Debbie had ran and got from her place. Caity was beginning to breathe on her own and get some color back. She had been cold as ice and Debbie had never seen anything like it, apparently the paramedics hadn't either. In the meantime, Caity had partially lost consciousness and cried as they drugged her again. Once stabilized; they put her on the gurney and asked Debbie if she could get her personal things, lock up the condo, and then meet them down at the ambulance. Debbie quickly grabbed her purse and a jacket as they passed her place that was just two doors down from Caity's and made it to the elevator as it opened for all of them. She got in while one of the paramedics assured her that Caity was through the worst and that she should make it once they got her to the hospital.

It was only seven minutes to Credit Valley Hospital but to Debbie it felt like a lifetime and it took all her strength not to call Jack and tell him off, except that she didn't want him showing up at the hospital and upsetting Caity more. What a way to spend Easter! Well he did it; he ruined yet another holiday for her friend and she had witnessed all of them. Debbie couldn't help herself from thinking that the best thing to happen to Caity would be if this ass-hole would just drop dead! Then again, death was too good for the bastard. He needed to suffer for this. It was too bad there was no way to hurt the heartless excuse for a man.

On that note, the ambulance came to an abrupt stop in front of the hospital and the back doors were flung open as the gurney was being pulled out. Everything was happening so fast that Debbie's head was spinning, but worst of all she heard them say that Caity was unconscious. It was a hell night and it was only going to get worse. Debbie was going to have to go through Caity's purse and get phone numbers and start calling the family. Life was shit and Caity was in the middle of the stinking pile.

Chapter 12

It was past two when Father O'Malley got up to leave as Stew's phone rang. Just a minute father I'll walk you out, just let me get this. As he said hello, he felt his stomach lurch as he discovered Maggy was hysterical on the other end ranting about Caity. Hold on a minute Maggy, count to ten, catch your breath and I'll come back to the phone in minute. He walked the old priest to the door and said he would get back to him on their conversation. As he slowly closed the door, Stew saw the taxi cab that was out front waiting for Father O'Malley.

Stew ran back into the den and wondered what the hell was up with Maggy as he looked over to see that Emma was passed out by the fireplace, he said; " O.K. Maggy; what's up?"

Stew could hear himself yell out "WHAT"? Oh my God, I'll be right there." Caity was near death and all that anyone knew in the halls of the condo was that she was yelling at some guy named Jack at the top of her lungs in tears when it happened. Stew didn't wait to hear the details but wondered if Jack had beaten her or something.

He ran to his garage and got in the car. Thank God he lived just a few blocks down from the hospital; he couldn't have taken any more tonight. All this was helping him forget the hopeless disgusted feelings he'd had earlier as Father O'Malley had spilled his guts. That information seemed a million miles away as he sped to the hospital. All he could concentrate on was that he had a fist around his heart worrying about this woman that consumed his world. His thoughts were about how his heart was hurting at that very moment, and that Caity was the first woman that had ever gotten to his heart in this way. Ever! He was shaking with a kind of fear that he had never known in all his years and all the weird things he had ever seen and been through.

He ran into the emergency room looking frantically for Maggy who said she'd be waiting in the main waiting room. God, this was worse than the first night he had met Caity when he and Maggy had to rush her in because of an asthma attack. Did the guy finally kill her with his stupidity, or his sick life? Stew didn't know, but Maggy was pale, flanked by her two boys for support, she ran to Stew and threw her arms around him crying her eyes out. As Maggy cried in his arms, a blonde woman walked over to them, Stew wondered who this was and tapped Maggy. "Oh Stew, I want you to meet Caity's neighbor, Debbie. She brought her in after Caity woke up the whole floor yelling at Jack."

"Hi Debbie", he shook her hand as he said that; "It's nice meeting you! Listen, I'm a private detective, and is there anything about what happened tonight that you can tell me, that may help me with my case?" Stew sighed deeply, looking at the two women. If anything, Caity had good friends, and they cared. As his thoughts were processing the information, in ran Caity's sister and her parents in a hysterical loud mess. It was going to be a longer night filled with more nightmares as if Stew hadn't had enough already.

No one here knew about Stew's meeting with Father O'Malley and he felt like he was going to burst just thinking about the load he was carrying before he found out about Caity.

They all sat side by side in the waiting room hoping that a doctor would come out soon to say that someone could see Caity; Stew leaned over and whispered into Maggy's ear. He had to talk to her about important things.

At that exact second the doctor walked solemnly into the waiting room. He looked of death and bad news and the group went silent as he approached them about Caity. Stew's heart leapt into his throat and waited to catch his breath as the doctor spoke.

Looking right at the group, Dr. Green looked down at the floor first, took a breath and said, " Caity has had a very close call, we have had to revive her twice and put her on life support, but the good thing is that she is finally conscious and covered in baked blankets because her body is ice cold. I have to say, it will be touch and go for the next four to six hours but we really think the worst is over and that as long as she stays calm, I believe she'll make it and be fine. More importantly I need to know which one of you is Jack?" Stew stood up and quickly said, " None!" The jerk left her in this state earlier this evening." As Stew had spoken in anger, the doctor was grateful for what he heard and said, "Good because the last thing that this woman needs is to be upset. If anyone is going to go in that room tonight they have to make sure they don't upset her. So, how about the parents go in and we can consider other family and friends tomorrow once she stabilizes. O.K.?" Doctor Green said as he led Caity's parents to her and left the rest of them tense in the waiting room.

A few hours later, Caity's parents had persuaded everyone to go home while they waited it out. As Stew and Maggy walked out with the two boys straggling tiredly behind them, Stew looked down and said, "How about coming to sleep at my house, Maggy? That way you and the boys can be there if a call comes in." Maggy squeezed his hand and hugged him while she whispered, "We got to go home Stew, the Easter Bunny is coming in the morning and the boys would be disappointed if he missed your house." Stew smiled and hugged her; put her and the boys in the great new car he'd bought her and waved good night. He slowly went over to his car, got in and drove home in a numb silence that drained him. He thought back to when hours earlier he had closed the door behind Father O'Malley.

He leaned forward and pressed his forehead into the heavy wood of his front door, trying desperately to gather his thoughts. Little did Caity know when she used the term "Catholic Cult" that she could never have been closer to the truth? Why in the hell had he let Maggy talk him into this case? Why hadn't it been just about a cheating bastard? Why was it that for the first time, Stew's job affected him?

How is it that for the first time in his adult life, Stew was unable to separate himself from his job and his life? His head was pounding violently and he pounded the front door with his fists while he cringed at the thought of having to share all of his findings with anyone, let alone, his sister and Caity. Stew even thought of all the legal implications. There was just too much happening in his brain for him to put things together clearly. Once he was inside his house, Stew threw his head back, and started toward the den where Emma had fallen asleep hours ago while he and Father O'Malley were talking. The priest had had quite a few glasses of scotch and Stew had put away a whole bottle of red wine, but even that wasn't enough to dull the senses. It would take an army of wine to help Stew sleep, as the time on the clock read early morning. He couldn't believe it was almost six, how was that possible? What time did that lunatic get here anyway? Nine? Ten? How much did he offer to pay Stew again? The check sat there on his coffee table in the den just staring right at him.

He was numb and felt sick but couldn't bring himself to even stand up after he'd thrown himself into the couch. Emma jumped up to rest along side him as if she sensed his unrest. She moaned a bit and kept nudging him with her nose. The only thing Emma wanted was to get Stew to pay attention to her and head up to bed. She was tired of waiting for their nightly routine, and finally gave up and went upstairs to jump onto her side of the bed and pass out. The house was so quite that Stew could hear the doggy snoring sounds all the way to the den. Poor thing, she was used to her routine and today was anything but normal to say the least. Hearing all those sounds gave Stew a calming sense of normal. He grabbed a bottle of his favorite red wine out of his vintage rack, picked up his glass and after shutting all the lights off, climbed up the stairs to the sounds of his snoring pooch.

Two glasses of wine later and a whole lot of scalp rubbing, somehow Stew fell asleep with the lights on and the empty glass at his side.

Chapter 13

The room was eerily dark and a weird grey at the same time. There was a constant humming of machines at all different levels, and almost irritating but yet rhythmic humming. The brightness in the center of her eyelids bothered Caity most. She was in a sense of semi- consciousness but mostly toward the unconscious state in a dream like manner. Her mind was wandering in and out of a strange darkness that was irritating and comforting all at the same time. She could feel the heavy weight of hot baked blankets against her ice cold skin and felt her stomach continue its little rhythmic shivers.

Oh God! She was sighing on the inside of her body where no one could see or hear her, she felt like some weird prisoner trapped in a dead weight of hell. Her limbs felt cold and as heavy as lead and all those weird feelings and ting-lings where the hot met the cold. Caity was too out of it to realize what she was feeling pain coming from the needles of the intervenes that was shoved up the tops of her hands. Worst of all, in this cold darkness of hell, she could feel the intense soreness of her chest.

She came in and out of dreams where people had beaten her with baseball bats on her chest and now the pain was terrible. She felt like she'd been beaten to a pulp and no one had been there to help her as she lay in her pile of pain. Jack was there too, she could see him standing over her in the dark, holding a large two by four, and Caity could feel the pain of where he had obviously hit her. She cried in her deep state, this time her parents sat there tense as they heard her begging him to explain why he had hurt her so badly. Begging him to tell her why he had picked her to use and destroy. Begging and crying for over ten minutes before she sunk deep into her state of sleep and unconsciousness yet again.

Caity's father who knew nothing about this guy Jack, figured once they got Caity stabilized, it would be time to sit down with his wife and find out what the hell was going on. He wondered if this guy had actually beaten the pulp out of Caity somehow, or was it just all emotional. Either way, neither was better but he was sitting in the room tense, irritated, worried, scared but most of all helpless. At that exact moment he saw Caity move again and prayed to God that she would wake up soon. From what he knew about these things, the longer you were unconscious the more it meant you may not come back. He didn't care what the doctors said; he just felt it to be that way. He was unconsciously rubbing his hands together grinding them as if he could find a solution though their rough motion. Pausing, he looked over at his wife, the love of his life for the last forty eight years, and thought about how lucky they always were to have each other.

He looked over again at his wife Francis, "Franny" as he'd called her from the instant he had first heard her very formal name. She sat there tense, pale and overloaded, and with all that he still had to ask the questions that were eating at him like a cancer inside.

"Francis" he started. She looked up and knew that when ever Greg called by her formal name he was usually very upset about something and wanted her full attention. Pausing, she looked across the bed at him dead on and let out a very heavy sigh as she said, "What?"

"Are you going to tell me who the hell Jack is? Or do I have to sit here wondering what the hell is going on?" His tone was irritated but he whispered so as not to upset Caity's subconscious. "Well?" He said again. "You can't sit there and tell me you don't know what's going on because I know how close you and Caity are and that she tells you everything. It's probably because of that age old Mother and Daughter thing that you two have, but none the less, I figure I haven't heard about or met the guy because he's probably not worth wiping my boots on. Am I right?"

Franny nodded and winked at him with a look of love she always had in her eyes when she looked at Greg. All these years and she loved him as much, no, actually she loved him way more than the day she married him. God they were lucky, she thought. In her mind, she was trying to put it all together in some sense of order for a way to carefully tell Greg about it. Greg, his touch still gave her goose bumps, they still chased each other around the house when the kids where out and they still loved to sit and talk for hours, usually while they sat side by side cuddling or just lying in bed naked touching each other. They had a deep relationship that Caity had always admired and dreamt about for herself, and it broke Franny's heart to know that Caity may never know this kind of happiness and peace between a man and a woman.

Looking right at him, Franny whispered, "Greg, why don't we go sit outside the room for a few minutes and chat. How about it?" Greg nodded, and started to get up out of his chair feeling like he'd aged twenty years today. Franny grabbed his hand and nuzzled his arm with her cheek as they walked out of the room with no change in Caity.

Caity was completely lost in her unconsciousness, surrounded by her deep darkness and intense sadness. She could actually see herself sitting at her computer at home. When did she get there she wondered. She watched as she realized she was about to write yet another letter to Jack. He had really upset her again and she wanted to tell him how she felt. Funny, it was the only way she could ever really tell Jack things because when they were together, he would never let her talk about the negative things. She felt suffocated, trapped, as if this darkness would never go away. She even felt an odd coldness that seemed to be warmed on the outer sides of her. It was almost cloudy in the room now as she watched herself almost through a Vaseline type of glass. It was blurry but Caity could feel herself move so she could see what she was about to start typing. Just as she could see the computer screen, Caity noticed words suddenly appearing. It was if she was talking to him but she could see the words on her computer screen clouded by a misty film all around it. Words were traveling through her mind. She could see Jack and her talking and she couldn't really tell where they were because it was almost like being surrounded by clouds.

All of a sudden she could hear herself talking louder and louder until she was sure that she was almost screaming at him. What made her so angry was the fact that he seemed to be standing there surrounded by these puffy white clouds but totally ignoring her. He was looking right at her but had no reaction on his face. Caity kept shaking her head, angry and frustrated that she couldn't get a response out of him. She paused, sighed and let out a deep breath and looking right into Jack's eyes started to tell him how she felt.

"*Jack, lies eventually catch up to you! At least I may feel like a fool for believing in you so deeply, but I can look myself in the mirror every day, you on the other hand should hide yourself!*

You said you humored me, another way of saying you lied through your teeth! Am I some sick game you've been playing????? Why?????? Well I know you will never tell me the truth anyway......you have obviously gotten so used to getting away with lies with me you just keep on dishing them out!.

I would never have imagined in my wildest dreams that you would have turned out to be such a nightmare in my life! All I can think of is that you couldn't tell me the truth because that would be admitting you used me. .Intentionally set out to hurt me over and over and over and over because you knew how my heart felt and it made it easy for you!

Tell me, .every time you spent an evening with me was it because your other woman was out of town? Why did you need me if you had someone else? Do you even know what type of guy that makes you???? I said it in January and I say it again, you have no credibility, you may be laughing and thinking to yourself, ya, but I suckered you again. but the joke has always just been on you! All I ever wanted was the truth. I lose nothing because there is nothing to lose for me. One day the impact of losing me will have an astounding affect on you!

I'll never understand why you have stooped to the all time low of HUMOURING me. You HUMOURED me! I feel so very BETRAYED!!!

Why didn't you just say you were seeing someone and that you called me because you were thinking of me? A real man may have missed my friendship but the truth is you were never a friend to me! All you ever did was hurt me!

I guess you have to keep up the "Fraser Boy" tradition. Too bad I thought you were very different from your brother, but I guess you truly are the eldest and the leader of the pack.

There are way too many weird things that happened that I can't explain. You know the tone you had the Sunday morning in August when we were sleeping in after swimming, the tone you used with Jane and the girls on the phone was because you didn't want them to know I was there beside you. You remember when you had me lay silent so she wouldn't know I was there.

The only times I have heard that tone from you are on weird occasions where I have called on a Sunday or Saturday morning and you pretend to be coming out of the shower, and looking back you never said you'd call me back in five minutes you always insisted on calling me back that night, hours and hours later, I guess you were with someone at the time and didn't want me to know either. Funny how weird memories come back to you when you think about it! I remembered that morning lying there and a cold shiver ran up my spine because I recognized that weird tone in your voice. Too bad I just ignored my gut feelings. They could have saved me a lot of heartache!

Being religious I actually bought into all of your bullshit about guilt, the church religion etc but mostly because of the only time we went to Church together and I thought you were going to have a heart attack right then and there! What I know now is that probably you felt guilty for lying to me. You really are a piece of work! You never saw me on a Friday night? Whose night was that?

What kind of heartless man makes love to a woman and tells her how much she means and then ignores her at a party just five days later? An absolutely heartless man!

Looking back you were right about one thing you said, why would I want you? Well I don't any more! When I really think about I guess I haven't for a long time now. I was living in the past of who you used to be with me. Keeping that memory close to my heart, instead of the real you, that horribly awful guy that once again proved his true colors. I missed the closeness we once had, the carefree feeling of just being myself around you; I missed so many things I couldn't see that they haven't existed for a long time. I missed things that were obviously just an act!

Remember that hand blown church I gave you to hang on your Christmas tree each year, let it remind you of what an awful person you were to me! I can spend a lifetime wondering why you got such pleasure in using me and lying to me or I can just forget about you! I now know in my heart that you are a cold hard bitter man that uses others to take out his frustration on.

I wonder how you think God is judging you for how you treated me for the last two years? I really wish I had never let you into my life!

You don't have to worry about pretending I'm dead, because my heart is, so it really doesn't matter anymore! No one can truly love someone and treat them the way you treated me.

Sadly I wish the guy you pretended to be, really did exist. I seem to be in mourning for someone that never existed and that in itself in incredibly unreal.

I wish I could say that I walk away with some precious memories, but instead each moment that was so precious to me was obviously just a sick game to you and that burden I must somehow learn to carry.

In the end I know that God loves me and that he has sent you into my life for a reason. I just wish I knew why????

Congratulations, you win the award for being the absolute worst man I have ever known. You are heartless and that is the only way I will remember you! I feel truly and very deeply BETRAYED!!"

Caity was dreaming, seeing clouds float around as she screamed at Jack. Her heart wasn't dead. She was still very deeply in love with Jack, but some how she felt comfort and a weird sense of relief for letting out her pent up emotions. Her whole heart belonged to Jack and the truth was that he was the reason that she lay there in unconsciousness; fighting for the very life she couldn't handle any more. She lay there shaking her head with someone seemingly whispering to her, asking her how it was possible for her to believe that he loved her when he treated her so very badly.

Dreaming about Jack and telling him off, made her heart beat so rapidly that it set off her monitor which was enough for a nurse to come in and check on her. The old nurse rubbed her brow wiping the sweat off it; she adjusted Caity's position in her bed, checked all her levels and fixed her bedding. This was a good sign she thought, every time she saw a patient in this condition and they were moving in their sleep they ended up coming out of it. If anything, this young girl was certainly having some real bad dreams though. After finishing adjusting everything and checking to make sure the intervenes was working, she quietly left the room closing it softly behind her.

Meanwhile downstairs, Franny and Greg sat quietly drinking their prospective coffees in the small and dimly lit cafeteria. They sat facing each other, not saying much but holding each other's hands softly as they sat in silence. Franny was wondering how she was going to tell all this stuff to Greg without him flying off the handle. How was she going to tell him that this had been going on for the last few years and that he had been completely left out? Franny knew it was mostly because Greg really had a bad temper when someone he loved was involved. He didn't handle difficult life things very well. Both she and Caity had decided it was for the best to keep it a secret from everyone until the relationship either became normal or ended. Franny knew in her heart that Caity had never expected it to be ended ever! That was the saddest part about all of this. Suddenly, she realized that Greg was speaking to her and bringing her out of her deep dark thoughts.

"Franny, when are you going to tell me what the hell is going on here? I know you think that men don't do well with women talk, but I think with all this, that it's time I knew what the hell has been going on in our daughter's life!" Greg looked down at his coffee when he finished speaking and sighed heavily enough that it echoed in the tiny room. Franny looked over and started to whisper talk as she spoke. "Greg, Caity has been dating this divorced, well, legally separated guy now for about two years or so. You actually know him, or at least I think you have met him at one time or other. He was Sandy's cousin." Greg looked a bit puzzled. "Come on, you remember, one of Caity's friends from way back, Caity went to the wedding. Remember, she didn't have a date and she wore that beautiful purple dress that she'd bought for her grad." Franny coaxed, she knew Greg could remember but that he was fighting it for some reason. "Greg, she said, "Jack was Sandy's cousin; Scott's brother or something like that. You remember they all came up to the cottage for that boating weekend and all the kids sat around that huge bon-fire you built." Greg nodded, he did remember. But for the life of him he couldn't get a picture of this guy in his head. Shit, how come he couldn't remember. Franny could see his frustration and paused.

"Anyway, when Jack got separated somehow he and Caity started talking on the phone a lot and one thing lead to another and they started dating. Unfortunately, Caity didn't find out that Jack had a lot of issues until she was in way over her head. The truth is, from everything I've heard of the story, I really think he loves her to death, but the sad thing is that I think the guy has just too many issues to make anything work in his life." Pausing yet again, Franny was trying to give Greg as much detail and as little info as she could. Which in fact she knew was impossible. Also knowing that Greg was an on again, off again atheist; she'd have to be careful about just how much information she included about religion.

Knowing that Greg was a smart and level headed guy who was never easily influenced by anything and anyone, he'd have a hard time understanding a forty something year old man letting the priest dictate his life. "Well?" She said sighing really loudly, "he is also this pretty obsessed Catholic that has to have an annulment before he can really get on with his life. Or at least that's what he's been telling Caity all this time, and Greg, you know how Caity is; she's a pretty religious girl that has that talk with God in the middle of the field type of relationship thing, and she'd totally have the patience for all of this stuff."

Suddenly Greg slammed his fist into the table, not caring who jumped in the cafeteria including the fact that his wife was completely startled. "Shit, Franny. What the hell are you talking about?" Greg was mad now, and more than a bit frustrated. A bit too loud, Greg asked in a deeply angry voice, how long has this thing been going on?" Franny was nervous, she knew that Greg was really mad and he'd probably see her as having lied to him all this time. She was tense but knew this finally had to come out. She'd hated keeping this from him; he was the love of her life, and she cherished every moment they had together. He still made her heart skip when he walked in the room.

Franny looked at Greg; she still had all the old urges. She loved putting her hands at the bottom of his neck where his hair stopped. She loved rubbing that area softly with her hands while she passionately kissed him. Boy how they could kiss. Franny loved kissing Greg. She loved how they always melted together when they did. In fact, it was exactly the kind of thing that Caity said she had with Jack. That, when they were together it was like there was no one else left in the world. Franny leaned forward and gently placed a quick kiss on Greg's lips.

Flopping back into her chair, she looked up at him and said "Greg, do you even know how much I love you? How much I thank God every day of my life for having sent you into my life? Do you even know how much I cherish you? How very lucky we are to have each other and the life we have shared? Do you even know that?" Franny looked at him with a huge question mark on her face. "Oh, for God's sake Franny! What the hell is wrong with you? Of course I know that. I know that my life would have been shit without you and the girls. Without what we have shared or we're going to share, it would have been a life not worth living. What in the hell is wrong with you? When have you ever had any doubts about that?" He said, waiting anxiously for her response. "Never!". She said as she took a sip of her coffee before she said the rest. "Actually, I just wanted to remind you of that so you know just how much Caity loves this guy, and from what I have heard, how much he loves her. "Can't be that much!" Greg responded. "Any guy that can leave a woman in this state and not be there for her can't give shit about her! This guy sounds like an idiot and our daughter is obviously completely out of her mind. I mean, for God's sake Franny, she was screaming at him tonight, waking up all the neighbors and he never turned around, just kept going. What kind of man does that to the woman he loves? No man I know, that's for sure!"

Greg was right and Franny knew it, but she hadn't realized it till this exact second. Franny also hadn't realized that he had heard the conversation that went on earlier between the detective guy and the neighbor. "I guess I underestimated how much you could handle, huh?" was all she managed to say to Greg. "Yep." He said nodding but reaching over to caress her hands in the loving manner she was used to. "Well honey, we've been through worse than this, and Caity is a strong girl that will make it this time too! And when all is said and done, we'll either welcome this guy as part of her life or I will kick the living lights out of him, but either way it will be a done chapter and on to other things". With that Greg stood up coaxing her to go back to Caity's room with him and Franny did that in a silent obedient manner. She always underestimated Greg's ability to handle things and all she could do was squeeze his hand in a silent appreciation of him. He knew what she meant and leant down and kissed her forehead as they headed back up to the room. Neither of them speaking, but saying so much in their silence and hand holding.

Chapter 14

While the life monitors kept track of Caity, and Franny and Greg headed back to her room, simultaneously at those exact moments just about ten minutes down the street; Jack was kneeling down in his bathroom, leaning on the cold hard tile floor, while he violently prayed to the porcelain altar. His vomit was green now with no content which meant he was actually throwing up what he believed to be his stomach lining, or at least that's what he remembered hearing on one of those health shows.

While he crawled into the shower, the sweat poured from his brow. As the hot water flowed over his face he felt his limbs go limp with exhaustion. He'd been throwing up since he got home from Caity's. Her panicked screams echoing in his memories all night. Her heartache was his. He ached to tell her everything. To tell her that the love he felt for her, scared the living hell out of him. That he had never felt this for anyone in his life and never knew that it could be so deep and strong. He needed desperately to tell her, how she scared him. How hurt he had been in his past life and how much he deeply needed her. But each time he had spent with her intending to tell her, he'd panic, fear running through him like lighting bolts jamming his body with panic, and always hurting Caity in the wake of it.

He threw his head back in a pause from vomiting hoping it would finally stop. The tears welled up in his eyes, and he was heaving gasps of despair as his whole body shivered with exhaustion. He loved her.

He deeply loved her. He needed her and he needed to go back there tonight to tell her. He needed to hear her soft voice whisper in his ear that she loved him. That was always something she did as she made love to him and he had always cherished every second. He loved the way she gave little kisses all around his face while his eyes were closed just eating up every moment of this intense intimacy they obviously shared.

Caity owned his heart from the very depths he never knew possible, and she was everything that he had always wanted. Oh God, why hadn't he waited to marry? Looked harder for someone to build a life with? Why had he settled for Jane? He had known she chased him from the very beginning. He had known in his heart that she hadn't loved him enough to make a life but yet he had settled, wanting a life with family and children so badly he had thought at the time, that not only was it worth the sacrifice, but all this talk about fantasy love that he had heard about was only really in the movies. That all people could ever really hope for was a type of compatibility.

Until Caity had come into his life; Jack had never known what real love was. His father had beaten them all their lives till he had finally had enough at eighteen and moved out in shear disgust. His parents had never had a loving relationship; if anything, it was a toleration of each other. He had known that his mother had had a lover for years, but never knew who or where. Even on her death bed she wouldn't tell Jack the truth although he had begged her for hours. He remembered the night his mother died. She was crying about how much she had loved some man and that he wasn't even going to be there for her in her last moments. She made Jack and Scott promise to find the kind of love they talked about in romance books and movies and she passed on with her secrets deeply intact in her mind and no one else's.

Jack was so upset about not knowing what his mother's life had really been like that for weeks after her death, he'd tried tracking information through all of her friends; he was no closer to the truth weeks later than the actual night of her passing. The strange thing was that Jack had always in this gut felt that the peace he restlessly searched for in his life, lay in his mother's dark secrets. With her absence he lost the ability in finding the peace that he desperately needed in order to go on with his life.

Jack was remembering weird things tonight. Like the fact that his mother had been so excited to hear about his split with Jane. That she had actually hated his father for something besides his beating of the boys, but Jack didn't know what that was. Sadly, Jack's father was a cold heartless man. His father always refused to talk about their mother and the past. It was completely, way too strange. Jack's father actually wanted to pretend that his mother had never existed. How strange was that? He never understood and wanted desperately to know the reason.

Jack was still lying on the cold tile floor of the bathroom when his phone started ringing. He was thinking the machine would get it but on about the tenth ring he decided he better pick it up in case it had something to do with the welfare of his girls.

As he picked up the phone, he looked over to see that it was already nine o'clock in the morning and it felt like hell had entered his house forever. Picking up the phone, he said, "Hello". Pausing and waiting to hear who it could possibly be on the other end. " Jack? Jack Fraser?", was all he heard when he responded with, "Yes, why?"

Stew was mad and just hearing Jack's calm healthy voice on the other end, irritated him to no end. "Look Jack, this is Stew Banks, you know me because you have followed me home and sat outside my house a few times. I'm the private detective that's working for Caity, and while we are on the subject, you unfeeling cold bastard, Caity is lying in a hospital bed while we speak; fighting for her life."

Jack went cold. His whole body was like ice knowing that he could really, for the first time, lose Caity forever. "What do you mean she's in a hospital fighting for her life? Where the hell do you get off calling me and what the hell does Caity need a detective for?"

"None of your damn business right now buster" was all that Stew could come back with. The important thing is that you don't try to see her at all, so she can at least survive this thing". Stew was just about yelling as he responded to Jack.

"Oh really, like some asshole private detective is going to tell me what I can and can't do." Jack replied pissed off enough to hang up but too curious to find out the rest of the information to let that happen. "So tell me, just how did Caity end up in the hospital and did you have something to do with it?" Jack was asking in a mean and derogatory tone half expecting to hear that this detective has somehow got Caity mixed up in something that almost killed her.

"What are you? An idiot? Or just completely insane?" Stew asked. "I mean really Jack, what did you think would happen to Caity after you left her in that state tonight?" The words were said before Stew could realize that he hadn't achieved setting up a meeting with this jerk and all he managed to do was give him too much information. "Me? I'm the reason she's in the hospital? Why? What happened? How could this be? She was just a bit upset? What are you saying? You think I caused this? Are you crazy? I love her! I love her to the depths of my heart and back. With all my soul! The kind of love that some crazy mixed up detective couldn't possibly understand." Jack said in condescending tone thinking that all this wasn't at all possible.

Stew was really mad now, wondering just how stupid could this guy be. "What do you think you idiot? When you got on the elevator and you heard Caity choking in tears, did you actually think she was faking it? What an absolute idiot you are, in fact; if it wasn't for her neighbor Debbie, Caity would be probably dead right now and I'd be phoning to tell you of the fact. Don't tell me that you are actually that stupid to believe that your little visit tonight with those comments were going to be forgiven. What in hell were you thinking?" Stew stopped and before Jack could comment because he was just too much in shock." Stew added, "That's only part of why I was calling, the other part is about a visit I had from Father O'Malley last night. I'm going to tell you whether you like it or not you had better get your act together and meet me at Smitty's on highway five, for breakfast in about fifteen minutes. You can refuse if you want to but I highly recommend that you meet me, trust me it's in your best interest."

Stew stopped talking and could hear Jack breathing funny. Actually it sounded as if he was half choking on his air. But the guy managed to pull it together and tell Stew that he would in fact meet him but he needed a half hour in order to get himself cleaned up and drive over there. Stew agreed and hung up. Jack heard the dial tone, placed the phone back on the receiver and sat down on his couch in a type of emotional shock. He was drained, hurt, heartbroken, sad, and his body felt like it had been run over by a tractor trailer. He was going to pull himself together and meet this guy, if only to get some answers of what had been going on the last few weeks, and with Caity, now!

Jack was tired, sore and hungry. He pulled into Smitty's parking lot sizing up the other cars knowing full well that Stew was already there by the familiar red BMW parked in the lot. Jack slowly got out of his car and headed to the restaurant with anticipation driving him up the internal crazy wall.

Stew sat at the table with his own anticipation of how exactly he was going to handle this, and in truth he hadn't a clue. Just as he was feeling the pressure of Jack's presence, Stew's phone rang. It was Maggy calling to see if he would be over for the Easter egg and goodie hunt around ten this morning. Stew told Maggy where he was and why, and after she let out a gasp he told he'd call her when he was done, but if it was too late to go ahead without him. He knew the boys would have a low tolerance for time this morning, putting a lot of pressure on their mother to get to the hunt.

At the exact second he hung up his cell, he looked over to see Jack go down in the middle of the parking lot. It looked exactly as if he had just been shot and he went done in a mille second. Stew jumped from the table spilling his coffee, cell phone in hand figuring he may need it to call 911 if in fact this was a shooting. Not thinking more about it, Stew ran to Jack's side as he laid on the cold pavement in the morning first rays of sun. The sweat was pouring from his brow and he was ice cold. A number of Smitty's workers were also around Jack, trying desperately to figure out what had happened. Stew yelled at one of them to call 911, but the kid said his boss was already in the process of doing just that. From Stew's new perspective, towering over Jack, it looked just like a heart attack. In fact, Stew figured that's exactly what it had to be.

Minutes later they could hear the ambulance pull up as Jack kept a type of semi-consciousness trying hard to hang on and complaining about the numbness in his arm and the pain in his stomach. According to the paramedics those where typical heart attack symptoms. Since Stew was the only one that knew this guy, they asked that he travel with them in the ambulance, and he complied. Once the doors of the vehicle closed behind them and the driver got in, they took off at full speed, the whole scene seemed surreal to Stew. He heard them talking on the radio and figured out that they were on their way to Credit Valley Hospital.

What were the odds? Stew just hoped that Jack wouldn't be in the room right next to Caity. That he'd be too busy to even know that she was there. At the exact second that Stew was thinking that, Jack reached out to grab Stew's arm and beg him to call Caity and ask her to meet them at the hospital. He was obviously delirious and had apparently forgotten their earlier conversation. Stew grew immediately tense and Jack looked at him in puzzlement and pain. How in the hell was he going to deal with this now? He didn't know but he certainly had every intention of protecting Caity. As for this guy, personally Stew couldn't have cared less even at this terrible moment. In fact, Stew was sickly thinking to himself that the best thing that could happen for Caity was for this guy to just kick off.

He couldn't help but think that the best thing to happen to Caity would be for Jack to kick the bucket and be finally out of her life once and for all. Then, immediately after those thoughts pounded through his brain, so did all the conversations with Father O'Malley. Suddenly sickened with too much information, Stew felt the motion of the ambulance and the weight of the information; Believe it or not, Stew suddenly felt sorry for this man who had treated Caity so horribly and yet had suffered so many travesties against him. What a screwed up world this suddenly looked like. What a complete mess he'd gotten himself in. Stew couldn't wait for all this to come to a head and finally be over, but judging from Jack's horrible condition, Stew felt the outcome may take an uncontrollable turn on its own.

The six minute ride to emergency felt like an hour and the thoughts that went through Stew's mind were incredibly draining. The first thing he would do when they arrived, once Jack was taken care of by the doctors; would be to go looking for Caity and check on her. There would be no way that he'd let her know that Jack was in the hospital too! The less she knew, the better; and he was sure if she did find out it would certainly affect her recovery.

Minutes later they pulled into the emergency area of the hospital, the back doors to the ambulance blew open and people were grabbing the gurney and rushing Jack into the hospital to be treated. From what Stew overheard, it sounded like they believed that Jack had a heart attack and they were rushing him in to emergency, in order to try save the life that appeared to be slipping away quicker than expected.

Stew got out slowly, thinking about all the events of the last twenty four hours and tried desperately to make sense of it all as he thanked the ambulance guys for working so fast. He hopped out of the back and headed inside to face whatever the day had to offer. First things, first! Find out Jack's status before going up to check on Caity. Then give Maggy a call, and also talk to Caity's parents about all this. Suddenly Stew felt old and drained and wondered just when life could get any more complicated.

It turned out that Jack made it just by a thread. He was resting quietly in intensive care when Stew left him and headed upstairs to deal with the second round of today's trauma. As the elevator doors opened to Caity's floor, Stew could see Fran and Greg sitting hand in hand in the cramped waiting room, flanked by Liz, Caity's younger sister by two years. They all looked up in a sort of anticipation as he entered the small archway of the brightly colored area. Fran was the first to stand up and speak to him and was probably anxious to know why he was there. "Mr. Banks, it's nice to see you again. I guess you thought you'd check in on us early this morning, huh?" She said as she approached him to shake his hand. "Yes Mamm, but as a matter of fact, if you have a brief moment I'd like to tell you all something."

Stew paused realizing he suddenly had Greg's full attention. Caity's father looked tired and drained and Liz was leaning on him half sleeping, half paying attention. Stew continued, "I don't know if you want to hear this right now, but I have to tell you some information that is certainly going to make you have a reaction. Good or bad, you really have to be aware of this. But first, tell me how Caity is doing." Franny jumped in and said they could see real improvements in her condition this morning, and that although she wasn't completely awake yet, the doctors felt that Caity would be totally coherent any time soon.

The night was tough and apparently she appeared to have had some real serious night mares, but other than that Caity's breathing seemed to be great, her heart rate was normal and her body temperature was back to where it should be. Stew sighed, "Thank God! Well that's the first good news I heard in twenty four hours." Stew sat down opposite to them leaning forward to rest his elbow on his knees and rested his chin in the palms of his two hands while he looked concerned and hesitant before he started to speak again.

"Well, I don't know how to begin so I guess I should just spit it out. Suddenly leaning back to speak, "First let me tell you that I think this information should stay in this room and under no circumstances should we let Caity know any of this. Right, now let's see." Stew was jabbering like a woman enough to aggravate Greg into a reaction of telling him to just spit it out before they all aged here. "Good point." Stew said. "O.K; well just so you know, Jack is in the hospital. Just so you know, he's not here to visit Caity; he's actually here in the intensive care unit fighting for his life. He just suffered a heart attack this morning and got rushed in." Stew could see the anger on Greg's face as he responded to the news; "You mean the bastard didn't die, it figures! He's gonna stick around and torment our daughter some more, isn't he?"

"Well, I don't think he'll be in any condition to torment any one for quite some time. When I left him downstairs, I didn't think he was going to actually make it. In fact, I think it's much better that he didn't pass on, that way he wouldn't be put on the "dead man's pedestal" that so often happens when someone dies. You know what I mean; we remember all the good things and suddenly don't remember one bad thing they ever did. I think it's really important for Caity to get on with her life now and not treasure the past in torment either." Stew felt more like he was giving a speech and less like he was comforting worried parents, and Greg said as much just as Stew had finished talking.

"Sorry Greg, sometimes I get carried away. It's just that it's been crazy the last few days, and to be honest with you two, I actually really hated this guy up until last night. It wasn't until Father O'Malley showed up at my door and told me a story that would make your hair stand on end; that I finally decided to have a little compassion for the guy. Believe it or not right now, he really <u>does</u> deserve a little, even though he treated Caity like shit. There is nothing that can really justify it. Let me tell you that I have a much greater understanding of the whole thing now, but it's still really confusing."

Greg stood up in disgust. "Let me get this straight, you want us to suddenly feel sorry for this creep who has been using and hurting Caity for the last two years, because of a load of bull shit some old priest had the nerve to feed you. Well you can forget it. Whatever it is, no one and nothing will ever justify any of it to me and as soon as she's better and on her feet I'm gonna talk some real sense into that girl before she ruins her life anymore." With that Greg stormed out of the waiting area and down to the cafeteria to calm down. Liz got up, quickly rubbed her mom's back in passing, thanked Stew for the info and followed her dad down for a coffee. Someone would need to calm him down and she knew she was just the person who always knew how to do just that.

Franny watched them exit and then looked dead on at Stew. "O.K, now that we are alone, how about telling me the whole story. I know you are carrying quite the load, including the fact that I saw the way you looked at Caity yesterday, so I know this is personal for you. So how about it Mr. Banks, are you going to tell me the details that Caity and I have been anxious to know for the last two years?" She looked up with pleading in her eyes and a needful expression that Stew was sure he had never ever seen on anyone's face in his entire lifetime. Fran had obviously been through every rough moment with Caity, living parallel through every heartache as she obviously cried on her mom's shoulders every time Jack hurt her. Now Francis Anderson wanted the much needed answers to the obviously millions of questions that were flowing through her mind.

Just as Stew was about to start telling her part of what the old priest had said last night, suddenly; there he stood, the chubby and round Father O'Malley. He looked like the type that could have played Santa at Christmas and was looking at Stew as if he'd seen a ghost having heard that Stew was about to spill out the whole story to this woman in front of him.

Stew stood up abruptly, and spoke as he rose. "Francis Anderson, this is Father O'Malley, Jack's Priest, Father, Francis," waving his arms in nonchalant gestures as if the formality was too much for him today. Although his gestures were introductory, Stew felt more personally invaded then anything. He hadn't expected to see the old guy here of all places, let alone intrude as Stew was about to tell his story to Francis. Stew could almost feel Father O'Malley's Catholic Church check burning into him, while it was hard pressed in his wallet. It was like a led weight in there, waiting for his decision on what Stew was going to do.

Not paying attention to their conversation; Stew could still tell that Father O'Malley was being polite with Francis, extending his condolences and prayers for her daughter's recovery. He heard father O'Malley tell her that although he was concerned about their daughter that he was really there to visit Jack. That statement brought Stew back to reality and out of his daydreams. Apparently, as the priest spoke he told them that he was listed in Jack's wallet as the person to call in case of emergency. At that moment, as Father O'Malley was speaking to the Andersons, Stew couldn't help but think that it was really too bad Jack hadn't had the decency to kick off in the parking lot earlier this morning. Instead, Father O'Malley was visiting him, while he was still hanging in there. How very sad for everyone, Stew thought as he looked around the room with a sense of sad reality.

Stew was internally drained, he'd never known himself to be so mean in his thoughts, and that was always what made him successful in his job. He reflected and realized that with all the winning characters he'd come across in the years, he'd never before spent his time wishing for someone to just drop dead or off the face of the earth, not like this, and never before. Stew wondered if he'd finally lost his edge. Was his career over? Or was this just one case that would haunt him for years but he'd keep on going? This was really the first time he had ever let it get personal, and he knew it was not only clouding his thinking and the way he did his job; it also went against everything he knew to be his basis for survival, as a successful detective.

Shaking his head trying to bring himself back to reality, Stew realized they were both speaking to him now. "Pardon me, Francis?" Stew sighed. "I'm sorry, I wasn't really paying attention". Fran knew that when she had touched his shoulder in order to bring him back to reality; Stew had been off somewhere in deep puzzlement, and his facial expressions totally highlighted his thoughts. "Well", she paused. " It looked like you were off somewhere, and we were just saying that maybe we should all grab some breakfast in the restaurant downstairs." Looking at him with pleading eyes that begged Stew to stay and go with them, Fran waited calmly till he agreed and then followed the two of them to the elevators.

As she stood behind the two men in the elevator, Fran's mind wandered to Caity. She'd checked in on her just before Stew had shown up and the nurses had said that it would take at least another hour for the sedatives to wear off but that she would probably be up and out today. That's if everything went as planned. Just then Francis let out an exceptionally deep sigh that caught the silence between the two men in front of her. With that, as if timed, the elevator doors opened just down the hall from the restaurant; and off they went.

Chapter 15

Caity felt the intense warmth on her face, and it comforted her. In her mind she was on her favorite beach in Punta Cana and it felt wonderful. In reality the nurse had just opened the blinds in her room, and as the hot morning sun moved across the sky it rested on Caity's sleeping face. The sun was streaming into the room and onto Caity's pillow. As it streamed onto the covers, it filled Caity with amazing warmth. So much so, that Caity started to stretch and take a big breath in as her arms reached above her head and her toes pointed out and tapped the cold metal foot board of the bed. With the coolness that she suddenly felt, on her toes, Caity slowly opened her eyes softly staring up at the ceiling; and for a few short seconds wondered where she was. Looking around she realized she was in a hospital bed now and suddenly all the horrible moments and heartache from last night came rushing back to her.

Suddenly, she felt a fist grip her heart; she could picture Jack getting on the elevator at her condo, last night. The warmth she had just enjoyed was all gone now, replaced by ice flowing through her veins at a speed which made her slightly dizzy. How cold and heartless he had been, and the worst part was that he had been so warm and loving, both in words and actions just hours before. What happened? Why did he do this? Did he really care about her? Was it all lies just to get her into bed? Did he really love her? Was it some kind of sick game? If he did love her, how could he walk away the way he did, cold and hard? Didn't he know what this did to her? Didn't he care that she was hurting to her very core, her very existence? Did he ever give her a second thought after he left her? Did he ever worry about her? Was he hurting right now or was he on with his life like nothing happened?

Was he just using her for sex because she was such an idiot the minute he'd say he loved her she was back in her arms? Was he making fun of her and laughing at how stupid she was as he left? Was he off making love to someone else right now? Did he do this because Caity was just a mistress in his eyes and he had a girlfriend outside of this? It certainly felt that way!

Was he still sleeping with Jane on the side even though he had said over, and over that he hated her? What was the truth? Was he really this religious nut case that let the priest tell him what to do or was he the best manipulative bastard the world had ever seen? I mean really, using your religion as an excuse to not commit to a relationship, what about the fact that he'd been sleeping with Caity over and over? How did that go over in confession? Did he even go to confession or was all the church stuff just another bunch of bull shit? What was the truth? How was she ever going to find out? Did anyone out there know? Would Stew be able to find out? What if she never got her answers? What if she had to wonder about all this stuff over and over for years to come? What if she never knew? What if there really was another woman that Jack was treating really wonderfully and it was only Caity he treated like this? What was it that made the other woman so wonderful, that Jack would do all this to her and not treat her right, but yet treasure someone else? How could there be another woman, if Jack needed to sleep with Caity, why would he have to if he had someone else? Maybe she was this church going nut too and she wouldn't sleep with him so he used Caity because he knew she loved him? What if there really was someone else!!????" Caity's tears were inside her and she wanted so desperately to have a good heavy cry, but for some crazy reason all she could feel was the bottled up tension of tears and they wouldn't come out. Her heart and head were spinning with unanswered questions and she felt tired and drained; all over again.

She had a million unanswered questions swirling around in her mind, while at the very same time she actually felt the sunshine trying desperately to warm her now shivering body. Her focus switched temporarily to wonder how she had got here. Who brought her here?

Who knew she was here? Was Jack here waiting for her? Had he come back off the elevator, heard her choking and rescued her? Would he bring her flowers and say he was sorry? Would he hold her and apologize for everything? Would he finally make everything normal for them? Would he finally start treating her right? Although, in her heart Caity knew that Jack would never treat her right; would never appreciate or respect her; she always had the same daydream. That he'd come back holding flowers, declaring his love for her and begging forgiveness. She was a hopeless romantic and she was hopelessly in love with a truly heartless, cold man.

At that, Caity's thoughts were suddenly interrupted when the door to her private hospital room, flew open. Looking over in anticipation, wondering who it was; in popped a large furry beige and pink rabbit's head, followed by two humungous floppy ears and about a three foot body, all trailed by Kevin…Maggy's seven year old. He was looking proud and all smiles as he whipped into the room as if he was in some kind of race. The door started closing behind him only to be stopped halfway and it opened again to show Chris, Maggy's ten year old. His arms were filled with an Easter Basket oozing full of colored packages filled with chocolates and candies and toys and stuff…all wrapped up with a lightly colored purple cellophane wrap, encircled with a large yellow bow. Suddenly the two little couriers with their big eyes open wide; were flanked at the end of Caity's bed, they were smiling and struggling to hold on to their packages. Not uttering a word they just looked at her, as if waiting for her to say something fascinating.

Caity was trying to think of something to say when seconds later the door opened again only to let Maggy in at full speed. She'd obviously been running after the boys but hadn't succeeded in keeping up with them. Her face was flushed and when she looked over and saw Caity sitting up in bed smiling at the boys, she lit up like a light. "Caity" she said in an excited high pitched sound. "You're up and about. I was half expecting you to be lying there half dead. Boy, am I glad to see you this way! So how are you feeling? Breathing O.K? Seen anybody this morning? Oh, listen to me; I'm off rambling so fast you can't get a word in edgewise. So? How are you? Maggy said as she leaned over the bed and planted a big hug around her friend as if she hadn't seen her in twenty years.

"I'm feeling pretty good, but my ribs are killing me" Caity slightly winced at Maggy's over generous hug. "Oh, Sorry Girl, just glad to see you are doing better! I passed a whole bunch of people sitting in the restaurant arguing. Looked like your parents and Stew, some girl that is probably your sister, and a priest of all things. Did they think you'd need one? Maggy said tilting her head to the side looking a bit confused. "A Priest? Really? Couldn't be, my Dad is a semi-atheist, and mom would never think to have a priest here, she knows how casual I am about that stuff. Wait a minute, was it a rounding older man, jolly looking, almost could play a Santa at Christmas? Lots of grey hair and wrinkles?" Caity asked, now assuming it could only be Father O'Malley. "Yep", Maggy replied, sounds just like the one I saw…but boy, they were in a real argument as I passed by. Stew was facing the window and he waved me on as if to say, don't come in here. Actually, Stew looked like he was in the middle of the argument as well. I don't know Caity, seemed a bit rough down there; do you know what they could be fighting about? Maggy sighed one of the Caity type of sighs, the loud ones that caught everyone's attention. Suddenly Kevin sounded out, "Mom, you're doing that sighing thing again, and you're not letting your friend talk. Mom, are you going to make us stand here holding these things all day? "Oopps, no honey, sorry, we got a little sidetracked" Maggy reacted. With that she walked over to the end of the bed, first taking the bunny and placing it at the foot part looking right at Caity, then taking the basket from Chris and placing it on the side table. "Now boys, how about you two go down to the restaurant and ask Uncle Stew to get you a drink, Chris …you make sure Kevin stays with you, and I'll be down shortly. That way Mom and Caity can catch up and chat". With out another second passing by, the boys were off waving their good byes and headed out the door to look for Uncle Stew.

"O.K. Caity, now that we're alone, what happened? Talk to me! Why not think of me as your stress councilor and your friend all at the same time and dump it all out?" Maggy was anxiously waiting to not only help her friend but also get down to the latest facts. She was still on pins and needles over what Stew hadn't yet told her and now all this happening with Caity, she thought she'd lose her mind in unknown questions.

Caity sighed as she always did. Life just seemed totally out of hand. By the time she'd finished telling Maggy what had happened last night, all her memories were back in tact as her mom was coming through the room door. Dad and sis were right behind, followed by Stew. God he was a handsome man and he always carried himself like the world had no issues. He was sure of himself and secure and the way he was around her family it seemed to Caity that he was the leader, and pillar of strength. They were all glad to see that she seemed back to normal. That was the thing about asthma. One minute you could be choking to death and land in the hospital and hours later you were all normal again as if nothing happened, except for maybe being tired and sore, that is.

Caity found out that she was being released from the hospital by the afternoon and that Mom and Dad had insisted she spend a few days at their place. The doctor was giving her three days off of work so she could just rest up and calm down. He'd also given her something to take at night for the stress and to help her sleep along with the standard asthma extra medicines that always were prescribed when your lungs got out of hand. Caity was looking at all of them standing around her bed and the one thing she noticed was that they all looked like kids that had just got their hands caught in the cookie jar. Looking over at Maggy, it seemed she was a little uncomfortable too. Best ask them what the hell is really going on here before she loses her mind. Also, she wanted to know about Father O'Malley and that whole incident downstairs.

Caity sat up straight in her bed fixing her pillows to hold her. "O.K. everybody. What is going on? You all look like you have a deep dark secret and the silence is killing me. Who is going to start? With that she waited to see who would be first to spill the info. Having really never been close to her sister she didn't expect her to say a word and in fact she noticed Liz slowly backing out the door hoping not to be noticed. "Well? Come on, do you think I don't know you all well enough to know that something is going on; and if you don't tell me and I find out later. I promise to never speak to you all again. This isn't funny. Have I got some horrible disease? Did they find out I was dying? And what was Father O'Malley doing here? Well?" Caity was growing impatient and her voice went up a full octave by the time she was done.

Stew jumped in before someone would say the wrong thing, and he started with; "The thing is Caity, just because the hospital is releasing you doesn't mean that you're back to normal yet and maybe it would make good sense to wait to tell you anything that may be on our minds." Greg Anderson was just nodding in agreement when he heard Francis open her mouth too fast to be able to stop her. "Jack's here Caity," was all she managed to spit out before both Greg and Stew had grabbed her arms respectively on both sides of her as if that would have stopped the statement from rolling out of her mouth.

"He's here? He heard I was sick and he came? And what, did you guys stop him from seeing me? Where is he now? Is he waiting outside the door to see me, to say he's sorry, what?" She was turning her head from person to person as if an answer would somehow magically appear on their forehead or something. Stew jumped in, "no, it's not like he's actually here to see you…in fact…..I don't think he had any intention of coming to see you once he found out you were here." Stew was looking right at her now, deep into her eyes and he's slowly made his way from the end of the bed to be right by her side and with that he reached out and held onto her hand as he knew he'd have to finish giving her all the information. "Actually Caity, I was meeting Jack for breakfast this morning to confront him on a few things and he had a massive heart attack in Smitty's parking lot before he ever got into the restaurant. Caity squeezed Stew's hand expecting to hear that Jack was dead. So far I can tell you he is alive and in intensive care, but none of us wanted you to know because we were scared you'd want to see him and he'd just end up hurting you again. As a matter of fact; I know that he can't have any visitors right now anyway, except of course for Father O'Malley who is listed as his emergency person to call when they went through his wallet."

Caity was dead silent; the room was silent with no one saying a word. Maggy was sitting tense with her eyes closed half trying to imagine how Caity would handle the news, Greg and Fran were holding hands standing at the end of Caity's bed and her sister was no where to be seen. Maggy's boys had come back into the room but were so affected by the silence, they hadn't made a sound and no one even noticed that they had left their chairs that were positioned just outside of Caity's room and were now towering over their mother who was hunched in the big old yellow vinyl chair that was right beside Caity's bed.

For everyone it seemed like the silence was endless but in reality it only lasted about a minute before Caity spoke. "Right. Well, let's get my stuff together and get me out of here. The last place I want to be is in the same hospital with that heartless bastard." And with that Caity jumped off the bed and went to her bathroom to put her clothes on and get dressed. When the bathroom door was closed, Maggy was the first one to speak.

"You guys all must realize that she's in denial, right? Do you know what I'm talking about? Maggy looked at Greg and Fran dead on. "Well I hate to be rude missy", Greg said, "but who are you and where do you get off telling me about my daughter?" Stew jumped in before Maggy got her back up. "Sorry Greg, I should have introduced you all. Greg and Francis Anderson, this is my sister Maggy and Caity's counselor". "Oh my God! Maggy?" Fran jumped in before Stew could finish. I've heard all about you. As a matter of fact, if it weren't for you I don't think she would have been able to get through the last few months without losing her job and probably her mind. It's so great to meet you finally!" Fran finished as she walked over to Maggy, as Maggy was just standing up, Fran hugged her as if she was a lost family member that had just been found. Greg was confused, "so when does our daughter need a shrink?"

"Oh, I'm not a shrink, Mr. Anderson; I'm simply someone who counsels people to put their lives back into perspective when they get overloaded. I'm really just a stress counselor". Maggy informed him as her boys jumped up and added simultaneously, "yep, our mom handles everyone's stress but her own, you should see how mad she gets at us when we play ball in the house and stuff like that, she doesn't counsel herself all too good but she says she loves her job, right mom?. The two little voices feeling so mature for joining in the conversation had brought everyone back to reality and a little giggle at that. They had all but been forgotten in the room till now and were a bright change from the drama of the last few minutes.

Just as everyone was settling down, Caity emerged dressed, and if that wasn't a sign, the doctor walked in and gave her the release papers, so she was free to go home. Hospitals were cramped and didn't keep you unless they had to and in Caity's case she was happy that she could leave and not think about Jack lying in some bed just rooms away from where they were right now. She was dying inside to ask how he was and if he'd make it, but she knew a fight with her dad would emerge from any attention she'd give to the subject. Caity could see that Greg's face was stressed and angry covered up by the worry he had over her. She'd wait till they got home and then make a call to the hospital herself. Part of her wanted to run to Jack and part of her wanted him to disappear. Most of all Caity felt guilty for the fact that she partly wished he wouldn't survive because she knew her life would continue in turmoil if he did. The biggest part of her and her heart knew that Jack was really a mentally messed up man, that he had deep dark secrets that continue to plague him and destroy all he touched. The worst part was that Caity couldn't bring herself to stop loving that man, the man he was hiding deep inside himself, the one that he'd shown her from time to time and then hide again behind the cold hard bastard. Caity was lost in her thoughts and everyone could see it.

Stew brought them all back to the present by asking if everyone would like to have lunch. It was his treat and one of his favorite places was just minutes from the hospital. The boys were the first to jump in and say yes, followed by Maggy, Fran and Caity. Greg, being a true old fashioned man was saying he'd only go if he got to treat, but Stew wouldn't hear of it. He put his arm on Greg's shoulder to steer him out of the room and chat, man to man, as they headed to the elevator. Their conversation couldn't be heard but Fran sensed that Stew would put some much needed sense in her husband, concerning all of this stuff. That meant that lunch would be pleasant and not a repeat of the breakfast fiasco that occurred in the restaurant downstairs

Fran, Maggy and Caity waited for the boys and grabbed Caity's stuff and Easter treats. Without much being said, they followed the men to the elevator, silently all in their thoughts while the boys jostled around touching almost everything in their path all the way from the room, right to the elevator doors until they opened.

Caity was the last to get in and as she turned around in the elevator to face the doors, she saw Father O'Malley just looking at all of them from down the hall. He was just silently standing there watching them all leave and he looked sadly and deeply into Caity's eyes as if trying to tell her something. Just as the doors closed between them, a cold fearful shiver ran down Caity's spine and she would have desperately ran out of the elevator and right to Jack; had she not been surrounded by everyone.

Chapter 16

Jack looked terrible. He was pale, appeared to be barely breathing, and was hooked up to so many machines the old man could barely hear himself think without concentrating on the sounds of the room. It was cold in here too, apparently that was a good thing for Jack, but Father O'Malley was shivering a little even with all his robes on. A nice old nurse walked in the room and gave him a hot cup of coffee. "No change yet", was all she said to him as she adjusted things around Jack as she appeared to make changes to his machine settings. For the first time in his life, Father O'Malley felt helpless. He had no desire to pray, in fact he was sitting their questioning his faith, his beliefs, the foundation of his life, the church, God, Christ and all that was holy. He was in a state of total confusion. How did his world get so out of hand? How had all of these things happened through the years and how had he not done anything right? He'd been involved in thousands of parishioner's lives always guiding them on the right and wrong paths to take. Looking back through his aged eyes, he'd probably given a lot of terrible advice and probably ruined hundreds of lives.

Father O'Malley was so grateful that he had a replacement priest in for the holiday. It was a strange coincidence; timing wise. Originally he had planned to take some weeks off in order to think and find the answers he so desperately looked for. He got up and left Jack's side and walked a short distance to the large picture window at the end of the hall, just outside Jack's room. As he approached the enormous glass pane, he looked down to see the Anderson's and the Banks' families leaving. They were all in a group, walking ever so slowly. Francis held Greg's hand while each of the girls walked on either side of them. Just behind them was that detective, Stew, his sister and her boys, who were each bouncing around full of energy as they walked.

Father Jason O'Malley stared, transfixed by what he saw. The Anderson's were a real family. The kind you saw in movies and on television. They were everything that Jack had always dreamed about having, and being a part of. A normal family! What must that be like to be a part of every wonderful day? Father O'Malley wondered! The Anderson's' were the kind of family that Jack's mom had always dreamed of being a part of. Mary Fraser was a woman who had spent her whole life dreaming about the type of life she wanted. She always fantasized about that special kind of love and bonds that family should have, the kind she craved for, for herself, but never had.

Looking back in his mind, while he stood there mesmerized by the vision of the Andersons Father O'Malley was remembering younger years when he was known simply as Jason O'Malley. He had been a confused high school student, an outcast of his piers, and had grown up in a highly abusive family. His father had beaten him regularly, his mother had spent most of her time hiding her bruises and crying herself to sleep at night. Jason's childhood memories were of constant sadness and sorrow. He remembered always dreading getting up in the morning and having to face yet another day of intense struggles. He remembered being obsessed with a longing for the type of family that he'd repeatedly seen in others at church on Sundays, or read about in the many books he read for escape.

At sixteen, the young Jason O'Malley had already lived an old man's life, and he'd decided that there was no such thing as real love. That the most someone could ever hope for was a kind of peace. A calm tranquility while you traveled your life path. At sixteen he was determined not to end up like his parents and actively began to pursue a role in the church; with his goal to become a priest, and hide in the world of his church. His faith had been extremely strong back then and his desire for calmness and peace drove him until he'd completed his goal. He was oblivious to the world around him at the hospital, lost in his thoughts as he stared off out of the window. The nurses at the desk nearby had a good sense of things and realized the old priest just needed to be left alone to his thoughts, although they did notice he made the odd sighs every so often that almost sounded like a moaning injured young lost animal.

For the most part, when Father O'Malley remembered the first ten years of his career, it was a life he lived in contentment. He'd appeared to have found the peace that he had dreamed about, and his life was based on a type of tranquility in the parish. For the first time in his life, as a respected priest; Jason O'Malley was looked up to and even appreciated by the parishioners. He had put a lot of thought into his work and his parishioners around him. The parish had provided him with a beautiful old home that he cherished beyond belief. Having lived in poverty for most of his young years, he not only belonged somewhere but had a home that he truly enjoyed at the end of a long day. He felt that although he did not have a lot of money, he had become a man of great standing and a type of wealth with his position as a priest in a well established parish. The Catholic Church of All Saints was located in a quiet suburban neighborhood outside of Toronto Ontario, and back then, life seemed to be complete and all that he could ever need.

He paused for a moment, and closed eyes while thoughts fell deeper into his past. His mind was transfixed on years gone by. Back then, Father O'Malley had been going through his life as if all was the way it should be; that was until the day that Mary Fraser walked into his life. She was a young, freshly married woman, kneeling in a pew for hours at a time, crying and lighting candles. Jack's mother had been a beautiful young woman who was sadly trapped in a loveless and hurtful marriage. She had been struggling with her strong Catholic beliefs of "till death do us part" and "what God has put together, let no man ..."

Father O'Malley sighed heavily, with a load of truly sad memories that could not be re-written. He remembered letting the new parish member have a few days of praying by herself and after he had felt that sufficient time had passed, he imposingly went to sit in the pew in front of her. Sitting sideways on the bench just about a foot over to the right of her; at first he just stared at her while she sat there, eyes closed and mumbling her prayers.

Mary Fraser had been an absolutely beautiful woman. Long dark brown hair that flowed in curls in the back while lots of little tendrils encircled her delicate face. She was unhealthily slim, which accented her high cheek bones. As he sat there remembering, he could picture her face, the soft pale skin against the dark hair and her most mesmerizing feature of all. Mary Fraser had the deepest aqua blue eyes Father O'Malley had ever seen. They pulled you in while they were accented with the longest dark eyelashes known to man. Father O'Malley remembered himself sitting in that pew dumfounded and speechless and it took him a few minutes before he even spoke to her. It seemed that Mary Fraser was using her eyelashes and blue eyes as a magnet to just pull him into her world and to this day he couldn't remember how their first conversation had gone, but he knew he'd never forget the way she had looked that day; and he never had.

She had been beautiful and vulnerable and she had made his heart skip in a way that he had never experienced in his life. Thinking back, for the first few weeks he remembered that he could barely speak when she was around and that he felt flushed and his palms were always sweaty. Even his hands were shaky but the worst part was that at times he felt like a silly adolescent going through puberty because of all things he found that his knees would go weak whenever he found himself standing too close to her.

Back then he knew he was in real trouble when he realized that he was in fact falling head over heels in love with Mary Fraser. He couldn't eat, couldn't concentrate on anything and worst of all he barely got any sleep because she was all he could think about night and day. It shook his world and it made everything look so very different, and worst of all, it was in ways he had never imagined could happen to him.

After counseling her for months on her troubles, mostly about how to deal with her cheating and abusive husband, he started listening to her talk in great detail about her dreams. They were always the same, she longed for a normal little family. Just a normal little happy life that you read about in stories. How she'd married Stephen Fraser in the hope of finding that security. Her husband had charmed her when they dated. He'd romanced her into believing they had the same dreams and that when they married, they would have the life she longed for. Stephen Fraser never mentioned that he needed a wife for his image in his corporate world, and that she was what the image required.

Mary had found out way too late that Stephen was not only a womanizer but also and extremely mean spirited man. When he was drinking, which tended to be almost every night of their marriage, Mary always dreaded what would happen. As a staunch Catholic, Mary Fraser couldn't see herself leave her husband and Father O'Malley insisted that she stick to her vows. But one horribly cold day in January, just four short months after the first day he'd met her, Father O'Malley suddenly thought of himself as simply Jason, a man who was head over heels in love, and during one of their deep long talks alone in his living room, he leaned forward and stole a kiss. It was a kiss so deep that he'd lost himself in her arms. Their worlds instantly collided and she anxiously returned the passion he possessed.

He remembered how afterward Mary had said that she'd been secretly attracted to him from the first day they'd met. Like it was a type of magic that she'd never known? She had never felt like this in her whole life and now it was like some amazing drug that she needed more of.

There were lots of hospital noises happening behind Father O'Malley especially at the back of him by nurses' station. Strangely enough he remained oblivious to it all; deeply lost in his thoughts of the past. Staring blindly out the window as if it were actually a large movie screen playing the harsh details of the movie of his life. He was mesmerized looking straight ahead and knowing that he couldn't go back in time, nor did he believe he could go forward either. The memories were all so real that he was back in time and he could visualize it all as if it was happening at this very moment in time. He sighed heavily and closed his eyes throwing his head back deep in his thoughts.

That cold day in January, began their lifetime affair. It was the beginning of many wonderful and troubling times for the two of them. They'd lived through self analysis, self doubts, amazing guilt and everything in between. In fact, their love had lasted right up until the day she died. Unfortunately, she'd died a cold bitter woman, deeply saddened that her dreams of a life with Jason O'Malley had never materialized. Her spirit had been broken years before as if it had been emotionally beaten into submission over the years of all the broken promises he had made to her. Strangely enough he could never understand her ability to keep up the hope that things would eventually work out; that she had always believed that he'd leave the church as he had promised thousands of times. But years had passed and he'd watched her disappointment grow and sorrow deepen. He'd been a coward and a hypocrite, but worst of all he had been mostly driven by material goods; of all things. Which in reality was strange and totally against his training.

Five years into their relationship, Mary found out she was pregnant with their son and she had been elated. He knew she thought that should have been the very thing to make him change his life, but he didn't. She was forced to seduce her unloving husband into sleeping with her for the first time since they first were married, so that he would think the child was his. Thinking about all this stuff now made Father O'Malley really sick to his stomach. It was like something out of a horribly bad soap opera, but instead it was real life.

Father O'Malley stood there remembering how scared he had been to find out Mary was carrying his child. In fact, he had been terrified that it would make him lose his position in the church. Strangely enough he never worried about losing Mary, he'd always felt that she would never leave his side. Looking back he couldn't remember how he felt about the child itself, just the impact it would have on his perfect life.

Mary hated her husband, and having to share her bed with him took a greater toll on her than Jason could have ever imagined. She'd cried in his arms for hours as if she'd been raped by a stranger, and in some ways it was as if she had. Sadly, their twisted lives continued along the same path and two more years had passed where Mary was raising Jack and praying for a miracle so the three of them would be together.

There had been many memorable and wonderful nights together because Stephen Fraser was rarely if ever home. At the time, Father O'Malley had been happy with the way things were, but he never told Mary, allowing her to hang on to her dreams and hopes for their future together.

As a priest, he had lived an extremely false life. In strange way he had the family he had always craved for while still maintaining his role with the church, and the financial support it provided. Looking back, Father O'Malley's remembered how his house had been his most treasured possession, and by not leaving the church to be with Mary, he got to keep all of it and her too. Truth was that although he had been deeply in love with Mary, he hadn't been man enough to do anything right by her.

The worst night he could remember was when Stephen Fraser came home from a business trip, drunk and in shambles. He'd accused Mary of having a secret unknown life and chastised her for their child that he said didn't look a thing like him. After throwing her across their living room, he'd raped her and left her lying on the floor. She'd been beaten and bruised and barely able to get up. But even after all that, Father O'Malley remained in the back ground without the inner strength to act as a true man should and take responsibility for the woman he loved and the child they shared.

Tears were streaming down his face now as he came back to the present and saw his reflection in the hospital window. He never looked in mirrors anymore because he couldn't bear to face himself and the pain and sins he saw there. Shaking his head in disbelief, he wondered yet again, how could he have loved her so much and yet repeatedly hurt her so very deeply. Why hadn't he taken the chance all those years ago? Where would they be now? Would Mary still be alive? Would Jack be healthy and happy with Caity and instead of lying in that hospital bed? Would he have known true happiness or would they have ended up in poverty and sorrow? Why? Why? Why? Why? Was all he had going through his head.   Placing both hands on his face, he shook slightly from side to side remembering how Mary had changed after all that.

She had changed a lot since their journey had started and it had been like pieces of her warm loving spirit were being destroyed bit by bit. Sadly, nine months after that horrible night, Scott Fraser, Jack's half brother; was born. Conceived in rape and to a man she despised, Mary had a difficult time loving that child. But she tried hard, and Father O'Malley made her work at it. Scott grew up always knowing that he was disliked by his mother, and that Jack was the apple of her eye, and as the child aged Jason could see that life for Scott was similar to the life he had had when he was young. Life was cruel he thought, it was unbelievably cruel.

Their affair continued and fell into a familiar pattern of a long term relationship. Strangely enough, he was able to get the church to hire Mary as his housekeeper and cook so it made it easier for them to spend precious private time together. As the years passed, he'd watched the boys grow up in a home with an alcoholic and abusive father who often beat them for no reason; and a mother who spent a great deal of time either crying or sitting off by herself in her rocking chair by the fire.

Back then, just when he'd thought life couldn't get any worse or more complicated, Father O'Malley was faced with interviews by the church. He'd passed, but had been fearful that they were investigating his secret life; instead they'd assigned him to mentor new priests in his parish. By then Jack was an alter boy and a very religious little chap, finding solace in the peace of the religious building, which for him; housed tranquility and safety from his home and his father.

Suddenly Father O'Malley could feel the blood rushing through his body as his memories took on the darkest turn in their history. His own son, his flesh and blood, was sadly and repeatedly abused by one of his priests in training. He had never been quite sure of exactly how long it had gone on for, but when Mary told him, the rage he faced inside him was the worst a man could ever know. Worse yet, when he brought the case to the higher ups in the church they demanded that he burry it. Buy off the parents with whatever it would take. Make them feel guilty as if it was their fault this happened and as the priest in that parish he was never to speak about it again. Jason O'Malley, as Jack's father was in shock. But Father Jason O'Malley was forced to do as he was told or lose everything he had worked all those years to maintain.

With all those horrible thoughts of the past wheeling through his mind, he stood there in the window's reflection suddenly feeling quite dizzy and drained. It felt as if he was just about ready to faint. He was standing there in the present feeling as though he was really in the past. Almost as if she'd read his mind, a sweet chubby older nurse came up behind him with a wheel chair. Lightly tapping him on the shoulder, she whispered, "I know it's been a long day already, why not sit in this while you're looking out the window. No one needs it right now and you look like the last few days have taken their toll". With that she held the handles and locked the brakes, while he sat down and put his feet up on the rests. They exchanged pleasant glances while she released the brake and rolled him a bit closer to the window, then just as suddenly as she had appeared she silently walked back to her station, and left the old man to his deep thoughts.

Father O'Malley was grateful for the seat. Life had taken its toll on him and he'd finally come face to face with all the terrible truths of it over the last few days. It was like suddenly waking up from some horribly bad dream, except that in this case there was no time left to fix the things he so desperately wanted to change. Mary was dead now; he hadn't been there by her side when it had happened, and carried that pain with him daily. Jack was near death fighting for his life while his love, Caity had walked out of the hospital without even stopping by to see him.

The way everything looked right now was that his big life of power and position was just one big mistake after another, and the worst part was that he'd not only messed up his life but he'd also destroyed the lives of so many others around him. He bent his head down as he was so ashamed of himself he didn't know what to think anymore. He'd messed up Jack's life. He'd given such bad advice to so many parishioners who had come to him in trust, looking to spend their lives differently through divorce and annulment and he had been a complete hypocrite with every last one of them.

Thinking about a few of them he remembered; one particular parishioner stood out in his mind. A young gentle but plain woman named, Mrs. O'Grady, who had come to him in such despair. She was asking if God and the church could forgive her if she left her husband Ralph. Ralph was a drunk and a gambler, and Father O'Malley talked her into staying with him regardless of all the hardships and pain. He'd watched them lose everything; Ralph had taken off never to be heard from again. Jane O'Grady and her three children ended up in a shelter somewhere until some of his parishioners took her in. He'd talked so many into senseless things by playing on their faith and the deep guilt he could use to manipulate them.

Remembering back he wondered just how many lives he ruined! How many lives were wasted in sadness for guilt and the old expression, "till death do you part?" How many people suffered by the advice and guilt he had given them when they could have gone on to be just as faithful to God, in good happy lives that have moved on.

Father O'Malley's saddest advice was actually to his very own son, Jack. He'd talked Jack into marrying Jane even though he wanted to back out just a few weeks before the wedding. He'd convinced Jack to take Jane back three times, even when he'd found out that she'd been cheating on him. Each time she'd promise to stop, and each time she did it again, he'd talked Jack into giving her yet another chance by reciting those same words, "till death do you part?" And oh ya, the big one; "What god has put together let no man…" Worst yet, Father O'Malley had even convinced Jack that he could only really be legally separated to remain a good Catholic because technically you were still married. So Jack obeyed and never filed for his formal divorce. How warped was that, he thought? He even remembered worse advice yet, was when Jack came to him to tell him all about Caity Anderson. How she had swept Jack off his feet and how much in love he was with her. That he wanted a formal divorce and an annulment so he could build a new life for himself, with her.

The truth was that it was the first time Father Jason O'Malley had ever seen his son with a glow in his eyes and a skip in step. He was fascinated, for through all the love that Mary Fraser had brought Jason, he had never had the freedom to express himself in that way; and he cried heavy tears of regret while watching Jack's emotions that day. Truly Jack was deeply in love for the first time in his life and the only person he ran to tell about it was his parish priest. Jack relied heavily on Father O'Malley as his father figure because his legal father was such an absolute disgrace. Unfortunately, instead of giving Jack advice as the real father he was, he gave him advice deeply entrenched from the Catholic Church's religious rules and regulations, especially after he'd found out that Caity Anderson wasn't even Catholic.

He shivered now as he remembered working Jack over mentally with guilt and all the things that played up the religion and his strong faith. Sitting there remembering how it all went, Father O'Malley had to admit he'd been a stupid and ignorant bastard to destroy the only real chance for happiness, that Jack had ever had. Did he do it because of his role as a Catholic priest or did he do it in reality out of envy? He himself was the ultimate hypocrite…who was he to judge Jack's life, let alone tell him that he should remain celibate for the rest of his life and forget this woman named Caity, worst yet because she was not of his faith. He really worked Jack over mentally so that the "Catholic Guilt" would eat him up like a cancer and slowly destroy what the two lovers obviously shared. It got so that after weeks of working him over, Father O'Malley could see that Jack could never see past the insurmountable guilt he carried over being separated, the marriage vows, the part that said he should remain celibate and couldn't go on with his life and worst of all, he'd made sure that the issue of Caity's faith was the greatest sin of all.

And so, now here he sat, the cause of so many people's grief including his own that he carried like lead weights on his back. He had spent the months since Mary's death, analyzing and re-analyzing everything in his life. Why hadn't he'd made different choices? Why did Catholic priests have to remain celibate? He took a breath thinking hard about that one, and the truth was he was caught in confusion. It was the very same confusion that some Pope himself had created. Well maybe not the present Pope but some Pope along the way. Hundreds of years ago, priests did marry, they were land owners and from what he knew of the story, the Catholic Church was scared of losing all the land to the priests' sons so they passed a rule that priests could not marry, and live a celibate life.

Strangely enough though, to this day there were some Catholic priests in Europe that still married. He sat there pondering the strangeness of that information. He knew that if he'd been allowed to marry he would have somehow married Mary all those years ago. How life would have been different for everyone. Even his parishioners, whom he cherished, would have benefited from his different perspective on life. Maybe as a happier more balance man he would have been a different adviser. Instead, he; like Mary, had become bitter over the years. He was cynical, and walked with a deep sadness in his step as if always at some funeral. He'd seen the changes in himself every time he looked at his reflection which was why he'd removed all the mirrors from his house.

Again, he fidgeted in the wheel chair in front of the window. He was so tired he couldn't get comfortable. As if reading his thoughts, yet again, that same kind nurse walked over to him and handed him a fresh hot cup of coffee. "I thought you could use this." She said and turned and was gone again.

If he hadn't known better he would have guessed she was an angel instead of a nurse, but in the window's reflection he could see her working away and being just as kind to all the others around her. He sipped his hot coffee, grateful of the warmth it filled him with. The way the light shone and the window reflected now, he could see himself even more clearly than before. Jolly looking like an old Santa

Clause character with his white hair and rounding physic, you would never have guessed at what the real story was on the inside.

He shook his head in disgust of himself. Here he sat, a hypocrite to his faith, a liar to so many he'd lost count, an accessory to many pedophilia cases that were buried secrets by the church which paid off families and worked with the strength of their faith, and a strong regime of guilt. Seeing himself in this light, all he could see was just a sick old bastard that should probably have been struck dead years and years ago. Instead he was forced to live and face all of his sins, over, and over, and over, again. He had come to new revelations in his mind that would help him cope with the reality of his situation. That when he left this world he could only go up to heaven because since the day he was born, he'd already spent every day of his life in a hell from which there appeared to be no escape. It wasn't till today, sitting here down the hall from his dying son that he realized all of this, and as he sat reflecting on his life; he was filled with an incredibly deep and painful regret.

It was true what they said; it only took a few bad apples to ruin it for everyone else. He knew if his story got out the affect it would have on the faithful would be profound. That the media would play through every living moment with a fine tooth comb and lives would be changed forever. Maybe some for the good, but most would be left questioning all that was good. It was the same when those stories of the priests taking advantage of young boys, hit the news earlier this year. Every priest saw it in their parishes, in their collections, in the interaction with parishioners. He remembered how people looked at him wondering if he too was one that had taken advantage of their young children, and he'd found it difficult to continue in his role throughout the peak of the scandals. There was no doubting the fact that publicity of stories had had a huge affect on the Catholic world and he knew that his story would be equally impacting for different reasons.

Funny, just at that moment he realized something about himself that over all these years he had never known. For the very first time in his life; he realized that he had always considered himself to be in the role of a priest, and had never once considered himself to actually be a priest. Maybe that was the key to all of it. Maybe to him, this role was simply something he acted at, like a stage actor. It seemed that the person inside him had spent the entire lifetime struggling to come out and just be. Maybe, at sixteen he had made the worst decision of his life and from there it all just spiraled from one disaster to another. Maybe he was just a good actor playing out a role in a story and now was the time to close the curtains and end the show.

Maybe, but just as he was about to finish his next deep thought there was a lot of commotion going on behind him at the nurses station. He suddenly looked back to see what was going on when he noticed a number of them running into Jack's room with all kinds of equipment and stuff.

Jumping out of the wheel chair he moved as quickly as he could for a man of his age, and headed to Jack's side, hoping and praying all the way that's he'd survive so that all the wrongs in his life could be now rectified; especially Caity.

Chapter 17

Caity jumped into the back seat of her dad's mini van. He always drove vehicles that carried a lot of people and stuff around. Thank god he had captain's chairs back here. She flipped it back at a 45 degree angle so she could relax and just stared at the beige ceiling as if she'd find all the answers of life, up there.

Liz jumped in the other side and was fussing with her purse and cell phone, while her parents seemed to be dawdling and chatting about something outside the van. She looked over across the parking lot and saw Maggy get the boys settled into her car and she too stood in the parking lot chatting with Stew. Caity wasn't sure where Stew's car was parked but she could see that they were deep in some kind of conversation. Closing her eyes and letting out a deep breath, she wanted to be anywhere but here. Looking back at Maggy, she was thinking how lucky she was to have such a loving brother. Stew bought Maggy a new car. What a great guy! What a great brother he was!

Caity was a little envious of their closeness. Liz and her were kind of close but as siblings went compared to Maggy and Stew, they were like weird acquaintances. When it came to Lizzy, Caity knew it was all about her hair, her friends, being seen in the right places with the right people, marrying for money and position, and of course, but worst of all, Lizzy had to always be the center of attention. Today must have been hard on her sister, with everyone centered on Caity! Who was giving Lizzy the attention she needed? No one....and that was obvious from the cell phone conversation she was having with one of her friends.

The front doors opened simultaneously and Mom and Dad got in asking the girls if they were all settled in. For a few seconds it felt just like they were young kids again the way their parents were with them but Caity figured that was just the way parents were, in their eyes you were never really grown up.

As Caity half listened to the conversation in the car, she realized they were heading to her parent's place to finally celebrate Easter. Lunch had been good but they needed to be home and in private now. Mom wanted to stop by the church on the way home but as usual dad talked her out of it; but it really didn't seem like she minded. She was just happy that they were all together and safe and sound. What difference 24 hours makes.

Fran and Greg held hands while they drove, Liz chatted on her cell and Caity was left to deal with the thousands of crazy thoughts reeling through her mind. Looking at the two sweethearts in the front seat, Caity wished that she and Jack were able to be like them. In fact, they had been. The very first weekend they had spent together was like that. Jack and her had held hands everywhere and always touched each other while driving and being together.

Caity remembered the first time that Jack had held her hand. They were walking around looking for a place to have dinner. Both of them were caught up in the nervousness of being together for the first time. She remembered how he looked down at her with a smile while his middle finger played with the palm of her hand sending her a sweet romantic gesture that sent shivers up her spine. She was in love with Jack from the inside, with the person he was in his mind and thoughts before they ever got to that first night they spent together. She was lost in her memories, how nervous he had made her, how he had made her heart beat, how she just loved the way he smelled in the crook of his neck and oh, how when they kissed it was like nothing she had ever felt. Caity was so in love with Jack by the end of that weekend that she knew she was changed forever. Until that weekend, she'd heard people talk about things like when you meet the right person you'll know, and then after the first time with Jack; she did.

Caity suddenly heard her dad asking her if she was O.K. "Ya dad, I'm fine, just a bit tired." She said as she shifted uncomfortably in her seat. "O.K. then", he said, "we're almost home and maybe you can put up your feet in front of the fireplace for a few hours till dinner. What do you think? Does it sound good? Greg asked hoping to create some normalcy in this anything but normal world. "Ya, dad, that sounds like a great idea." Caity said. Fran jumped in and started telling them about the dinner she had planned, with cold cuts, and potato salad, and all kinds of goodies, colored eggs and her specialty of home made cinnamon buns. Those were the girls' favorites. She also said that they'd called everyone and told them that they'd decided just to have a quite dinner with the girls and cancelled Easter with the rest of their friends and family.

"Mom", Caity said, "You didn't have to do that, we could have still have had everyone over. You didn't have to do all that for me". But Fran said that she just wanted a close family time for a change and that it would be good for all of them to have some quality family time. As she spoke, Greg squeezed her hand as a confirmation that he felt the exact same way. As couples went, they were usually always in sink when it came to doing things. That's what was so amazing about them!

Caity's thoughts went back to Jack and the way they were in the beginning, before all the stories of guilt, the church, and oh the stuff that Caity hated the most. When he'd say to her that Father O'Malley told him this, and Father O'Malley said he had to do that, and Father O'Malley, blah, blah, blah.

Oh how Caity hated Father O'Malley for being such an awful person, never mind what she thought of him in his role as a priest. She was suddenly so glad that she wasn't Catholic. Before she got together with Jack she saw all Christians the same, she never designated them by what type of Christian they were, but instead saw them all as heading in the same direction to just slightly different tunes. But now, sadly to Caity, all she could see of Jack's religion was that it was like some unholy cult. A weird cult that controlled and manipulated the minds of the weak thinkers, creating a life that was built on horrendous guilt and fear. Caity knew that Jack had a lot of fear, he feared God, he feared the church, and he feared all kinds of ridiculous things.

To Caity, religion was supposed to bring joy and happiness to your life. In Jack's case, he would constantly be in turmoil, the man inside him that she had fallen in love with, the wonderful man that she missed seeing; he was the one that wanted so desperately to get on with his life and start again to find happiness. That man hiding inside Jack was fighting with the other half of him that was controlled by his guilt and fear; which drove him to live in a controlled life of his own personal hell. When the guilt became too much, he'd become this horrible, horrible man that was the complete opposite to the man she was in love with. She was in love with his inner spirit which he hid, and especially the person she knew he really was deep inside his heart. He was always frustrated, angry and usually screaming that he couldn't do this; that he wasn't allowed to get on with his life, that he couldn't live with the guilt. It was a cycle that had repeated itself over and over again through the two years. Each time the distance between them grew a bit greater; and today Caity realized that it was if a huge brick wall had just been erected between them, as a permanent destruction and prevention of love.

Caity could still hear his words that he'd said to her that last night. They echoed in her head while the tears rolled down her face. Caity wiped them away with a tissue as fast as they fell but knew her dad hadn't missed seeing them in his rear view mirror as he pulled into the driveway. Their eyes met in the mirror and he gave her a knowing wink as he said, "Hey girls, how about we open a nice bottle of red wine and sit and relax by the fire. Well?" He wanted normal back so badly and he just waited for someone to say something. Caity jumped in since Liz was still wrapped up in some cell phone conversation. "Dad, that's the best idea I've heard all day" and with that she opened her door and got out heading toward the front door to her parents house, which was her safe haven.

Chapter 18

While the Anderson's were settling in for some quite time, the Banks' were heading into Maggy's humble little home. Maggy was unsettled by the events of the last few days, and like all holidays the last few years, she missed George. Her husband of ten years had passed away two summers ago in a fluke car accident on the way home from a golf game. Maggy was always grateful for the fact that at least he was enjoying himself the afternoon before he passed away. It didn't seem to matter how much time had passed; Maggy loved him more now than she had ever had. As if sensing Maggy's thoughts, Stew wrapped his arm around his sister whose face was like a window into her thoughts. It was amazing how the woman ever got into a car, since she lost both her parents and her sweetheart in two horrible freak car accidents.

Stew was grateful they had each other and the boys; and they went in to get the festivities for the boys, under way. After the last few days, and the light lunch he just ad, Stew certainly could use a good home cooked meal. The group of them had just spent 3 hours at the restaurant mostly chatting about family memories and drinking a lot of strong coffee. "So what's for dinner, lady? He asked as they followed the boys inside. She looked up at him smiling and proud of herself. "Remember what mom used to always make for the holidays, hmmm? Well, I made her exact menu this year. I figured we needed something homey and couldn't think of a better way of doing it". She locked the front door and set her purse down as she checked her message machine by pressing the play button.

Like a cold bucket of water being thrown on the two of them, and ominous voice was speaking very slowly in a message but was direct in the content. The man did not identify himself but said that Maggy was to contact her brother as soon as possible and have him call a 555-1295 and ask for a man named "the Deacon". Maggy stopped the machine and looked as Stew who was now standing right beside her with the same dumbfounded look on his face. What in the hell was this about? They were both standing there wondering the same thing when it suddenly occurred to Stew that it really bothered him that this nut case not only knew about his sister but that he knew where she lived and what her number was; and that was very unsettling!

They looked at each other checking to make sure the boys were in the other room and too pre-occupied to hear their conversation. Maggy looked a bit pale and almost scared. "What's that about, Stew?" She asked in a somewhat shaky voice. "I don't know Mag, but somehow I think it has to do with Father O'Malley, the shut up money; and Jack and Caity". He rubbed his butt pocket to re-assure himself that his wallet was still there, and all Maggy could spit out was, "What? How? What money? What the hell is going on, Stew?" She was panicked and nervous and so unsettled that she had this crazy urge to grab a baseball bat and search her house to make sure no one was in there hiding. It's what the voice message made her feel like and she felt strangely violated. She leaned really close into Stew's face and whispered carefully so the boys wouldn't here? "Do you think we need to search the house to make sure there is no one here?"

"Don't be silly Maggy, that's just an intimidation message to get me to move as soon as possible and who ever they are; they are obviously impatient right now. Don't look so worried and confused. I'll make you a deal but first, let's have that great meal and some Easter fun for the boys. Then you guys can come and stay at my house for a few days while I wrap all this up. I promise, once we get to my place and get the boys all tucked in for bed you and I can sit down for a night cap and I'll tell you the whole story, and just for peace of mind I'll turn on the gate and house alarms tonight. O.K? Do we have a deal?" When Stew finished all he got from Maggy was an accepting nod as she headed off to the kitchen to get to work and gestured to him to go in and keep the boys occupied.

While the Bank's family members celebrated at Maggy's, the Anderson's sat tense in the dining room pretending nothing's wrong. But everything was. Caity was anxious and tense and lost in her thoughts, not wanting to discuss any of it with any of them. All she really wanted was to go home and be alone with her sad thoughts and lose herself in her self-pity. Thoughts of Jack haunted her every second that she sat with them, and the one thing that she really wanted was peace. She hadn't had that luxury since she spent that very first weekend with Jack; almost two whole years ago. Realizing that it was Easter Sunday and that Jack had never spent one holiday with her, not even her birthday! Those thoughts upset her so much that her face and chest took on strong red shading as if she was suddenly flushed.

Fran looked over at her daughter knowing the cause of the flush on her face but wanting to give Caity some much needed space, piped out with, "Caity, maybe you should stop drinking wine dear, looks like it's giving you quite the bit of color". Fran smiled a re-assuring knowing glance at her daughter and Caity went along with the excuse not caring if they had fooled the others, or not. "Yes, I think you're right mom, good thing I'm not driving tonight; and with that thought, who is driving me home tonight?" Caity asked looking from side to side to her mom and dad.

Greg wasn't stupid and he knew his daughter would need a bit of time and probably a little confidential dumping time with her mother, so without another thought, he jumped in and asked Fran if she could drive Caity home since she hadn't had any wine and he'd already had a few glasses. Greg had given up the idea of Caity staying with them for the next few days the moment he realized that she was way too tense around them right now.

Fran loved Greg for being so in tune. She winked at him as she got up and ushered Caity to the front door. While they pulled out of the driveway Caity let out one of her famous big sighs and looked over at Fran and whispered, "Thanks Mom! You have no idea how much I needed to go home and just be alone with you for a few minutes. "So, what do you think about everything right now? What do you make of what Jack did last night? Do you think he's o.k.? Has he just gone off the deep end? Or do you think he's just some real manipulative bastard? Mom, what do you think?" Caity was panicky and talking fast and appeared to expect that Fran would just jump right in with her opinions. "Well first of all, it's hard to know what the hell to make of any of this stuff.

Did you know your detective friend Stew, was just about to tell me this big story when Father O'Malley interrupted us. I don't know what he was going to say but he did say it was huge". Fran was paying attention to her driving so she was looking forward and couldn't see her daughter's facial expressions but could hear her stressful breathing. "The first thing I want you to do though, is take your medicine so I don't have to worry about you choking to death again….O.K.?" She stole a quick glance at her daughter who was nodding in acceptance and simultaneously taking out her medicines.

Chapter 19

Incredibly, when Father O'Malley sat down at 8:30 p.m., he felt a weight start to slowly lift from his chest. It was as if he could feel all these incredible energy forces coming together. He had often heard people tell him about feeling this way. But never in his life had he ever experienced anything like this. It was a type of over whelming psychic feeling that there were huge positive changes of electricity taking place in the atmosphere. It was kind of like wisps of winds circling him forewarning him of incredibly big and positive changes. He had no clue of what they would be….jut that he was sure of the positive energy and that these events were in the making and they were not only huge…. but…that they were meant to be.

He stopped and paused for a moment; as if he was trying to listen to something. It was almost as if he expected someone to whisper to him what to expect and what was going on. It was almost as if he half expected an angel or some mystical figure to stop by and tell him something. He held his breath, paused to listen and then shook his head in dismay. Obviously he was now losing his mind……but at least he was aware of it. Shaking his head in dismay, he tilted his head to the side with a half smile noticing his son was looking so much better…..while he was thinking of all the wonderful moments he missed over the last forty six years. All the moments he could have shared with him as father and son, were now wasted in the past with no real future. How sad, and with that he leaned forward and placed his hand on Jacks and begged him to get better.

Father O'Malley paused again, gave his head a good shake as if to get everything out of it and took yet another deep sigh. In reality, he did feel good inside because of the events of the last few hours. Jack showed huge signs of improvement and the doctors said it was looking really good for a full recovery if everything kept up in this direction. Remembering that awful scare that he had this afternoon. Everyone was running into Jack's intensive care room and it seemed like forever till he had reached the room. When he'd gotten there it was only to find that the team had been running to the poor ill man in the bed next to Jack, and not his precious son. For that he had thanked God a thousand times today! What a relief it had been, especially remembering the fear that had shot through his body like a lightning bolt those few long seconds it took him to jump out of the wheel chair in front of that window, and run to Jack's side at the best speed that an old chubby priest could do. It may have been only seconds, but it had sure felt like an eternity till he found out what was happening. Hours ago, running to Jack's room, was the first time in his life that he really felt that Jack was his son, and was consumed by an uncontrollable fear that he'd lose him before he had a chance to claim him.

Sitting there next to Jack's bed, Father O'Malley's mind wandered but his body and mind still felt like there were powers at work all around them. He felt such a strong force of energy at work all around him, and he felt weird and odd; but for the most part strangely happy; for the first time in years. Pausing, and taking another deep breath, he had to admit to himself, how strange this all was.

While Father Jason O'Malley sat diligently and quietly by Jack's bedside in the hospital, just a few short miles away, Caity and Francis Anderson had decided to head back to the safety and warmth of the Anderson home. After a ton of tears in the car; and a hot Starbucks specialty coffee, Francis had managed to convince her daughter that a few days of good old family R&R would be just what the doctor ordered; and luckily, Caity agreed. Francis also promised that no matter what, while her father was off at work tomorrow, they'd track down Stew Banks and get the whole story, and also check on Jack's condition; not necessarily in that order.

While Caity and Francis went off on their travels and Father O'Malley sat by his son decidedly spending the night; just minutes down the road from the Credit Valley Hospital Stew and Maggy were getting settled in at Stew's home.

Maggy's boys were excited, viewing this as a great new camping out adventure at Uncle Stew's. The alarms were all turned on and Maggy was sitting with Kevin and Chris around the big center island that sat in the heart of Stew's huge kitchen. She was dishing out double fudge chocolate cake and milk, with the boys propped up on their elbows looking like they were just about to jump into the cake if they had to wait even a moment longer.

As Stew walked casually into the most unused room in his house, he couldn't help but smile as the sudden inviting warmth enveloped him. His adorable rambunctious little nephews looked like two cowboys with a mix of chocolate and milk mustaches, and just like young boys they were getting more on themselves than in their mouths. True to form, Maggy was worried about messing up the always immaculate room.

"Don't worry about a thing sis, this room looks better when it's lived in" rubbing her back to re-assure her that he wasn't in the least bit upset by the mess. "Thank God Stew, because your house is always so perfect I feel nervous all the time. It's like I'm going to break something every time I'm here. Really, you live in something right out of House and Home magazine, and sometimes I feel that we are just the weird country cousins". Maggy was giggling as she spoke and was thinking how unlike him all this was. When he was a boy, her brother was just like her two sons. No one could even walk into his room without stepping on a ton of things between the door and the bed. As if he read her thoughts, while he sat down to enjoy the cake and milk with them, he mumbled, "Guess it makes a big difference when you have a full time house keeper and dog sitter, huh?" Maggy just smiled and nodded stuffing down a big piece of chocolate cake as he spoke, but mostly, she was just enjoying being around the adult company at this time of night. The boys didn't really talk much about anything and Maggy missed sitting around a hot coffee or glass of milk and just talking about grown up things.

Stew would have video taped this time they were spending together, if he could have, the house usually felt so empty with just him and Emma; but tonight it actually felt like a home. He had missed having noise in a house, missed his parents and their family life, truth was, suddenly Stew was missing so many things he couldn't capture all his thoughts. Maybe it was time he settled down and got his own family. He wasn't getting any younger and lately he felt oddly lonely; something he wasn't used to feeling.

"I'm going to go up to the look out room while you put the boys to bed. How about we meet up in the den after.......what do you say?.....Half an hour enough time?" Not expecting Kevin and Chris to jump in and beg to go up there with him, he ended up promising them that they could play up there tomorrow after a good night's sleep tonight and a hearty breakfast in the morning. They agreed and were off and running out of the room, anxious to go to bed so they could get up to their new adventure in the morning.

As Maggy rose to follow them out of the room, she tapped Stew on the head and said "thanks", smiled and walked out after the boys.

Stew followed behind her, heading up to his absolutely favorite room in the house. The "look out room" as he called it, was a large ten by ten room situated at the very peak and center of the house. Its walls were all floor to ceiling windows and it stood like a huge but functional non-rotating turret in the very center of his roof. It even had a beautiful glass window carved into each side of the four slanted shingle roofs in order to better see the stars at night and the sun by day. Stew remembered having to order special remote control blinds which he used when the sun got too hot in the day. Stew loved all the features of the room and he had often sat up there to collect his thoughts. He's always thought it would be an awesome room for an artist to work in, and to him it was his special and very private sun room. Most people had rooms like this off their back door but this was way better than any of those that he had ever seen. Since it was at the very peak of his house, and his house was situated at the top of a tall hilly incline overlooking the deep valley of Mississauga, he always had a beautiful view. He had a full view all around, and in the evening with all the city lights glimmering below him, and the stars above, the room took on a special magic of its own.

It was in the sun room, where Stew had first realized that Jack had been following him and had been sitting outside the front of his home, just waiting around in his car. Because of the reflective glass, Jack had never known he was being watched because when Stew didn't put any lights on up here, he could not only see for miles but actually watch what was going on around his home, and not be seen. Tonight there was no one out there. No car, no reflections, nothing. Thank God for that, Stew thought. After listening to that message from the so called Deacon character, Stew was a bit worried that he was dealing with some psycho nut that could hurt someone. At least here with all the alarms switched on and Emma to guard them in the house, they were all safe for tonight. Tomorrow he'd contact his friend at the cop shop and start tracking down this Deacon guy.

He sat there with his camouflage binoculars looking around the area. Like all the rooms in his house, he had big comfy chairs in this room too. The sun room was filled with unique but comfy outdoor furniture and it was really neat to sit up hear in the middle of winter and pretend he was down south. Even though it was spring and Easter time, not much was in bloom yet so he could see areas that in the summer were blocked by some of the neighbors towering trees. When he was up here, he always felt that he was in a special bit of paradise and always pretended he was down south at some Tiki bar by the beach. All he was missing was the sand. He had the fake palm trees and greenery, the temperature was set just right and light Caribbean music played softly from his stereo.

Stew was sitting on one of his two raised bar stool chairs that he had had custom made just the way he felt they aught to be. They were oversized arm chairs that sat high on stands with wide foot rests and the best soft fluffy cushions that money could buy, actually he had had those custom made as well. The two bar stools had special features built into them designed for how he used them up here. They swiveled and tilted and were exactly what he needed for observing at night. With all the lights off, and the door downstairs closed, he could sit here and see for miles while no one could actually see him because of the way the window panes had been designed. Lost in his thoughts he was suddenly startled by the sudden flash of light that came in from the door at the bottom of the swirling staircase. Maggy had opened it and after closing the door behind her, she carefully walked up the twirling stairs in the dark, twinkling glasses and a bottle that she carried with her. Once she got to the top, the room was actually pretty well lit from all the outside surrounding lights of the city below them.

"Hey there, are the kids tucked in and asleep? Stew asked. " You bet, "Maggy sighed heavily and said "finally, it took a little while but they are passed out cold on the big Queen size bed with Emma tucked in nicely between them with her head on one and paws on the other". That picture in her mind made Maggy giggle and thought that maybe it was time she got the boys a dog like Emma. It would certainly add a lot of company to their little home. "I went into your wine collection and picked out one of my favorites, hope you don't mind?" She looked right at him knowing that he wouldn't but somehow just needed to hear it said. "Are you kidding? That's what it's there for kiddo; that was a great idea! This way we can just sit up here, unwind and talk without the kids overhearing in case they wake up". Stew thought that he and his sister were so much alike when it came to thinking of things like this. If she hadn't brought up a bottle, he'd of gone to get one. Maggy looked right at him and said. "Did you know that you've been up hear for over an hour? Were you lost in your thoughts again?" Maggy was hoping to get the conversation and information flowing and knew that the wine would certainly help in that department. "You know Mag, time always passes quickly up here for some reason, but you got to admit the view is breathtaking, isn't it? Maggy nodded as Stew leaned back in his chair noticing that Maggy looked around and he could tell that she couldn't believe how absolutely wonderful it was up here. Like a mini little paradise, escape place.

"You're so lucky to have a place like this Stew, It's unbelievable. The thing I like best is that it makes you feel like you're on holiday somewhere instead of in the heart of the city" She paused but just had to know. "Was this the reason you bought the house, the room I mean, was this the deal maker as they say?" Maggy was prodding him as she poured the two glasses of red wind and passed him one, leaving the bottle on the raised bar behind them. While she waited to hear what he was going to say, Maggy was holding her glass in one hand while using the other hand to hold on to the left handle of the chair. She placed her back against the chair and kind of jumped up to position her bum in the soft cushion, while shimmering from side to side to get comfy. All that and she never even spilled a drop of her wine. Smiling to herself, she leaned forward, sniffed the wine and holding the glass with two hands, she carefully sipped a taste of her choice bottle.

"I guess there were a lot of reasons I bought this particular house, but you're right, this room really did close the deal. Even when it was empty I could picture it decorated just this way". Stew was remembering telling his agent that no matter what....he had to have this house, and in the end with some heavy bidding, he'd got it. He took a sip of his wine and realized that the crazy job he had and sometimes hated, actually got him all these types of wonderful things, which made it all seem worth it in the end.

While they sat there in silence, sipping their wine and enjoying the quiet, just a few short miles away, "the Deacon", as he called himself, sat in his car, patiently waiting for two people. One was for Stew to call him on his cell phone so that they could set up some kind of meeting and the other was for Father Jason O'Malley to show up at his home that was attached to the church.

Dressed from head to tow in his Bishop's garb, right down to the jewelry, his scrawny thin fingers tapped on the seat beside him, while he occasionally looked over at his cell phone on the seat as if looking at it would make it ring. Where the hell was Father O'Malley? He should have been home hours ago regardless of the fact that he had a replacement priest in for the holidays. Worst yet, why hadn't that detective, Stew Banks called him back yet. You'd think after a message like the one he'd left on his sister's answering machine they would have enough fear in them that the call would be coming in faster than this. He'd purposely left an intense message at Maggy Bank's house in order to force Stew to act faster, but for some reason it didn't seem to be working. He'd left that message over five hours ago and here he sat, still waiting for that damn phone to ring. The Bishop swore like a trouper and his code name of "the Deacon" was actually starting to bug him...but it was too late to change it, so he'd just have to go through this whole mess with a lowly title instead of the one he had.

He sat there in his car remembering back to what seemed like a thousand years ago. Father O'Malley was a young priest; he'd been a cop and was gently forced off the police force because he was gay. Jason as he thought of him, helped him start a new career in the church, and it wasn't long before he was making a way for himself. The Deacon then, but now a bishop.....had been nothing but trouble to Father O'Malley in those years, especially after he'd discovered that he'd abused Jack Fraser as an alter boy, making him his young lover and convincing the young boy that this is what God had expected of him.

The worst part of all was when he had discovered that Jack was the real son of Father O'Malley and Mary Fraser. If he had only known back then, despite the strong attraction he'd had for Jack he would have chosen a different boy and avoided the whole mess that this turned out to be. Now he sat there as an internal detective for the church, a problem solver and a Bishop. He'd been forgiven by the higher ups as immediately as the story had come out, but the relationship between him and Father O'Malley was damaged for life. He'd gone away for years and this was the first time he'd been here since the events had taken place. Shaking his head and then leaning back on the head rest he felt overwhelmed by the past, and the future; He needed to burry all of it to ensure that the press never got wind of this one. How he was going to resolve this was already set in motion, but he knew he didn't have much time; but most of all, what ever he did it had to be effective and permanent.

Sitting there in the big new comfy Oldsmobile, he was sure that no one would notice him under the shadow of the huge oak tree just down the street from the church where Father O'Malley's parish home sat, just to the side of the property on the side where he could see everything. It was a bright night with the moon half hiding behind some clouds, but the tree hid him under its branches which stopped both the light from the moon and the street lights. As he threw his head back and felt himself get drowsy, he knew it was going to be a long night. Without realizing it, he closed his eyes, and leaned his head back on the soft head rest of his Oldsmobile. With his car seat at the slight incline that he had set it at earlier in order to be comfortable, "The Deacon" slowly headed off to unconsciousness in a deep resounding sleep.

It was just past ten when Maggy and Stew broke their relaxed silence and started to talk about all the events the people of the last few days. Stew told Maggy every single detail that he knew about, Jack, Father Jason O'Malley, the church and all of the players, Jack's mother Mary, his brother and everyone else in between. During the lengthy story, they'd finished a second bottle of the same red wine that Stew found behind the bar in the sun room, as well as a whole pile of snacks and munchies that he'd kept up there in the fridge and cupboards.

It was dawn, and the sun was just beginning to rise with a slight purple orange haze to the East, and Stew and Maggy were tired. It had taken them all night to plough through all the gory facts and details of the last forty six years, or so. Actually to say they were tired was an understatement. Stew and Maggy were both emotionally drained, but for different reasons. Maggy, who had already been in turmoil over the last year because of all the events and cases that she'd worked on and through at her Catholic parish, now sat there overloaded from the story that Stew had spent most of the night purging. She had questioned her faith and all it stood for way before today, but now, with Father O'Malley's and Jack's life stories, both separately and intertwined, Maggy knew that not only would she never be the same, but that she could never go back to being the religious person she'd once been. She doubted if she would ever attend a church mass again, or for that matter even enter a church again, without thinking about all of this. Time would tell, but the way she felt she was sure her life had been altered for ever. She still believed in God and Christ, and knew man was to blame for the situations that had occurred, but she also blamed the church and its management for how it buried these things, how the innocent were left to suffer, and the guilty were forgiven. As far as she was concerned at this very moment in time, she couldn't see herself involved deeply in religion ever again, nor would she let her two precious boys even remotely near a church.

As for Stew, his reason for being changed forever had little or nothing to do with the corruptness in the Catholic Church. It had everything to do with Caity Anderson and the huge impact all this would have on her life and her heart. The truth was that Stew hated it all! He knew the burden was on him to be the one to tell her all this. That his sister Maggy could never get through it all in one piece. He also was faced with the intense realization that in the short time that he had known Miss Caity Anderson, she'd managed to slither through the tiniest hole in his huge protection wall and made her way right to his heart. In some unimaginable way, Caity Anderson with her big gorgeous blue eyes and her bright as day smile, grabbed his heart in her palm, and owned it. In just a few short days, she'd achieved what no woman had ever achieved till now. She'd captured his mind, his heart and his body, and worst of all; sadly, she was deeply in love with another man.

Stew knew that no matter how it played out, that after he'd tell her all of this info that he'd found out; he was sure that she'd hate him for it. Not for the facts, but for not keeping some of it a secret; and mostly he knew she'd hate him for the impact all this unbelievable information would have on all of their lives.

The impact would be huge and everlasting but most of all it would be devastating. When Jack found out all about his mother and who his real father was, Stew doubted if he'd ever be any good for anyone, but mostly he'd never be able to have a meaningful relationship with anyone, especially Caity.

There was still another side to all this. If Jack died now and didn't recover and find out any of this before his death, Caity would need years of therapy to get over him and the sadness she would carry for him for his sad life that he had led. It would take her years to realize Jack was simply a man and he certainly didn't belong on any special pedestal that Caity would be sure to place him on.

Without a doubt, this was the messiest case Stew had ever worked on. It was deeply entrenched in a strong and high powered church that would appear to stop at nothing to silence it's errors and hide the truths to ensure certain continued patronage from it's parishioners who where the income providers for the riches in the Vatican and elsewhere. Interestingly enough, this was the only case he wasn't getting paid a dime for that is if you didn't count the "shut up Money" the church had given him in a check which had been to ensure that all the secrets remained just that, secrets. Funny Stew thought, didn't they realize the first rule of life. That when more than one person knows a secret, then it no longer is. And the truth was, just when you least expected it, the truth was always discovered by someone, and it almost always came out.

Stew knew that after all he'd found out, he couldn't live with himself if he kept it all a secret and that the check was merely proof to use when it came out in the press. The way he felt right now was that he really had no options. There was only one way out of this complete mess and the only way out would be to leak the story wide open to the press, and just deal with the aftershocks as they came. He knew it would be just like a huge earthquake had hit their world, followed by one hell of a big clean up.

No matter what, he was only sure of one thing. The next few days or weeks ahead were going to be a living hell, and the sooner he got it over with the better. Unable to wait a moment longer he jumped out of his chair ready to spring into action.

He looked over and Maggy, who was now sitting on one of the lounging chairs, had since fallen into a deep and peaceful sleep while he had been alone and off with his deep thoughts. First things, first. Stew called Emma's dog sitter, who in fact had been a professionally trained nanny by trade and the only one who had passed his tough interviews when he'd been looking for a caregiver. She agreed to come over within the hour to baby-sit the boys so that Maggy could get some much needed sleep.

With that achieved, Stew felt a new burst of revitalization hit him. He was suddenly filled with life's nervous energy, and couldn't wait to tie up the lose ends and deal with the last of characters, "the Deacon". After that, he'd be off to the press and out with the garbage that had waited so long to rear its ugly head. He paused, hoping that he was doing the right thing, but feeling in his gut that he was.

Chapter 20

It took just about an hour as promised for Nanny Brown to show up, and although Stew had already started making breakfast for the boys, she came in and took right over. Maggy was still fast asleep in the sun room on the lounger and Stew made sure the blinds were closed, he adjusted the temperature and put a light blanket over her while she slept so deeply that she heard nothing.

He whipped back downstairs to the kitchen on his way out and made them all promise not to disturb her until she woke on her own. Knowing that everyone was settled and that the alarms were on, he headed for the big old front door, with Emma tight on his heals behind him. Emma loved to go with him to work on his adventures and he sometimes took her along. Today it seemed like she was asking to go with him, poking his leg with her nose and pawing him with her front paw to stop him from walking out. Her big black head and black as night eyes tilted sideways as if in a questioning glance and she was doing her usual mumble wining noises she always made when she wanted something.

"No Emmm, you're needed here. I'll feel better if you guard everyone for me today, and besides, I have a lot of running around to do today. O.K.?" Stew spoke with her just like he was talking to a young child. His tone had been soft and caring and filled with the love he had for her. As he spoke and hummed in her right ear, he gave her a few ear rubs and a head tap. As if she totally understood every word he'd just said, with that she licked his hand and strutted off to the kitchen with a bounce in her step and her tail proudly wagging. As Stew watched her, he suddenly wished he was a dog.

Emma had a happy go lucky walk and with her tail wagging and that joy in her step, she was oblivious to the horrors the day would bring. To a dog, the world was simple and disappointment usually only lasted a few seconds till your next ear or tummy rub, and then they were off to do something else. Unlike the complicated and often hurtful humans, dogs made life simple. It was too bad that life couldn't be simpler today, and every day for that matter. As he closed the front door behind him, he smiled at how lucky he was to have all of them, his sister, the boys, Emma and even Nanny Brown. He had a good life, and it took his dog to continually remind him of it. Thank God for Emma, he thought as he backed out of the driveway and reset the gate alarms.

Chapter 21

It was a beautiful sunny spring day; the air was crisp but warmed by the early morning sun. There was soft misty dew spread across the landscape, like a soft cake frosting. Driving along the silent sleepy streets at this early hour was peaceful and filled with a calmness that was always treasured. Father O'Malley couldn't remember the last time he had ever felt so at peace with himself. Having never felt this way inside, it brought him a joy and lift of spirit that he had never known in his life. After spending the night by Jack's side; and making sure his son was doing well before deciding to go home and get refreshed, Father O'Malley felt that it had been the longest night of his life. He had been hunched over, leaning forward on the edge of Jack's bed the entire night, with his forehead resting on his folded arms; he had just lain there and thought a million things.

    He'd thought of everything that he'd lived through in the past but mostly he'd spent the night deciding on what would be the best thing to do for everyone involved. After playing out every scenario in his mind, he reflected what he thought the repercussions were going to be, in his very near future. He knew full well that the fall out from what ever he decided to do; would be major. Looking back on his long sad life, filled with regrets and pain; he'd come to the conclusion that there was only one thing he could do. Once Jack was strong again, he'd find the right time to tell him the whole story from A-Z. Knowing that once Jack knew he would be able to take control of his life, for the first time ever.

In his heart, he wasn't sure Jack was the type of person who had the strength to handle the load of information he would deliver. He also knew that it would eventually mean that Jack and Caity might have a small chance for happiness after the storm cleared. Father O'Malley could feel his heart beat and skip in happiness as he drove. The thought of doing something really good and right for a change made him feel a relief inside he couldn't ever remember feeling before, in his whole life. Today and the rest of the week would be incredible! First things first!

Once he got home, he'd rest up, shower, change and eat. Then look up the Anderson's and head over and tell them everything. Maybe Caity and her family could help him tell Jack? Maybe that would be the easier road on everyone? As he headed round to go into his driveway, he was so caught up in his thoughts he didn't even notice the Bishop's car parked just down the street from the church. Mentally putting a plan together for his decision, he stopped for a minute with the car parked in the driveway, and paused to enjoy the scenery. He'd done a lot with this old place. The garden would be the best it's ever been, this summer! Driving in and admiring the early tulips that had recently shown their beautiful faces with the warmth of an early spring, and remembering that he'd planted tulips everywhere this year. Their rainbow of colors along the house front stoop looked amazing in the rays of the early morning sun, and looked like something right out of House and Home magazine.

Thinking that he should probably take a picture of it all for when he got too old to plant, and enjoying every moment of spring's glory, stepping out of the car he paused to enjoy the moment. Walking down the brick laid path to the front door, he felt a skip in his step. Ah, so this is what life is like when you finally find peace? So this is what people meant when they had told him about being so happy inside they could dance. What a feeling, he thought. What an absolutely amazing way to feel. No weight of life but just the exuberant knowledge that life was going to be just the way it should and that you were somehow going to be a part of all the excitement! Wow! If only he'd known this feeling as a young man, a feeling of hope, of dreams, but mostly of a brighter tomorrow. If only he could have known that feeling of hope, he probably would have done so many things differently. He paused at his front porch looking softly at the beautiful array of flowers, while he was lost deep in his thoughts.

Looking up at the old oak door, he realized he'd have to hire someone to put a coat of varnish on it this year, the weather being mostly the sun, sure did beat up the wood panels. Just then he remembered he had a visitor staying with him. The replacement priest would be inside waiting for him. He hesitated at the door with a type of sadness knowing that he wouldn't have the peace of being alone with his thoughts when he went inside. Instead he knew he'd probably have to sit and chat with the man.

With that Father O'Malley looked over on the porch at his big old wood rocker. It sat out on the porch from very early spring to the latest day possible in fall. He had spent a lifetime sitting in that chair watching people, and chatting with them as they passed. Mostly though, he'd spent hours alone simply just rocking back and forth while gazing into the garden. Right now his favorite chair was a wonderful invitation for him to be alone with his thoughts just a little longer; so he headed over to the edge of the porch, plopped himself down and let the sun warm his tired face.

He wasn't rocking but actually just sitting with his elbows resting on the arms, feet flat on the floor, and head bent slightly back so the rays could calm his excited heart. With his eyes closed he could smell the sweet sent of his awakening garden, and enjoyed the happy array of the birds singing to themselves in the morning air. Slowly opening his eyes to the sky he started to rest and calm down from all the busy thoughts he'd had the last few days and could suddenly feel himself start to doze off to a restful place.

A sharp crack sound, almost like that of a large tree branch snapping, turned out to be a gunshot. It was instant, its aim direct, and efficient; and in one fast second ………..the job was done.

Father Jason O'Malley was shot once through the forehead forcing his body backward into a strong rocking motion. The mission was complete, and with that the big new Oldsmobile drove off in a screeching furry.

Chapter 22

Stew couldn't believe what a beautiful spring morning it actually was. The sun was shining and the crisp air was still warm enough for him to have his car window down as he drove. As he pulled up to the stop light at the end of his street he was suddenly faced with the fact that he really didn't have a plan for today. In his mind he went over the list of things he had to achieve today; and although he felt like he was on a mission, the truth was that he really wasn't quite sure where the best place to start, but he knew he had to start with something.

This was all foreign territory for Stew. Normally he was always put together with both his plans and his thoughts. Today was starting out pretty strange. He was sitting there in his car at a street light and really had no idea where he was headed.

As the light changed he made a subconscious turn right which was off in the direction of his favorite cop shop where his pal Charlie Randle worked. Charlie; now there was a story. Charlie had been a cop forever, but most importantly, he'd been a young cop when Stew had first met him. As a kid, Stew got himself into normal teenage trouble stuff, and Charlie was the only cop that had a soft spot for him. He'd always bailed out Stew, mostly because he believed that he had been a good kid that just got a little to adventurous or curious at times. It was Charlie that got Stew through his Dad's death, and it was Charlie who encouraged him to pursue his dream to become an ace detective.

Through the years their friendship grew to be more than just friends; actually Charlie was Stew's extended family. They had reached a point where they were comfortable old pals that drank together, laughed together and sometimes had time for the old game of golf which they both really stunk at. Stew totally respected and trusted Charlie, but most of all, Charlie was the only rock Stew had, and in some ways it was the same way in reverse for Charlie. They always bounced cases off each other relying on the other's perspective which almost always paid off. Charlie had a pride about Stew. After all, as a young cop, he'd stuck his neck out for the kid too many times and his sergeant had always hated him for it but he'd done it anyway. He'd been thankful that with all that, Stew had finally made something of himself and he'd said as much to Stew as often as he could.

As Stew thought about Charlie, he pictured the overweight, rough edged personality as a bit of a Robin Hood type cop. He was shorter than Stew by at least a foot and he made up for it in personality. Charlie couldn't seem to keep food off his shirt when he ate and he didn't care if anyone liked it either. He was a great cop no matter what his clothes looked like. Charlie had been promoted a number of times and had solved too many cases to keep track of. The force had gotten used to his rough edges and over looked his shortcomings long ago because of his success. As Stew pulled into the parking lot, he could see Charlie standing in the window looking down, a phone attached to his ear and his arms were fraying in all directions. That was usually the way, Stew saw him every time he pulled in and he knew that Charlie was just being Charlie.

Stew had been to the cop shop so many times that all the guys not only knew him, but were like old family. He loved coming here and joking with the guys, he loved the way he was so accepted here, it was like he was one of them; but most of all he just liked being a part of something. In his line of work he was always alone and this place made him feel like he was a part of a greater thing. Today the gang picked up on it the minute Stew walked in the door. Stew wasn't himself, not in his body language, his fake smile which had not always been sincere in the past, nor could he hide the way he seemed to carry a lead weight on his back. Even Lorraine, Charlie's assistant, who Stew always flirted with and teased; was ignored as Stew headed straight for Charlie's office door.

Charlie was waiting in his office wondering what was taking him so long to walk up from the parking lot. When Charlie had seen him through the window he'd known something big was up. Usually Stew had smugness to his walk but Charlie had noticed that this morning Stew walked with his head down and a heavy load in his step. Something was definitely wrong with Stew, and if Charlie was a betting man, and he was; he'd say it was either a woman or one god awful ugly case. Just as that thought passed through Charlie's mind as he downed the last drop of his almost cold coffee, Stew knocked his usual one knock on the open door, tilted his head sideways and asked if he could come in. "Are you busy, Chucky?" "Na, never too busy for you Stew, come in and shut the door behind you. You look awful this morning like you're carrying quite the load on your shoulders today." Charlie answered in with the usual banter they exchanged every time.

"You know me Charlie, I can handle just about anything, but I'm working on the ugliest case of my career right now, and I've suddenly realized that I am head over heals in love with the wrong woman". Stew said in a heavy voice sighing as he plopped himself down in one of the two very worn out leather chairs that were positioned in front of Charlie's very old and worn out wood desk.

All Charlie managed to respond with was "thought as much by the way you looked getting out of the car". And just as he was about to continue, a young desk cop barged into the office in a total panic. He stopped dead in his tracks realizing that the sergeant wasn't alone but when he realized it was Stew, went into announcing in a panic mode that a priest in Mississauga was just shot and murdered in cold blood, right on the front porch of his parish home. Stew leapt out of his chair, knocking it backwards to the ground as he had to know what priest and where.

The young cop looked right at both of them, some priest named Father Jason O'Malley of St. Mary's Roman Catholic Church, just five minutes from the precinct. "He was shot right through the head while he sat on the porch in his old wooden rocking chair. The other priest said that at it made him rock back and forth for quite a while after it happened. Also chief, they have an eye witness on the scene. A jogger witnessed a brand new Oldsmobile speed off right after the shot, he got the plate numbers and when we ran it, you'll never believe this". The young cop paused, but no one said a thing waiting to hear the last bit. "The car belongs to a bishop in the Catholic church. Chief, can you believe it? A Bishop Sir, Serge? Did you hear what I said?" The young trainee was excited and scared but couldn't believe the story. As he went to leave the office after having delivered the message, he turned at the door looking at both stunned men and said, "Oh ya chief, they need you to get down there right away sir," and with that the young cop turned and left them to their shock.

Charlie looked at Stew and he couldn't believe how pale Stew was and it seemed like he was even a bit in shock. He moved quickly as he had been trained to do. He grabbed Stew's elbow as he headed for the door to his office. "Come on, we'll take my car with the cherry on top, that way we can get there fast, and while I drive, how about you tell me what the hell this is all about". With that they kind of walked and ran at the same time out of the office and straight to Charlie's' cop car.

Once they were strapped in with their seat belts and Charlie was in the process of maneuvering out of the light and through street lights with his lights going and the siren blaring, he looked sideways at Stew while he drove and said, "O.K. – what the hell does this have to do with you?"

It took less than ten minutes to get to the scene, during which Stew gave Charlie the shortest version possible of the story…but Charlie got enough of it to work with. When they arrived they'd noticed that cops were everywhere, the scene was already taped off and it looked a mess.

Stew's mind raced to Caity, what if she had something to do with this? What if she killed Father O'Malley? Stew panicked and couldn't breathe at the thought and then he realized, she couldn't have anything to do with it, a Bishop was seen at the scene and Caity hadn't been told the story yet so she couldn't possibly have any motive to hate the guy this much. He suddenly calmed down and switched on his detective's mode. Charlie looked over at Stew, saw the change in him, and while he smacked him on the back, he said "finally, you're back with us. Good, 'cause I'm gonna need all the help I can get on this one." With that the two men walked up to the crime scene. Father O'Malley was still sadly sitting upright in his rocking chair, strangely, he had a weird peaceful smile on his face as if he hadn't known what hit him and he was still in the last thought he'd had before he died. His eyes were eerily open and the blood that was splattered all around him suggested an instant death. The bullet entered his mid forehead but blew out the back of his head and chair. It was a sight Stew knew he'd never forget and wished he'd never seen. All he could think of was the poor troubled priest who had sat in his living room just days before, confessing all his crimes and needing Stew's help; was now dead. Today; Stew was helpless and couldn't fix anything, and suddenly that paper in his wallet was burning a hole in his backside.

Without saying a word to anyone, Stew turned when they started bagging the victim. He headed straight for the right side of the house that was full of tulips and blooming spring bushes, and there he lost his stomach to the day's events. He would never be the same strong sure detective he'd been till now, but one thing was sure, he'd help Charlie and the guys get the bastard and put him away for life.

With that, Stew told Charlie not to wait for him, and he headed down the street on foot to be alone with his thoughts and get a cab back to his car at the precinct. The day was going to be even longer than he'd thought, but right now, he needed to see Caity; and that's exactly where he was headed.

"Wait" Charlie yelled behind him. "Where ever it is you're headed, you'll have to put it off for a few more hours. I need you at the precinct to help me weed through all of this shit. Come on Stew." Charlie was yelling after him, which made Stew stop and turn around. He paused, looked back at the crime scene and then at Charlie. Realizing Charlie was right, that what he knew would be very helpful right now, he let out one hell of a big sigh and yelled back. "O.K. You got a deal buddy, but not more than a few hours." With that Stew gestured Charlie to head over to him, locking his feet where they were with no intention of going back there to take another look. Charlie nodded, got to where he was standing, whacked him on the back, and they headed straight for Charlie's car. "Another shit day in paradise, eh Stew" Charlie hummed as he got in the driver's seat and looked over at his pale friend. All Stew could do was nod, flip on his seat belt and whack the dash as a kind of, let's go Charlie, and with that they were off.

Chapter 23

Stew walked into the precinct behind Charlie Randle and was amazed how busy it was. After all, this was a suburb city in Ontario, not the heart of New York City, but yet, to Stew it looked as busy as any downtown major city cop shop. He guessed that with today's murder of a priest and the mornings' big drug bust in a fancier part of Mississauga, this was probably the most action this cop shop has seen in a while. Stew couldn't wait to get through the doors and into the quiet of the interrogation area. That would be where they would hopefully get their much needed answers. Charlie handed him a cup of strong black coffee and a couple of aspirins. "Take it" was all he said as he went to his desk to get his note pad. "You looked like you were gonna lose your stomach back there", half yelling at Stew in a loud voice as he rummaged through his desk across the room, and answered his phone at the same time.

Stew looked down at the two aspirins in his palm, wondering what they would do for his queasy stomach, but without another thought, popped them anyway using the strong black coffee as a chaser. "So, you think I'm getting soft on you, eh…..Charlie? Looking over, Stew couldn't wait to hear his friend's reaction. "No, just too personally involved this time buddy and it's written all over you. Anyway you look at it. It's gonna just get uglier as the day wears on, and you know that's a guarantee!" with that Charlie walked over to Stew, whacked him half gently on the back and added "let's get going. The jogger is in room number one and they just called to tell me they picked up the bishop a few minutes ago. We got him while he was still sitting and having a coffee in his car. They are in the process of bringing him in so when we are finished with the witness, we can get the murder's statement. All in all I hope we have this thing wrapped up in a few hours. You know Stew, the press will be the worst part of all this. They'll be on it like a dog with a new bone." With that, Charlie looked dead on at Stew and asked, "How about we interview them together? You might be so close to all this that you can ask questions that I'll never even think about. O.K.?" Charlie half asked and half told Stew what he wanted. Not in the mood to say anything at this point, all Stew could do was nod in agreement and after downing the last drop of his horrible coffee, he stood up to follow Charlie to room one.

As Stew stood up, he half rested his back side against a desk and he felt a bit weird. His gut feelings were ringing off the hook about what he saw this morning. It was like all this was way too easy. Something wasn't making any sense. This whole murder wrapped up in an hour thing was just too easy. There had to be more to this. As he thought about it all, none of it added up. Just then he heard Charlie ask, "You all right Stew?" "Ya, just a little tired, that's all. Let's go and get this over with." And with that Stew followed Charlie thinking that he'd better stop wondering and start paying attention if they were gonna get to where they needed to be on this stuff.

Just before Charlie opened the door, Stew grabbed him by the shoulder stopping him from entering the interrogation room. In a very soft whisper, he looked right at Charlie who was roughly a foot shorter than him, leaning forward so they could look dead on at each other and said, "Charlie, tell me something. Why in the hell would a bishop shoot a priest in cold blood, right outside the house attached to the church? Why wouldn't he drug him to death in his sleep or something more secret where the church could do a cover up or something? Why would he make it so public and so dramatic especially if the church likes to bury these things? They don't like any negative press especially these days with all those priests they have had to forgive for their sins with young boys and everything. You've seen the way they are trying to bury that and let the public know as little as possible. Why would a bishop want this kind of publicity? What is the motive? Don't you think that if he was trying to bury the secrets that Father O'Malley was a part of they would have done something very discreetly to silence him? Maybe even move him to no man's land, but murder him in cold blood in his rocking chair on his balcony at the church? That just doesn't make sense to me. It doesn't add up, does it?"

Stew knew he had Charlie's full attention and was watching his eyes add up all of Stew's questions. With a big pause and some heavy thought, Charlie looked right at Stew and said, "I knew I needed you on this on, all good points! We'll have to really ask a lot of the right questions if we are really going to get to the bottom of this, come on, you lead buddy!" With that they walked into the room to the waiting jogger seated at the table, coffee in hand and wearing nothing but an expensive jogging suit and brand new running shoes.

Chapter 24

Caity was sitting at her parent's kitchen table. Oh how she loved this house! It was an oversized two story family home, with six big bedrooms, 4 bathrooms a two car garage sitting to the back of the property at the end of the back yard and a beautiful in ground pool surrounded by an ten foot privacy fence. No matter where she went, when Caity came here, it always was the only place that ever felt like home. There was warmth in this house that Caity didn't quite know how to describe or for that matter duplicate in her life. She assumed it had to do more with the people in it than the actual house, and knew that if they had grown up in a shed it would still have the same feeling for her. Caity had always dreamed of recreating the same warmth in a home of her own with the man she loved, but as she sat there, she doubted that her dream would ever come true.

Thinking about all the things she loved about her parent's home, the kitchen was really her favorite part. It was one of those kitchens–den combinations. A beautiful open concept room that like everything in this house was oversized. It took up the whole back part of the house from end to end, while the family room took up the whole left side the kitchen and eating room took up the whole right side. It was great; you could actually stand in the kitchen cooking and be a part of everything that was going on, including watching a movie with the gang while doing dishes and stuff. She and her mother loved the way it was done. The only thing that separated the work space from all the rest was two well placed 4 foot walls that broke up the work area from the table, chairs and couches in the rest of the room. The best part in Caity's mind was the wall to wall windows and three sets of sliding doors that led out to the patio.

It was a marvelous spring morning. The sun's rays beamed into the room and sprayed the table and chairs with streams of warmth. Caity was sitting facing the back yard and was enjoying the warmth of the sun on her face. She was thinking about Jack and couldn't wait to find out how he was doing. Mom and her would have to drop by the hospital today and see for themselves. Somehow she'd managed to park that intense hurt that she felt the last night that she'd seen him. She was thinking of all the good things while wondering what could make him suddenly turn into such a mean monster at the strangest times. After all the things they had been through together, if it didn't work out now, Caity knew in her heart it never would. Mostly she knew she couldn't take anymore. She needed the stability and security that a real relationship had. She couldn't continue being turned on and off like a light switch in a busy room. The truth was that this morning she was feeling confused about how she felt about everything but in the same respect she was excited by the thoughts of her mom and her going to see Stew and getting the real story of why all this stuff has been happening to her. She just hoped and prayed they'd be able to get a hold of the man today. She'd call Maggy in a while and get her to track down Stew for them, and then head out.

Caity sat there with her eyes closed facing up to the sun as if the warmth would remove all the heart pain and sadness. Maybe she thought, maybe there were really good reasons for Jack to have been acting the crazy way he had the last two years. But if there were, would they even make the situation better or would it get worse? Maybe once she knew the story she'd be able to make better decisions and handle things differently. Lord knows, she was tired of bursting into uncontrollable tears all the time. Until Jack came into her life she had never known such deep emotions, but in reality, she'd never known such a deep love for anyone, either. Jack was the first man that Caity had real love for, the kind of love that lasted for a lifetime, the kind that kept two people together no matter what problems they had to face. Caity knew that this was the kind of love that was not only a once in a lifetime chance but that it was also the kind she knew would take her an entire lifetime to get over.

　　Just as she was caught up in all her day dreaming, as she was leaning forward on her elbows to sip her coffee, Fran silently entered the kitchen walking softly in her wooly socks; she went over to her day dreaming daughter and lightly and slowly touched Caity's shoulder with a motherly worry rub. Caity looked up at her mom while parking her deep thoughts and smiled, "Hey Mom, how come you're up so early?" Fran looked down at her, tapping her shoulder blade and she headed for the coffee pot. "I could say the same thing to you, honey. What ya thinking about dear?" Fran asked as she poured her coffee and leaned back on the kitchen counter looking straight at Caity.

　　Fran knew that she'd remember this moment for ever, standing here in her stocking feet, and old pink bathrobe, she was admiring how beautiful her daughter looked in the sunlight. She also noticed how sad and deep the lines of worry were on her young face. Strangely, Caity always sat in the very same chair that she had since she was five. There she was in her favorite chair; favorite spot at the table, still wearing her teenage years worn out flowery blue bathrobe which had certainly seen better days, but had a strange happiness about the print. Caity even had on those strange teddy bear slippers that had that big fury head on them. Fran remembered trying to get her to throw those things out years ago, but she hung on to them like everything else.

　　"Well Caity". Fran said, "Are you feeling a bit better today? We have lots of interesting things to do once we get your father off. What do you think....are you up to seeing Stew and hearing the whole thing?"

　　Fran was sure that Caity wasn't aware of the fact that although she was in love with Jack, Caity certainly was affected by Stew. Fran had noticed how nervous Caity was around Stew or how she actually floated with all the special attention he paid her. Fran knew that her daughter was probably taking notes and wishing that Jack would treat her that way, but she was sure there was more to it. Fran suspected that if Jack wasn't in the picture, Caity and Stew might end up dating.

　　Caity looked a bit puzzled and asked, "What do you mean Mom? Of course I'm up to it, what are you worried about? Is it another bad asthma thing? Well before you say anything...the steroids they've got me on have done the trick and I can feel that I'm using my lungs better again". Caity wanted to let her mom know so she wouldn't worry, but she'd missed the mild implication that Fran had made about Stew.

Fran smiled as she put down her empty coffee cup and came and sat right across from Caity at the warm sun drenched table. "Absolutely nothing is worrying me now dear, you know me; information is always better than not knowing something! Besides, you finally have a peace about you in your face that I haven't seen in a long time, and it suites you!"

Chapter 25

As they entered the interrogation room, Charlie made the intros; while Stew's mind was wondering back to when Father O'Malley had been sitting in his family room just a few short nights ago. They had shared drinks together and a detailed conversation about the priest's life. Now that same old guy was dead, shot dead by a bishop of all things, and this jogger was the only witness to the whole mess. Great! What the hell was coming next?

While day dreaming Stew only caught the guy's first name and realized he should have been paying better attention. Having been part of these things so many times, he knew that the first few minutes were intros and the set up of how things were going to go and Stew already knew all that.

Looking at this witness, Stew felt like something didn't fit. The guy had a brand new jogging outfit, and those damn running shoes couldn't be any whiter. Except for the green stains from the morning's wet grass, they looked like they had just come out of the box before the morning's run.

As Stew kept thinking, he suddenly realized that Charlie was getting to the tough questions and started to pay attention. Charlie was asking the regular boring stuff, age, employer…..what the guy did for a living. He was in his late sixties, sixty seven to be exact. A retired widower and he said he was out trying to get in shape. As the guy sat there, he looked really nervous, not the type of nervous that Stew was used to when people didn't know what was going on, the type of nervous that was serious. The guy even sat grinding his hands together as Charlie spoke to him and asked him general questions. Maybe, Stew thought, maybe he was one of the parishioners of the church and the whole scene had been too much for him and now he was in some kind of shock. Weird thing was; if this guy was a jogger, he certainly didn't have the body of one. After all, he was pudgy, a bit bloated, his legs weren't thin or muscular at all, and even his arms were weird. Just then Stew decided that the questions Charlie was asking didn't make any sense, so he interrupted the chit chat of the guy's background and jumped in and asked "Charlie, do you mind if I start with a few questions of my own first?" Looking at Stew by his side, Charlie knew his friend had something on his mind and said "Stephen, Stew is going to go through the important stuff and I'll take the notes." With that, Charlie made a little gesture to Stew to go ahead, using his pen as the go ahead gesture, and then looked down at his note pad preparing to write it all down.

"Stephen," Stew said the guy's name, pausing as if there was more to a name than just someone's attention. With that Stew asked him key questions, like how long he'd been jogging, had he just taken up the sport. And how well did he know Father O'Malley, or did he even know him at all?

Stew found out really quickly that Stephen became even more nervous for some reason, but couldn't put his finger on it. He found it made sense when the guy said he'd actually just started jogging this morning. That it was really his first time out, trying to get in shape on the doctor's recommendation.

Well, that explained the new outfit. What a bummer! You decide to get in shape and your first morning out jogging get to witness a gruesome murder of your parish priest, Stew said as he continued probing. It turned out this Stephen guy had been a parishioner most of his life. Great, now the witness had personal ties to the scene, even better! As they talked about sports, the church, and the priest, Stew suddenly had to know if Stephen had ever met or seen the bishop before this morning, and with that, suddenly the witness became weird. He looked from Charlie to Stew and back to Charlie. He didn't answer the question but actually was speechless as if trying to decide what answer he should give them. Before he could say anything, Stew held his hand up and said, "Say no more. So you actually know the guy, right? Stew asked again in that way, that all Stephen could say was "Yes".

He bowed his head down and placed his forehead in his hands as he rested his elbows on the table. "Sorry, we know this is a lot for you to take in this morning. Your parish priest was shot dead by your area bishop, but we are just trying to get to the bottom of all this. Is there any reason you can think of as to why the guy did it? Did you ever see them argue or anything? Do you know something that could help us with the investigation? Stew threw a pile of questions at the witness hoping to get him to open up. "No, not really" Was all that Stephen guy answered.

"So, now that we got that figured out, how about you give us a detailed description of the events you witnessed. How the guy got out of the car with the riffle. How he did it. Were you too scared to move? Did it all happen too fast for you to realize what you were watching? Where did he take the shot from? All that kind of stuff." With that Stew stopped talking so the witness could give them the detailed account of what he'd seen.

Stew listened with a skeptical ear. Apparently, the Bishop never got out of his car. He'd taken the shot though the window, and then drove off in a mad furry. Stephen said he'd stood there mostly in shock and fear, watching the events unfold as he stood on the sidewalk just down from the whole chain of events. He also said he'd thought about hiding behind the nearby bushes but couldn't remember why he hadn't. He was also pretty sure that the bishop had been so caught up in what he was doing that he hadn't noticed him across the street and down from where he'd been parked. Apparently the bishop's car had been quite a ways down the street from the church and enough of a way that Father O'Malley hadn't seen him.

Strange, you'd think that the priest would have seen something. The car, maybe even noticed the bishop sitting in it. Anything! You'd think that the way things were the pieces would make sense, but the dead priest looked like he hadn't expected anything or anyone as he's sat rocking on his baloney. He actually had the chair at the right angle to have noticed something, and you'd think that if he'd seen the bishop down the street he wouldn't have remained in his chair rocking. Wouldn't he have gotten up and headed toward the car? Who the hell knew what the truth was? Stew certainly didn't feel like they were getting what they needed from the witness.

With that, the three of them were suddenly sitting silently in the room when Stephen asked if they were done and could he leave. Just as Charlie was about to release him, Stew piped up with, "I can understand that it's been a really rough day and all, but we just have to step out of the room for two minutes and confer. Routine you know. When we come back in you'll be allowed to go. Till then, can I get you another coffee or something? Shouldn't be long, ten minutes or so. O.K?" And with that Stew and Charlie stood up to step out of the room as Stephen nodded and said he was fine with that.

The second Stew closed the door behind them; Charlie grasped his arm and asked "Stew, what's going on? You are starting to treat the witness as a guilty suspect. You know better that to get that way. So what the hell is up? Charlie asked appearing a bit impatient with Stew. Either because he couldn't read what was going on or because he thought Stew was taking over and exceeding his bounds.

"Calm down Charlie, let's go to your office so I can fill you in. Can we hold this guy for a while? Or at least until we've interviewed the bishop guy? Can we?" Stew was anxious and was obviously on to something or thought he was. Charlie looked at him and said, "We can probably hold him till we interview the Bishop, but not for long. Stew, the guy's a willing witness for Christ sake and you are acting like he's the murderer or something. We're gonna have to be careful to maintain his rights and all that. You know that we can't make him stay unless he agrees." Charlie was doing his cop job now.

"He just agreed. Besides, I don't think he's innocent. The guy isn't telling us something. I don't know what it is, but the pieces don't add up. Don't you feel that Charlie?" Stew needed to get Charlie's take on the whole thing. "Ya, I felt that too! I just can't even imagine what to ask him to find out!" With that Charlie shrugged his shoulders and led Stew down the hall hoping that the Bishop was already in and ready to be interrogated.

Luck was definitely on their side! The guy was booked and in the second interrogation room, waiting. The two were like anxious school boys on the road to discovery and they walked in a hurried pace toward room two and the bishop. Grabbing Charlie and holding him dead in his spot outside the room, Stew looked at him and said "Charlie, think about the crime scene. The witness said that the bishop's car was parked a ways down the street and couldn't really be seen by the priest, that means he'd have to be a hell of a marksman to make the shot dead on in the forehead with the angle the priest was at that would be impossible. The bishop would have had to drive his car up to the front of the house and take the shot with the priest seeing him do it. There's no way at that time in the morning, that Father O'Malley wouldn't have stood up when he saw the car pull up. Even if he didn't, tell me how the bishop would be able to stay in the car, whip out that long barrel and take a clear, marksman type shot. It just doesn't add up." When Stew finished talking, Charlie smiled right at him. "You see Stew, that's exactly why I brought you along. You're thinking before I do. I would have had to take all the info back to my desk and pour through it to come up with that this morning. I guess I'm just getting old, or you're really into this case. Either way, let's go in and find out what this old geezer has to say for himself."

As Charlie was about to open the door, two men walked up to him introducing themselves as lawyers appointed by the church, for the Bishop. Charlie and Stew shook their hands and invited them on in to the room with them. Christ, Charlie thought, it was going to be one hell of a day! And with that he also thought, with all his swearing he should be going straight to hell in a hand basket, or something. Good thing he was an atheist, he couldn't take much more of this shit!

It had been one long morning, and it wasn't even eight yet. They had the interviewed jogger, Stephen, held in at the precinct for a few hours longer while they interviewed the bishop; lawyers and all. Then they went back in and interviewed Stephen again. When Stew and Charlie were finished they were drained and withdrawn by what they had found out. They were disgusted with religion and the way it had all come down. By the time they were through, the bishop was free and the jogger was being booked.

Stew sat down at Charlie's desk and put his feet up leaning back in the chair. Charlie had thrown himself on the old black and cracked leather couch that has somehow ended up in his office. What a day, what a life, and who in the hell would believe it. It turned out that the jogger was Jack's father, Stephen Fraser. The bishop was the instigator but never actually pulled the trigger, but he was certainly responsible for Stephen Fraser pulling the trigger.

What they found out today was sick and disgusting. The bishop had paid a full visit to Stephen Fraser just two short days ago, he admitted as much. He even admitted that he confided in Stephen telling him the whole story of Father O'Malley, Mary Fraser and Jack. His explanation was that as his bishop he felt the poor man needed to know. In Stew's eyes, the bishop was no better than the devil himself. He purposely gone to see Stephen Fraser, he'd purposely told him the whole story of his dead wife and son's real father, knowing full well that if he wound up being the sucker enough, he'd set out to kill Father O'Malley. The bishop had even admitted as much to them. What made Stew mad was that they didn't charge him as an accessory to murder. The fact that the cops didn't charge the bishop for some how being the cause of such a senseless death, seemed really irrational to Stew. Charlie was frustrated and tired as he watched Stew sit as his desk, just as frustrated and just as tired, as he was.

The bishop had told them that just two short days ago, he'd been to Stephen Fraser's house, knowing full well that the man wanted complete revenge for having been wronged his whole life. He knew it would take at least a day for the man to pull himself together enough and all he had to be told was that Father O'Malley had had one reliable habit, that was; in sunny weather, he always sat rocking in the wee hours of the morning. He loved to take in the splendor of his garden and the joy of just sitting in his old wooden rocking chair. Today was a good day for the bishop. He'd thought as with most cases he'd worked on in the past, that it would take days before justice was done. Sitting in his car he had realized that it was a great morning when he'd seen Stephen Fraser suddenly jogging along the walk across the street. He'd had new runners on and was set on the visual of Father O'Malley on his rocker. The bishop had said that he hadn't known what to expect next, but knowing human nature and the way he'd wound up the guy, it was only a matter of time before the deed was done. Stew sat there remembering the highlights that the bishop had told him. Father O'Malley was gazing into the garden on a perfect sunny morning and hadn't even noticed the jogger on the other side of the street.

Stephen Fraser had planned the murder well, he'd hidden a rifle in the bushes across from the church, he knew that when the cops saw that he was jogging they would never assume that he would be able to carry the murder weapon, he took the shot, and was done. Then he took off;

hid the gun, and was back in time for the police to arrive. The bishop on the other hand drove off the minute the priest was shot, claiming that he couldn't afford any bad publicity for the church. During his statement, his lawyers were always advising him not to continue with that thought or this one and they were always interrupting, but through it all they managed to put the pieces together. The old guy even laughed when he'd heard that Stephen Fraser was trying to pin the murder on him. They hadn't found a murder weapon in his car and according to the where his car was it would be a near impossible shot.

The green grass stains explained the hidden riffle in the bushes and the fact that the man was guilty as the day was long from the first minute Stew laid eyes on him. Something still didn't make sense. Where was the murder weapon now? It wasn't anywhere in the area to be found. In fact there was no trace of anything like that ever having been hidden in the bushes. Still worse, Stephen Fraser's hands had no apparent residue from shooting a gun, on his hands or body. It was like he had never shot one and that didn't make sense either. The bishop's lawyers made sure he was questioned and held for as little time as possible making it a record interview and release. Stew couldn't help but feel that the early hours of the morning had somehow made the interview seem a little distorted.

In the meantime back at Caity's parent's house, Fran was enjoying the calm warmth of the sun and Caity's new peaceful existence. The silence was broken by Greg rushing into the kitchen, dressed in his cool blue pin strip suit and his favorite crisp white cotton shirt and navy tie. "Hey girls, what are you guys doing up so early? I hope you're planning a nice relaxing day and just doing fun girl things. Remember what the doctor said Caity, you should rest up and keep your stress down." Greg was moving at full speed through the kitchen, pouring a hot coffee into his car take out mug, while looking for his brief case. Fran and Caity just stayed sitting quietly at the table while he rambled on about his busy day and then whipped out the back door to the car.

"Dad's kind of hyper today huh Mom, is he stressed over a new deal or something, or is it me?" Caity was hoping it was a business deal and that she wasn't the real reason he was stressed since she was sure the last thing he needed was something else on his plate. Fran paused, taking a moment to think about the question. Letting out a heavy sigh she responded with, "Well it's probably a little of both......but I really can't tell this morning. I know last night we talked for quite a while about you and I got him to agree not to be too demanding on you today."

Signing deeply all Caity could say was, "Great! That's a relief." And before she could say anything else her dad ran back into the kitchen and flew to the T.V. set that was sitting in the corner, turned it on, and said; "You guys are never going to believe this. I just heard it on the car radio and thought that maybe one of the morning shows were covering it'. And at that exact second there it was on the screen, the day's top story. A Father Jason O'Malley of St Mary's Roman Catholic Church in Mississauga was shot dead on his church balcony while sitting in his rocking chair earlier this morning. The reports said that the suspect was a church bishop of all things and that they had a jogger as a witness. As the reporter went on with the story and videos from the scene were being played. Fran and Caity were speechless. They sat there in shock just as glued as Greg was and soaked up the story on the morning news show.

All Caity could feel was relief, she suddenly had a terrible sense of relief that the old guy was dead. The priest that was repeatedly responsible for making Jack go nuts with guilt and who had talked Jack out of their relationship so many times that it drained Caity to think of it. She suddenly felt drained and she could feel the blood rush from her veins. As she heard the gory details on the news she wondered why a bishop would even think of killing a priest let alone Father O'Malley who by all accounts was doing exactly what the church had instructed him to do.

The story was clearly a shocker for the news team and the city, when murders were reported it usually had to do with drugs, gangs and not some local half hero of a priest. You could cut the air in the room with a knife and one of the only things you could hear were all three of them letting out deep breaths that appeared to have been held when the story first came out.

When the reporter switched to the weather, Greg turned off the T.V. and looked at his two girls. "Can you believe that? Fran was half turned in her chair so she could see the screen better and Caity was just sitting there shaking her head in disbelief. "You know Dad, the world is full of nut cases and this just goes to prove it; again". Caity said while getting up and heading toward the coffee pot to get yet another cup of caffeine. Greg came up to her and gave her a big "Dad type" hug. "Are you O.K. kid? You know that old guy was just a bastard in a priest's suite. Be thankful he's finally out of Jack's life!" With that he hugged her again while tapping her back and signaling Fran to come take over so he could head off to work. The dinner conversation was certainly going to be interesting tonight when he got home; that was certain.

Fran came over and did the group hug thing and looked at Greg. Winked and said…. "You better get going dear, you're going to be late for your big meeting, and Caity and I will be just fine with our girly girl day". With that she gave him a soft quick kiss on the lips and a lovingly little tap on the bum and off he went.

Caity giggled "That's what I love most about you guys! All these years of marriage and you are both still as cuddly and romantic as the day you got married. You know Mom, I often day dream what it would be like for Jack and I to be together always. I know, we'd have exactly what you and Dad have, and that's what makes me so very sad. To know that Jack would throw it all away for some advice some old bitter priest, who is now thankfully a dead one at that!" Caity was trying to put all her emotions together but wasn't succeeding.

"Mom, I'm going to take a shower and get ready to go out. Then I'll call Stew and Maggy and hopefully they can meet us for lunch or something. O.K?" Caity wasn't really getting permission, just confirming that her Mom was on board. Fran nodded and started to make some toast for herself. "I'll be ready in about forty five minutes Caity, you shower first and I'll be right up". With that Caity left the kitchen and raced up the stairs to get on with the day.

Fran stood there at the counter; worried. She didn't know what the day would be like but she knew she was worried about Caity's mood swings, acting like nothing was really wrong when she heard about Father O'Malley. Alone with her thoughts the phone broke up whatever direction they were headed in. Knowing that Caity was in the shower and would never hear the ring, and that Liz hadn't come home last night and thank God Greg didn't know; Fran reached over to the phone and picked it up.

It was Maggy; she was on her way over having left Nanny Brown with the kids and the dog. Fran hung up the phone realizing she had only a few minutes to get dressed before Maggy arrived and decided she'd get washed quickly to freshen up and put on slacks and a lazy long sleeved white v neck t-shirt. It was one of Fran's favorites and it gave her a comforting feeling wearing it. Just what she needed for what she knew was about to become another day from hell.

It had turned out to be a disgusting morning for Charlie and Stew. The bishop had been smug with them and said that he had been happy with today's events. Worst yet was that he'd done nothing to hide his joy. He had even bragged about being a great study of characters, and that if you could read people you could predict their next move. According to the bishop the death of Father O'Malley was the best thing that happened to the church, and he didn't hide his opinion. He may as well have pulled the trigger himself as he described the scene from early that morning.

Chapter 26

Maggy arrived just ten minutes after she'd hung up the phone with Fran. In that short time Caity had showered and dressed and Fran was not only dressed but she'd already been back to the kitchen and put on a fresh pot of coffee, when the door bell rang.

Caity ran to the door to let Maggy in and hugged her at first sight. "Thanks for coming; I guess you heard all about Father O'Malley's death, huh?" As Caity urged Maggy in and closed the door behind her, she absent mindedly took her coat and hung in on a hook close by.

Ushering Maggy toward the kitchen, Caity was excited with a happy energy that Maggy had never seen since she'd known her. Too bad that today's events would take that brief happiness from her, but at least, Maggy thought; she'd be the one to tell her and be there for her when she'd heard too much.

Maggy felt the warmth of the house immediately. From when she first entered at the front door all the way down the light honey oak floor hallway into the beautifully open concept sun drenched kitchen. It was a happy feeling type of kitchen that just filled you with thoughts of happy family moments that must have filled the room over the years, and Maggy paused in the door way and took it all in.

"Boy Fran, you really have a beautiful house!" Maggy said as she walked over to the kitchen table and sat down in Caity's favorite chair and let the sunshine envelop her with its warmth. Maggy suddenly got a cold shiver dreading what was to come.

"So Maggy, you didn't tell me what you thought about all the news this morning. What do you think about Father O'Malley's murder? Can you believe it? Huh?" Caity persisted trying to get some kind of response form her friend. They were both seated at the table, facing Fran as she worked at the counter to make the coffee and set up a plate of munchies. Maggy could see the tense worried look on Fran's face, knowing that she was waiting to see what Maggy would tell them, and obviously wondering how Caity would react to everything. Maggy had said she knew the whole story now, but Fran wasn't sure Caity would be as strong as she hoped. Maggy watched Fran and told them that they both had better be sitting down when she shared all the details of the man's life; but in her mind she was also thinking that she'd leave the news of Jack's death; till the very end of it all.

As Fran brought the coffee and treats to the table, Caity looked up at both of them and said, "This is going to be a great day. The man who brought Jack and me nothing but heartache is out of the picture, and although I didn't want to see him dead I can honestly say that I don't even feel sorry for him. And after we find out how Jack is doing and I go see him to see if this will make a difference in everything…. today will not have been half bad. What do you think? Eh? Caity asked as she looked from Fran to Maggy and then back again. "Look I know you are both against me ever seeing Jack again, no; don't even try to deny it!" Caity said waving her hands to prevent them from saying anything until she'd finished. "But, I really need you two to do this for me. To be there for me. To help me because after the last two years of hell that I've been through, Lord knows I need it! O.K.?" Caity stopped and looked at them as Fran tapped Caity's hand as she sat down next to her and replied; "Dear, that's exactly what Maggy and I are! We're here for you, and you don't even know how much! Right Maggy?" Fran asked and Maggy nodded.

Realizing that the atmosphere was getting tense, Maggy jumped in and answered. Well, how about first things first. Stew told me the whole story last night and I thought it was time you knew it all too! If anything it will certainly answer quite a lot of those questions you used to bring to me in our sessions. You know Caity, I have to tell you that the whole story is way worse than we could have ever imagined. It's so bad, that I'm not quite sure exactly where to start, except in the beginning of Father O'Malley's life. Let me say this, I can tell you that the whole story will not only be overwhelming but a little hard to take." Maggy paused and Caity looked at her and told her that no matter how bad it was, that she needed the truth more than anything right now. That after living in the dark full of strange questions, today was the day she'd be freed of it all. Little did she know how true that was?

It took a few hours, two pots of coffee and a lot of sickening details before Maggy finished telling them everything she knew about Father O'Malley's life, and the truth about Jack being his real son. Fran felt horribly drained and sick to her stomach from hearing how pathetic it all was and what a waste of so many lives that were driven by deep secrets and dark sadness. Fran looked over at Caity and realized her daughter was not only overwhelmed but she was breathing really poorly. Almost only half breathing. She wasn't even taking full breaths. "Caity!" Fran said panicked, "Your chest's purple, hurry, go take your asthma medicine before you have a bad attack." Fran was panicked in her voice and urged her with a lot of worry. When Caity ran out to get her pump, Fran explained to Maggy how that Caity's chest always went purple as a pre-cursor to an asthma attack. They could always tell when it was going to be a bad one by how purple the little area in her shallow of her neck, would get. The second that Caity was out of ear shot, Maggy told Fran about Jack. She was shocked and horribly saddened for Caity.

The impact of this would be felt for years to come, and all Fran could think about was how Jack had ruined her daughter's life the last few years; and now this! Maggy was quiet. She knew that she was going to have to tell Caity about Jack once the medicine kicked in, because better she get the news in a controlled environment, than to get it by surprise somewhere. They sat their waiting in silence. By now the sun had moved across the room and the day had half passed. Caity came back in looking a little better having taken both her asthma medicine pumps. Fran had poured her a hot coffee while she was gone and as soon as she sat down she took a sip of it to warm her chest.

"What's up?" Caity asked, looking at the two of them like they were little kids who'd just been caught with their fingers in the cookie jar, just before dinner. "Well, come on, I know you two, all too well! Maggy what did you tell Mom while I was gone? Well?" Caity was getting impatient and a little nervous thinking they were keeping something important from her. Maggy spoke carefully and detailed, explaining Jack's health condition before she told her that he'd passed away this morning, just shortly after Father O'Malley had left. Maggy spoke slowly and kept sighing while Fran held her daughter's hand all through the details and the final outcome.

Caity was silent. She said nothing, didn't shed a tear and had no reaction. She was either in shock or had not quite processed all the information. Fran tapped her hand and stood up and hugged her daughter as hard as she could without hurting her. "Caity, you know that the Lord works in mysterious ways honey. You and I both know that Jack would never have been able to handle all the news about his mother, his real father being Father O'Malley and all the stuff in between. Caity, you know how screwed up he was with the religion thing, and now, having heard the whole story about him and even his being abused as child, you got to know that all the stuff you went through had nothing to do with you. Jack really did love you! He really did! There never was never really another woman, but you can see why it felt that way with how the priest was making Jack feel so guilty about you….can't you honey?" Fran said holding Caity softly from behind as she remained in her seat …quietly listening to her Mom, while Maggy sat there silently listening to the soothing attempts of a loving mother with her child.

"Caity, all this time you were blaming yourself for not doing things right. That it had to be something you did and said. All the times that he broke up with you, you were always carrying the entire burden. Now you know Jack was being manipulated by a sick old bastard priest who I hate to say, deserved everything he got this morning." Fran sat down; pausing to take some breaths and hoping that with her silence she'd get some kind of reaction from her daughter.

Caity let out a heavy sigh as the tears started to roll down her face like a faucet had just burst. Grabbing a tissue from the center of the table, Caity cried and blew her nose for over half an hour while Maggy and Fran tried desperately to comfort her; there was not much they could do but wait it out.

When Caity had calmed herself, and the tears subsided enough that she finally talked about how she'd lost the love of her life. How much at that moment, she couldn't hate or detest anyone more than

Father O'Malley. How she didn't know how she'd go on. Why things couldn't have turned out differently?

That she knew that if Jack had lived, he'd be more screwed up than ever, and they wouldn't have worked out anyway. She finally realized that Jack had been honest with her when he'd told her he'd loved her but couldn't deal with any of it. That his religion had not only consumed him but had become his cult. "The Catholic Cult," as Caity had always referred to it. It's what probably killed him in the end. The guilt that Father O'Malley had placed on him was probably the cause for his heart attack and all of his pain. That in her mind, Jack's religion had destroyed so many lives. Caity didn't understand any of it. To her, religion was supposed to bring joy to your life. Instead of bringing joy to their lives, it ruined them. It controlled life to the point where Jack was at odds with his religion and what his heart wanted. That type of religious affect is what Caity simply referred to as a "cult." A cult controls life and destroys it. To Caity, it was the "Catholic Cult" that destroyed Jack and their love; forever!

With that, Caity stood up and said she was fine; but what she really wanted was to be alone right then and there. Maggy and Fran disagreed. They stood up and convinced Caity to go with them to Stew's house and get out for a while. Maggy needed to check on the boys and she thought they could use the distraction. Caity protested quite a lot but after much convincing and hearing about Emma and Maggy's boys. She got her purse and got into the car in a numb state of shock. The truth was that she was in total fear of her new reality. Caity suddenly realized a very deep sadness that consumed her to the core of her very existence and yet she had to continue to go on.

Chapter 27

Stew couldn't hide his excitement. He felt like the whole world suddenly looked marvelous; but in a harsh reality is seemed actually quite sick that he was this happy. Even after the day of hell, interviewing the jogger, then the bishop, then the jogger again only to find out that the guy was Jack's legal father and he'd been set up to kill the priest. If that wasn't soap opera material, Stew didn't know what was. When Maggy had reached him on his cell to tell him about Jack, he hated to admit it because he was sure it made him seem like a bad guy, but in reality it was as though a huge weight had been lifted from his back. He started the morning by tossing his cookies at the church, and was wrapping up the day with a skip in his step and a new look at life. Maybe there was a God after all! O.K., so he always knew there was. He'd been raised Catholic for Pete's sake, but he'd spent the last few years doubting it all. Now, he felt like the devil himself had been dealt with and that everything was suddenly right again in the world. He knew Caity wouldn't see it that way right now, but maybe in time she'd be set free.

As Stew sat in his car in the parking lot of the station, he paused a few more minutes to put the whole day in perspective. He had to admit that this was even too much for him! Today's events were probably too much for most people. The strange thing was that he felt like the case wasn't closed at all. Instead, he had this nagging feeling in the back of his neck, that he missed something. That some how all the pieces they had didn't really add up. Stew let out a very heavy sigh and threw his head back against his head rest and shut his eyes for a few seconds. They had a witness. So it was that bastard character; the bishop. But in reality, the bishop was still their eye witness and the courts would certainly see a Bishop in the Catholic Church, as a credible witness. That was for sure!

They had a very suspicious Stephen Fraser from everything to his stained running shoes to the fact that he didn't deny any of it. Fact was, Stephen Fraser didn't deny it or admit it; either. The priest inside the house told the cops he hadn't seen anything and wasn't even sure he'd heard a shot. The thing that was eating at Stew was the fact that the guy who shot Father O'Malley had to be a crack shot. It was someone who had been shooting for a long time, because this was not a one time lucky shot. The guy who did this was a marksman. The priest was shot, dead on; perfectly through the middle of his forehead. What bothered Stew most was that they couldn't find a murder weapon! The other thing that bothered Stew, was, how could the Bishop had been so sure that Stephen Fraser would make an attempt today. More specifically; at that exact time in the morning?

Was it a coincidence that he was sitting in the car that early in the morning, just waiting; or did he know something in advance? What if Father O'Malley hadn't gone home to change? What if he'd stayed at the hospital that morning? Was Caity or anyone else capable of doing this? Christ! Why would he even think of Caity in that way? What if Stephen Fraser was innocent and just taking claim to something he'd wished he'd done? Just then Stew wondered if Father O'Malley had called Father John to tell him he was on his way back from the hospital. Stew made a mental note to check with the nurses' station.

While wild and crazy thoughts floated through Stew's mind in the parking lot, Charlie came out walking to his car that was parked right next to Stew's. Instead of going straight to his car, he went right up to Stew's driver side window, leaned in and asked him what he was still doing there.

"Hey Charlie, I think we got the wrong guy in custody for the murder." Stew said in a strong and positive tone, as he sat back up in his seat, leaning forward looking right at Charlie while he rested his hands-on the steering wheel. Charlie shook his head, reached in tapping Stew's left hand and said "Buddy, you're losing your edge.

We've got an eye witness and Fraser never denied doing it. We have it all right down to the suspicious new jogging suit. Why don't you go home, have dinner with Maggy and the kids and just forget all about this shit! Really Stew, I think you need a good vacation! Now get going!" With that Charlie tapped the car door, and walked over to his own car and got in. He waved to Stew as he drove off, giving him the signal to get going, to which Stew waved back and started his car.

He wasn't halfway out of the parking lot when a lightning bolt of thoughts hit him so hard he pulled over to the side and slapped the car into park. Idling, he smacked the steering wheel in frustration. Why hadn't he thought that before? Why not run a check on the three guys? The Bishop, the replacement priest Father John and Stephen Fraser. They could see if any of them were registered for, or ever had been registered for fire arms etc. What if one of them was a marks man after all?

Pulling out his cell phone he dialed Charlie. "Hey Buddy, turn your car around and meet me back at the station, Pronto." Stew said with excitement racing through his voice. He'd wished he taken the speaker from his ear because not only was Charlie swearing at him but he was yelling at the top of his lungs, too! Something about wanting to get home to dinner; Stew heard his grumblings which only really lasted a few seconds. After he calmed down, he took a deep breathe, and agreed to come back in but threatened Stew that it had better be good!

Smiling to himself at what an ornery old guy Charlie really was. He parked his car, got out and headed toward the main doors of the station. Seconds later in sped Charlie; drove in with his cherry on top flashing; sirens going and at full speed, he whipped into the parking lot and parked his car. When he got out he slammed the door behind him and walking faster than normal, he caught up to Stew, grabbed his elbow, turned him sideways to look at him and demanded; "O.K. Cough it up Buddy! What you got? And it had better be damn good!" Stew looked right at Charlie, grabbed him by the shoulders and said, "Charlie, you booked the wrong guy! I need you to run a check on all three of them, the Bishop, Stephen Fraser and Father John, and find out who has ever had a gun license etc. You and I both know that the shot was that of a marksman, an ace shooter. It could never have been a one time lucky shot. I'm sure of it; and I know if you think about it, you'll agree." Charlie just shook his head sideways as he answered him, "Stew, are you out of your mind? What religious guy, like a bishop no less, is going to shoot a gun? Right there, with that thought alone you can count out the two kneelers as suspects. I'll bet we find out that this Fraser guy has you wasting another evening of mine, chasing some kind of crazy whim of yours. For God's sake Stew, Get Real!!" Charlie was pissed; but Stew knew that his curiosity would get the better of him if he didn't check.

They went back up to Charlie's office to make the calls. While waiting for answers, Stew's cell phone rang. Absently picking it up without checking his call display first, Stew answered it expecting it to be Maggy.

A deep male voice was on the phone instead. "Well, did you forget to call me? You don't know who this is right?" Pausing and not hearing a response from Stew the guy continued. "It's the Deacon, didn't you get my message?" With that, Stew went cold. He felt his blood race, suddenly worrying about Maggy and the boys. Truth was, in the midst of all this chaos, he'd forgotten all about the guy. "Ya, as a matter of fact Buddy; I've been a bit too busy today to play your bullshit games! What the hell do you want anyway?" Stew said as he sat down into the old leather sofa in Charlie's office, and he could feel the tension growing in his shoulders and neck. Charlie was so busy talking to someone on his phone that he didn't even look over at Stew...or he would have known on the spot that something was up.

"So, what is it that you want?" Stew said, sounding very impatient with the guy. "I have to meet with you to discuss a certain matter of a check, no less. Turns out you have something I need back. Where can we meet?" The Deacon was direct, but Stew could tell that he was also very nervous. Almost sounding a scared or even worried. With that Stew said. "Well actually you're a bit too late for that; I gave it in as evidence this afternoon. I no longer have it, so I guess that makes it that we no longer have a reason to meet."

Stew said as a matter of fact; hoping that the guy didn't have any inside contacts in the cop shop. Not knowing who he was, or for that matter what his relation to the church was; if he was even a Deacon, or if that was his code name. Stew didn't know and was trying to stall to try find a way to meet the guy anyway. The guy sat on the other end of his cell phone, not saying anything, but Stew knew he was still there because he could hear the guy breathing. At that second, Charlie hung up his phone loudly, half slamming it down and then slamming his hand on the desk. "Well if I'll be a monkey's ass!" He said to Stew suddenly looking up and realizing he was off the phone. Charlie stopped talking and did the hand signals for who are you talking too. With that, the guy hung up and all Stew had left was a dial tone and his call display indicating the caller had blocked his I.D.

"O.K. I can't wait to hear what you found out, and before you ask me, that was that Deacon fellow on the phone. He wants to meet me to get the church's check back, which I told him I handed in as evidence this afternoon. I was just trying to figure out if I could meet with him anyway and he hung up." Charlie was obviously excited about his new facts and he dismissed the stuff about the Deacon with a few sweeps of his arm "Guess what?" Charlie started, "You were right again, you old son of a bitch! I've been a cop forever and I can't believe that my mind never thinks like yours! Not even after all these years. Turns out that the Bishop, Bishop McDuff used to be a cop of all things. He was an ace marksman in his day but he left the force because they all found out the guy was gay. Can you believe it?! Besides that, Father O'Malley is the one that helped him leave the force behind and got him in as a trainee in the church. He worked his way up to where he is now, and became the Bishop within not time at all. Now isn't that a piece of interesting crap?" Charlie said as his phone rang again. "Let me get this Stew and then we can put a plan together with this new info."

Charlie picked up his phone, and judging from the conversation, Stew figured it was one of Charlie's detectives coming in to the office for some reason. Stew had to laugh when he heard Charlie say, "Ya, I got Stew in my office, and you know what that means, he's making me miss another good home cooked meal. Hey how about you stop by Starbucks and get us some of those Carmel "crapiatas", or what ever you call them. You know Stew, he lives on those dam things and I could use a really good coffee treat. Oh ya, Frank; make sure it's got all the caffeine in it and fats, I don't like that decaff shit! Oh, and get the super size ones. What are they called Grande or something or super Grande or something thing like that. Oh and Frank, get yourself and your partner one too. I'll pay for the whole lot although it'll cost a small fortune, ya, ya, go on, see you back here." And with that Charlie hung up the phone to look over at Stew who had broken out into a deep smile and an under the breath giggle.

"Carmel "crapiatas" Charlie? You make me laugh. You love those things but yet you hate to admit it and you are always razzing me about them. Go figure, Charlie, you are mellower than you think buddy." Stew said as he had walked over to him and smacked him on the back of his shoulder blade. Leaning forward looking right at Charlie, Stew asked, "So what did you think about this new info? Was it worth me getting you back here for it? I'm dying to know!"

Charlie buckled and agreed, he also sat down with Stew and went over a list of scenarios as to what they thought could have really happened. A few minutes later Frank got there with their super sized specialty coffees and they continued to go over what they thought they knew and what they thought they needed to do next. It wasn't going to be easy to put the pieces together unless something gave, but they did think that the Deacon character had some type of tie to the murder. They also waited to have the results about Stephen Fraser and the replacement priest; Father John.

Three hours later, they found out that there were no records anywhere for Stephen Fraser to have ever owned or shot a gun legally, and that Father John as he called himself, the supposed replacement priest; didn't exist anywhere and certainly not with the church officials.

Stew and Charlie went back to the crime scene to find out that Father John had completely disappeared without a trace. The only people that knew he had ever existed were the cops that interviewed him on site this morning, the dead Father O'Malley and of course the Bishop. It turned out that replacement priest that the church had actually sent, went by the name of Father Robert O'Grady, and no one had seen or heard from him in over a week. Even when they called the Bishop, he denied knowing a Father John and claimed the same story as the other administrators of the church.

Now they had another problem; where was Father O'Grady? Charlie called the precinct from the crime scene and had them run a full check on a Father Robert O'Grady while the investigators combed the house, the church and the grounds for evidence.

It was past two in the morning when one of the detectives found the body. One of the dogs they'd brought in took only ten minutes to become obsessed with the gardener's tool shed. It took a few minutes but when they finally got the door pushed open, the stench was enough to make them all toss their preverbal cookies.

Stew and Charlie, laid ten to one odds that they'd found Father Robert O'Grady, and once they got forensics in to do their job, they'd get their answer soon enough.

By four in the morning, Stew and Charlie were running on empty. They'd drunk enough coffee to keep Brazil in economic wealth and besides being buzzed on caffeine; they were grumpy and tired but mostly emotionally drained.

The last twenty four hours had been filled with death and corruption and they still weren't any closer to finding a murder weapon or for that matter, the murderer. All they did have was a second murder and probably the wrong guy being held in prison. Stew aggressively rubbed his forehead and scalp to try and alleviate some of his frustration. He and Charlie had been sitting on this cold curb for hours while the detectives combed for more evidence. The whole neighborhood appeared to be out, mainly because of the bright search lights the team used, but mostly because of the incredible shock of the new of the double murders right in their back yards. It just seemed to Stew that everyone standing there appeared to be uneasy and drained.

Stew looked over at Charlie, just the sight of him made him realize that the day had taken its toll on the old guy. "You know Charlie, I know you're beat but a thought just came to me." Stew said as he watched to make sure that Charlie was listening. "See that crowd over there bud, I was wondering if we'd find our murderer amongst them?" Stew could see Charlie's eyes getting bigger as he continued, whispering so no one would over hear him. "You know what they say at a fire, eh Charlie? How the arsonist always returns to watch the fire, maybe the murderer has returned to watch for what evidence and things we find? What if the guy is standing right there in front of us? How can we find out?" Stew paused hoping that Charlie would have a suggestion.

Slowly looking over at the crowd and then back at Stew, Charlie said, "You know Stew, what if I get the guys to pretend they are doing a routine questioning of the crowd, they could confirm people's addresses and the like. When they start doing that,   the minute they go over there the guilty guy will probably try to back away from the crowd without being noticed, so he can disappear, and if no one does that; then we can be pretty sure he's not hanging around. If the guys find someone in the crowd with an address far from here, then we can check into it ...even if they claim they are visiting a friend in the neighborhood. What do you think? Worth a try?" Charlie asked, looking at the background behind Stew as he whispered back. Stew looked over at the Church and the lights then back at Charlie in case anyone was watching them, and then he whispered back, "Let me position myself in a spot where I can observe, unwatched. Give me about five minutes and then get the guys to do that.....we may just find our guy tonight if we get lucky." And with that Stew stood up and headed off to the side of the house that wasn't very well lit. He went in a side door and up the stairs to a room with a view of the street and the crowd. Sitting there in the dark, he waited for the gang to go into action.

The idea had been a good one, but it turned up absolutely nothing. No one appeared to run off, and everyone in the group lived within a few blocks of the church. Even the members of the press all checked out to be legit. So much for their brilliant brain storm! By six thirty, Stew and Charlie decided to call it quits. They were beyond exhausted and needed sleep more than anything. Knowing they'd get a call if anything big was discovered, they got up and headed to their cars.

As Stew drove home, he realized just how exhausted he was. His body was aching and his head was pounding, as he headed round the corner just down the street from his house, Stew wondered what was happening on the home front? As he pulled into the driveway, he could see the chimney with the fire place going and as he got out of the car he could swear the cold air was filled with the warmth of a freshly baked apple pie or muffins or something like that. He inhaled deeply as he headed toward the front door, noticing the strange cars parked on the curved driveway in front of the house.

Chapter 28

As he came through the front door, Emma came bounding at him. She'd missed him, that was for sure, and she made no bones about hiding the fact or licking him to death as he tried to close the door.

With all the commotion came the two boys in their flannelette jammies and Maggy following behind them with an apron tied around her waste. 'Hey you! Were in the world have you been all night?" Maggy asked, obviously worried about him the whole time that she hadn't been able to reach him. It was just past seven in the morning but the house smelt like a mid day cooking session.

"I was out with Charlie trying to figure out what the hell has been going on and who is responsible for everything. By the way, whose cars are sitting on the driveway?" Stew said curiously as he got mugged by the boys and the dog all at the same time. Maggy giggled at how Stew was so loving with the three of them making, sure even Emma got a love hug in between the two boys. "Greg, Fran and Caity all came over in different cars last night. Greg was supposed to only stay and hour and Fran said she'd head out to get some errands done on her way home, and Caity was determined to stay and wait for you till you got back. Well, we sat around opening wine, talking about a million things, with Caity crying through most of it, but to make a long story short; Greg drank way too much to drive so he's in your bedroom passed out cold. Fran slept on the couch and Caity spent the night on the rug in front of the fireplace with Emma as her pillow. Nanny

Brown is asleep in the guest room that I was supposed to be in, so the boys slept in the big guest room, and I passed out in the sun room all night. How's that for a full house?" Maggy asked looking at Stew who seemed to have a hard time wrapping his brain around it all.

"Oh." Was all he said. "Anyway Stew, as far as I know; everyone except for me and the boys, is still asleep. Oh ya, before I forget, there was a big Buick Regal parked in front of the house all night. Navy Blue. I thought it might have been an undercover cop car that you sent to protect us, but it took off about six this morning." Before Stew could say anything, Maggy added, "Don't worry, I got the plate number just in case. Well actually, I got most of it. I think I missed the last digit. Those binoculars you have work well, it's just that the angle was a little tough." Maggy said trying to get Stew to stand up and follow her into the kitchen because she could smell her apple muffins at a point that they just might start burning.

As Stew entered the kitchen, he couldn't remember when the room seemed more inviting. Living alone he wasn't used to the warmth that encircled him. The coffee smelled amazing and that stuff that Maggy had in the oven was making his stomach loudly complain at how hungry he really was. Maggy pulled an egg soufflé and apple muffins out of the oven. The cooked bacon and sausages were in the warming oven and the coffee pot had just announced its last spurt to say the coffee was ready. Stew grabbed a cup and headed over to the big round table. He had two types of chairs in this room, the tall fluffy high chairs that sat around the eating counter, and his eight big favorite wicker ones that encircled the glass table. Like everything else in his house, these chairs came with a cozy soft padding for your back and seat, and even the arms were covered with a soft restful padding.

Stew sat back in the chair that faced the sliding doors and the yard. The spring sun was as brilliant as it was the day before, but for some reason it looked sad to Stew. Even his tulips were up to greet the garden and they all seemed a bit unhappy. Stew shook his head realizing he was beginning to lose it if he actually thought his tulips were sad. Looking over at Maggy who had already put food on plates for the four of them, poured her coffee and had the boys tucked into two of the high chairs around the counter. She served them their breakfast and then placed a huge plate of goodies in front of Stew; got hers and sat down in the chair next to him.

"What about the others? Do you think we should wake them for this? Stew asked. "No, I'll warm it all later or make fresh. I think they all need their sleep right now. It wasn't exactly an easy night for the Andersons'." Maggy said as she was grateful for the calmness of just sitting down to a warm breakfast, and was hopeful that Stew would fill her in with the latest.

They had sat there for over an hour. The boys had long gone into the sun room to watch TV where they wouldn't disturb anyone. Stew had told Maggy all the details of the day before. She looked shocked and drained. As they sat there drinking coffee they both couldn't help but wonder as to who would turn up dead; next. It just seemed like a never ending road of death and destruction.

As Stew leaned his head back in the chair, having finished all the coffee he could drink and the two helpings of breakfast, he looked over at Maggy and said in a very sad voice. "You know Maggy, I have the feeling that we are not going to find any clues to the murders and that this is going to be one of those unsolved cases that everyone talks about for years to come. Worst of all, if that does happen, the lack of closure will be terrible for everyone, and especially you know who." Maggy didn't comment on what he'd just said, but she nodded acknowledging the fact that she knew what he meant and thought about all the parishioners in that church who wouldn't get the closure they'd need. "Why are you so sure, Stew?" She asked. He looked at her shrugging his shoulders and said; "Because, it's a huge gut feeling I've had all night. This wasn't something that just happened. The way it looks to me is that this was in the planning for a very long time. That who ever did this was waiting for the right time and waited to make sure that there was no trail that would be easy to follow. We don't even have a murder weapon for either of the murders. There appears to be absolutely no prints anywhere, which means they wore gloves the whole time. The detectives are going to have to pray for a piece of hair or something, and if the guilty guy doesn't have a record and DNA on file, it will be useless without a suspect. I don't know Maggy. It's the first time in years that I feel this way about a case but the truth is I'll bet I'm bang on."

Maggy could tell that Stew needed sleep to think clearly, so she got up and went to the side cabinet where she knew he kept his medicinal stuff. Poured him a good size glass of cognac and got him to take it up to the sun room with him to get some sleep. It was the only room in the house that would be quiet enough for him to pass out, so she told him to send the boys down and they could watch TV in the kitchen.

When Stew was finally alone in the sun room, he settled into the covers that Maggy had used the night before, and before passing out, took a few minutes to call the station and run a check on plates that would have those numbers and be attached to a navy blue Buick Regal. Knowing that was done, Stew placed his head back on the pillow and wrapped himself in the blankets and passed out cold.

Chapter 29

By the time Stew woke up six hours later, all the Anderson's had eaten and left; not wanting to disturb Stew's rest. Nanny Brown was off at the park with Emma and the boys, and Maggy was in the den reading one of her romance novels. He'd found out that the precinct had called and they had narrowed down the Buick to be one of four in the city. One of which belonged to none other than Bishop himself.

Stew wasn't sure if he should be worried about the kids being in the park today, but since they could see the play ground from his kitchen windows, he felt less concerned than he should have. He sat down at the kitchen table pouring over his notes and making new ones, while ever so often glancing over at the playground. Stew couldn't put his finger on it but he felt very uneasy as if waiting for a bomb to go off. Something was really bothering him, he was tense and worried but didn't really know why. Without even thinking, Stew got up and stood in front of the sliding doors to watch the boys play. Nanny Brown was sitting on the bench with Emma flanked by her side. In a split second, Stew's hair on the back of his head stood up and without even stopping to think about it, Stew threw the door open and flew off the back patio and through the back garden gate to get to the park and the kids as fast as possible. His timing couldn't have been better, as he approached the sand box play area, Stew could see the dark trench coat sitting not more that fifty feet to the left of them. Why hadn't he noticed the guy when he was in the kitchen? It was probably because the kids had held too much of his attention. He didn't often feel fear, but at that very second, Stew was scared and felt panicked needing to get the boys to safety as soon as possible.

He quickly commanded Nanny Brown to get the boys and Emma back to the house and lock the doors.

Reaching into the back of his jeans waste band he made sure his gun was ready for use; and casually walked over to the gruesome character on the bench. He knew exactly who he was and as he got close enough to talk…Stew stopped, standing directly in front of the old man in front of him, who remained very still in his spot on the bench. Stew just stood there waiting for the Bishop to say something.

"Hello Stew, did you think I would stop trying to contact you?" My inside contacts at the precinct tell me you never did give the check in as evidence and I'm guessing you still have it on you. Why not just give it to me and we'll call it a day on this nonsense, once and for all. Bishop Arthur McDuff paused while waiting for some sort of reaction from Stew. It was just passed one in the afternoon but with the shadows from the nearby trees along with the dark trench coat, Stew couldn't tell if the guy had a gun on him or not. His hands were almost completely covered by the dark material and his bulkiness hid everything beneath it.

"So, what are you going to do now? Shoot me too? Is that the plan? Stew asked him while moving his gun to his side just in case.

"Are you out of your mind, young man? The Bishop responded, "I'm a man of God, I don't use weapons. Put your gun down so we can talk, like two grown men with a very serious problem." He added as he shifted slightly on the bench, but not enough for Stew to be sure about him not having any weapon on him.

While Stew was dragging it out in the park, Nanny Brown and Maggy had already called Charlie who was on his way with a few cars as back up. They'd set the house alarms on and were standing at the large sliding doors, transfixed on the sight of Stew and that creepy looking guy, watching them talk. They knew Stew so well that they could see the tension throughout his body. Maggy was so scared that her eyes started to tear. Nanny Brown kept it together because she knew in her heart of hearts that Stew was in his element and that he'd be just fine.

When the phone rang, they'd both jumped, and Maggy ran and pounced on it hoping that it was Charlie and that he was calling to say he was close by. It wasn't him though....in fact it was the hospital, the nurses' station to be exact. One of the nurses was just calling back because Stew had called yesterday. Apparently, Father O'Malley had called the church house to let the replacement priest know that he was on his way home to change and take a brief nap before coming back. The nurse, Anne was her name, said that she remembered that Father O'Malley chatted with her about it afterward and that he didn't really like the new guy but had to work with him because that was God's way. She also remembered something he'd said during the conversation as well. Something about the fact that he wouldn't be longer than a half an hour but didn't understand why it was such and issue as to when he got home especially at that hour in the morning.

Just as Maggy was hanging up the phone, they heard it. A single shot rang out echoing in the house. Nanny Brown was pressed up against the glass of the sliding door and Maggy ran to it ready to run out of the house. Of course, Nanny Brown stopped her, they had to stay in the house till the cops came, since neither of them could do anything at this moment. The worst part of the next few minutes was intensely painful and felt like an hour. Both Stew and the man had somehow moved out of sight range and they couldn't see anything. Maggy ran up the stairs as fast as she could to the sun room to be able to see what was happening. When she got there she died in her tracks. There on the cold spring ground lay her brother not even moving. In the distance was the man in the dark trench coat running but limping and he appeared to be bleeding badly. In seconds cop cars appeared everywhere and in a blink the man was thrown to the ground and they were all over him. Maggy rushed back down to find the sliding doors thrown open and Nanny Brown running toward Stew at record pace. Maggy was right behind her running faster than she thought possible. When they reached him Stew looked up and asked, "What the hell is wrong with you guys?" The two women stopped in their tracks and couldn't believe he didn't even seem hurt. "We thought you were shot! Were you shot? Are you O.K.? "Are you bleeding? Talk to me Stew!" Maggy said as she knelt beside him trying to pull him up and examine him at the same time. "I'm O.K. Really! It's one of my rules. When you hear gun fire, drop down and pretend you were hit till you can find out where the shots are coming from. I think they hit the Bishop though" Stew said as he sat up to assess the situation.

It turned out that the Bishop had been shot in the leg but hadn't done the shooting. The cops were all over the area searching for the shooter. Stew didn't know what was worse, not knowing who was shooting or being a member of the clergy on a week where they all seemed to be a target.

Chapter 30

After it was all over and the cops were gone, Stew sat with the women in the kitchen trying to make sense of everything. It had been a few hours since the whole thing had happened. The Bishop had been shot in the leg and was lying comfortably in a hospital bed under police watch. The shooter, turned out to be a hot headed father of some kid that had been molested by some priest that the Bishop protected. From what they found out from the guy, the church buried the whole event and paid off the family enough to shut them up for a while until his teen age son decided to commit suicide a few weeks ago. Apparently the guy had been stalking the Bishop for weeks and thought he would take his shot today.

He was a terrible shot, and Stew ended up being lucky that he wasn't hit by mistake. As they sat there, the cops were making sure that the day's shooter wasn't in fact responsible for the two other murders. But when the results came in, the bullets didn't match and neither did the gun types, plus; the guy had an alibi for Father O'Malley's death but they couldn't be sure about Father O'Grady's death until forensics finished their job.

Maggy was quiet and just sat there. Nanny Brown stood up and announced that she was going home to have a bit of normal for a while. They saw her off at the front door instructing her to call when she was home safe, then they locked the door and set all the alarms for the night. Stew knew he couldn't leave Maggy and the boys alone tonight, and he really didn't want to go anywhere, anyway. Ten minutes later Nanny Brown called and announced that she was home safe. The minute she hung up the phone rang again, it was Caity. She'd heard about the shooting on the news and just had to call.

Maggy chatted with Caity for over an hour on the phone while Stew settled in the family room with the boys and a good old fashioned comfy fire. They were watching some cartoons when Maggy finally joined them. She plopped herself down on the sofa, and sighed, looked up at the ceiling and told Stew that she needed for life to return to normal too! He nodded and tapped her on the arm, wrapping her in his shoulder and kissed her on the forehead. "You know Maggy, I'd be lost without having you and the kids around, but I agree with you. My life is too chaotic for you guys to be around all the time. Besides the boys have been grumbling about how they miss their friends and stuff. How about we get you all home tomorrow, safe and sound; but just for a little extra piece of mind I'll install a good old fashioned state of the art security system and pay for it. O.K.?" Stew asked. Maggy nodded grateful to have him look after them. "You bet Stew, but can you really have it installed tomorrow?" Stew smiled and said, "Are you kidding me, of course it will. You're forgetting that when you're in the detective business, you're connected in all the right places and especially getting security installed."

Stew half laughed out loud squeezing Maggy's shoulders in an attempt to get her to relax about all these fears she had developed over the last few days. He'd known that it had been his entire fault that she felt that way, mainly since that first call from the Deacon. But now that they had the Deacon in custody at the hospital, or really to be exact the Bishop who just called himself the Deacon. Stew didn't feel like Maggy and the boys were in any more danger. In fact, he was thinking that the sharpshooter had probably already left town a long time ago. He had probably been a hired hit man, nailed his target by first getting rid of Father O'Grady and then his real target, Father O'Malley. Now that the man had been silenced and couldn't do any more damage, the guy's job was done and he was gone. Hired hit men never stayed anywhere any longer than the hit which made it so hard to track them and catch them.

Stew was so deep in his thoughts that he hadn't noticed Maggy had fallen deeply asleep leaning on him. He carefully placed her head on the couch arm, stretched her out and covered her with one of the throw blankets. He got the boys bathed and ready for bed and by ten o'clock he'd called his contact who'd confirmed he'd meet Stew at Maggy's house at nine tomorrow morning. Heading back into the family room after the boys were fast asleep, he sat down in one of his big arm chairs by the fire and reflected on life.

The last week had made him realize that in fact he wasn't really living. He was surviving and working, but when it came to the important things like love, family and a life. Stew sadly realized he didn't really have much of a life. Even though Maggy had lost the love of her life, the boys made her a family, so that even if Stew wasn't involved in their lives they would have a life. Unlike him, without Maggy and the boys in the house and his life, the house would go back to being a big old cold building. Thankfully it had Emma in it! Stew leaned forward to rest his head on his palms while his elbows rested on his knees. He couldn't get over how empty his life really was; and that the last few days with everyone around and people to come home to, he'd been more fulfilled than he had in years.

Stew sat in front of the fire for most of the night, just thinking and trying to make plans to put life back into his world. Emma sat at his feet, every so often nudging him for a rub and resting her paw on his foot as if to say he belonged to her. He loved Emma with his whole heart, as if she was the kid he'd always wanted. Having tucked the boys in tonight, Stew realized he'd better get started to find that special woman in his life and hurry up and have some great kids or he'd miss out. Kevin and Chris were really great kids and Maggy was doing a great job in rearing them. They were secure and happy and didn't feel like they were missing out on anything.

Stew leaned back into the chair, staring at the embers of the fire as if he'd find the answers to his problems just resting there in the remainder of the fire. He was drained and tired yet again. He'd had about all he could take of this "Catholic Cult" thing and wondered if he had never promised Caity and Maggy that he'd investigate all this....where it would have gone. Stew was sure the murders would have still occurred but it would have been harder to know why with out his involvement and the confession of Father O'Malley. The cops knew a ton of stuff because of him, and had he not been involved they would have probably just had two mystery murders. The thing Stew had to come to terms with is whether or not to take it to the press. From his past experience he knew that if the true story of the priest and the parishioner made it into the press, those hungry dogs would probably be able to dig up more in a day than he could in a month. What he also knew was that if he went that route, the damage would be irreplaceable for the parishioners and the church.

He still had the check in his wallet and didn't know what to do with it. He'd have to talk to Charlie tomorrow and ask his advice on what he should do with it all. For the first time in his life, Stew didn't know what to do. What was right? Which turn to take? For a man that always did the right moves and the right things, he didn't have a clue what to do next; and that really scared him!

Chapter 31

It was a gorgeous sunny day in June. Not a cloud in the sky, there was a slight warm breeze to take the edge off the seventy six degree weather. The birds were singing to the sounds of the earth and Caity was silently sitting on the grass trying to take it all in. It had been over a year since Jack had passed away. For her, it had been of one of the longest years of her life. She'd shed more tears than she'd admitted even to herself, and had spent untold hours at Jack's grave thinking about what might have been and remembering what had been and why hadn't it been different?

She thought back to his funeral. Stew and Maggy had gone with her. The church had been packed with his work associates, and very few friends and family, but few of them had known him well.

Jane had brought the girls, whom she'd dressed in bright Barbie pink and it had looked more like they were going to a fancy party or wedding rather than their father's funeral. Caity remembered how shocked she had been when she'd seen them walk into the church. She hadn't been alone in her shock. It almost seemed like everyone in the pews took a breath in when Jane and the girls walked in. Jane was herself dressed in a bright floral sun dress and was flanked by her boyfriend who had apparently joked about how easy it would be for them to marry now that Jack was out of the picture. As Caity remembered Jane's callousness, she shivered as a tingle went up and down her spine in disgust.

Sitting in the sun, remembering back to that horrible day, Caity thought about how Jane had been a real piece of work for the entire funeral. She'd come to Jack's funeral flaunting her new and vividly oversized engagement ring, laughing and joking with everyone she chatted with. She'd said horrible things to a lot of people including Caity and made sure that everyone knew of her upcoming marriage the following weekend. Caity continued to think back at how horrible the whole event had been and she'd heard through some of Jack's colleagues that days after the funeral, Jane had either sold or thrown away everything that Jack had ever owned, making sure that there were no memories of the man for his girls to treasure in the years to come. Jane clearly wanted to wipeout the fact that Jack had ever existed and it had appeared that she'd done a very good job of it. Besides the fact that the girls were going to be legally adopted by their future new step father; and that their family name of Fraser would be legally wiped off of their records. Jane had even gone to the extreme by burning all their pictures and negatives so that no one could take them out of the garbage.

Caity let out a very heavy sad sigh. She remembered how Jane had paid for Jack's funeral out of obligation, but it hadn't been fancy, and she almost got away with putting him in a pine box, but her mother of all people talked her into an economical acceptable casket instead. Jane refused to have a lunch afterward so Maggy and Caity had made one at Stew's and had invited a select few from Jack's work and family. One of the truly saddest memories that Caity had was when Jane stood at the grave sight just after the priest had finished, she stood up flinging a yellow rose on top of the casket and declared that it would be the first and last time she or the girls would be at Jack's grave. With that, she grabbed the girls hands while they looked to be the saddest little faces Caity had ever seen, and headed straight for her limo. Caity couldn't believe that Jane's fiancé never even got out of the car at the grave site, but instead just sat in the limo with the door open, and chatted on his cell phone through out all of it. How sick they both were, Caity thought. She'd felt deep sadness for Jack's daughters who were now being raised by two of the shallowest people Caity had ever met.

Truth was that Jane had remained true to her word. Were it not for Caity's almost weekly visits, Jack's life and grave site wouldn't be remembered. Sitting there in the warm breeze, with the sun on her face, Caity looked at the beautiful silver and black marble grave stone. It had cost her a months pay, but it had been worth it. Jane had made it clear that the four inch by six inch marker that the cemetery had provided to mark the site, was sufficient. But she told Caity that if she wanted to be an idiot and waste her money on Jack's gravesite, she was welcome to it. Jane laughed at Caity as she said it, making it very clear that she thought the girl was a fool, and adding that Jack had often told Jane that Caity had been simply his little "call girl" for sex and nothing more. Those words often haunted Caity, but she really believed that they were the words of a very screwed up woman, and not the words of the man that Caity had come to know and love.

Looking at the grave stone now in the sunlight, Caity's eyes began to fill with tears. As always with Jack, she loved him more with each passing day. It was true about love, you carried it with you always, and you couldn't stop your heart from feeling something for someone whether they were with you or not!

She closed her eyes remembering only the good moments while trying hard to block out all the awful ways he'd treated her when his guilt had consumed him. The warmth of the sun brightened her face and brought her to a quiet place where she dreamed of being in his arms, cuddling him to sleep and sniffing his neck where he always had a dab of his after shave. Thinking back to those moments Caity remembered how safe she felt when he'd be cuddling her and she would sniff his neck. It was incredible how the gentle blend of his cologne combined with his scent made her sniff and sniff until she'd gently fall asleep. Suddenly a soft breeze touched her and she shivered slightly as if Jack was there with her.

It was amazing, after all this time she could still smell him. God, she missed him! She'd mourned for the dreams they had talked about but never fulfilled. She mourned for her lost love and the part of her that would never be the same. Sadly she often mourned for herself and the lost spirit that had once made her who she was. The year had changed her into an empty shell that often wandered about in overdrive, but never really felt much of anything.

Opening her eyes as she sat there at the base of his grave site, she looked at the beautiful grave stone that had Jack's picture encircled by a gold heart frame. The stone had the year that he was born and the year he'd died, and the inscription was written from Caity's heart and read, "Love finds you and holds you in my heart for Eternity," followed by an X and an O to symbolize a kiss and a hug from Caity.

How sad to know that Jack's girls had never been back here since the funeral. Caity knew that because she'd become close friends with the old grounds keeper. Jack would have been devastated to know that his girls, the loves of his life and whole existence in life, had never been back, probably and mostly because Jane never brought them. She must have totally discouraged it! Caity thought of all the sad truths that she now knew about Jack's life, and the one thing that she was truly grateful for was the fact that he had died before finding out about his mother and Father O'Malley. In her heart, Caity knew that the news, would have destroyed him from the inside out, and thought he may have been alive were it not for his second heart attack. In reality, his life would have become a waste land of emotional despair. Looking back to all the details that Stew had shared with her, Caity knew that Jack had never been a strong man emotionally; and that perhaps, in truth; maybe everything had happened for the best.

It had taken her over a year to come to terms with everything, but in her heart she knew that if Jack had lived, they probably wouldn't be together. Or if they were together, her life would be filled with the sad truth of Jack turning their relationship on and off like a light switch, turning it into one ridiculous roller coaster ride.

Caity sat their realizing that with each visit she'd become more and more at peace with everything. That today; for the first time in the years since the first weekend that she and Jack had gone away together; she had begun to dream about meeting someone and falling in love again. She was starting to hope for tomorrow and dreaming about leaving the past behind her.

As she sat there day dreaming listening to the breeze travel across the cemetery, Caity suddenly noticed sounds of a car pulling up. Looking over, she realized it was Stew's red BMW. Boy it had been ages since she'd seen him. She and Maggy were as close as ever, but even Maggy hadn't seen a lot Stew over the last year. Apparently he had buried himself in work, taking on case after case while still being totally consumed with solving Father O'Malley's Murder. To date, it still wasn't solved and it still occasionally ended up on the evening news when ever a negative story of the Catholic Church appeared. Initially the press had had a field day with the two murders, but as days passed and other stories seemed more interesting, the two deaths drifted into occasional crop ups of news tidbits on slow news days. Her eyes were fixated on Stew as she sat there lost deep in her thoughts. She watched him closely, as he got out of his car and started to walk toward her.

Strangely enough he hadn't changed at all since she'd last seen him just after the funeral. Still tall and incredibly handsome, he had a walk that showed that he was sure of himself. As he got closer, Caity took off her sunglasses and laid them on the grass as if to get a better view with unprotected eyes.

Stew knew Caity's habits; he'd watched her from afar all year. Her weekly visit always seemed to be on a Saturday, unless it rained in which case it would be the first sunny day there after. He stopped and stood just to the left of the grave stone unconsciously leaning on it in a relaxed way. "Hi Caity, it's been a while. How are you these days?" He asked sounding a bit edgy or nervous and Caity wasn't sure which. "Fine I guess Stew. How'd you find me? Or were you coming here for your own reasons?" She asked; mostly to make small talk and get the conversation going. Stew smiled. "I am a detective you know sweetie, and it's not like you're not predictable. Besides, I couldn't wait to see you and let you know the latest." Stew teased by not telling her what the latest was.

"So, what is it?" Caity was very curious and knowing Stew, it had to be big if he came all the way out here to tell her. "I tell you what, how about we get some lunch and I'll tell you about it over a good meal. Want to follow me or would you prefer I drive and we can come back and get your car later?" Stew asked hoping she'd want to ride with him.

We'll take your car, that way we can talk on the way." Caity said as she hopped up after picking up her sun glasses, and wiped off the grass and stuff that stuck to her pants. As she started to walk to catch up to Stew who was already heading to the car, she walked passed Jack's grave stone, she kissed the tips of her right hand fingers, and touched the top of the stone and whispered; "See you later Jack." It was Caity's way ever time she left him. In her heart she always needed to kiss him one more time. Since she couldn't have his kiss and hugs anymore, it was the best she could do to feel close to him.

Chapter 32

The way Stew drove they got to the restaurant in record time. They hadn't said a word in the car, instead Stew had blared the radio with one of Caity's favorite songs, "Angel" by a guy named Shaggy of all things. Stew whipped around corners so tight he'd made Caity giggle. Laughing and giggling with the wind in her face brought a temporary happiness in her eyes that made her sparkle with a look that Stew had never seen.

It was good to see her without that usual sadness that had become such a complete part of her daily existence. Stew looked over at her as they pulled into the restaurants parking spot and thought to himself, what a waste of such a wonderful woman! Sometimes it seemed that Caity had died with Jack and although she was still on earth in body, her heart and mind were dead to the world around her.

Maggy had told him that Caity's career had actually suffered and she'd taken a demotion at the TV station. He also knew that besides going out for work and doing the odd grocery run and stuff like that, Caity rarely went out except her weekly visit to the florist on the way to the cemetery. It couldn't have been healthy for her the past year, but Stew knew it was all probably part of the grieving process.

Stew smiled at her, coaxing her out of the car even though the song hadn't finished yet. As he walked her to the door he'd wondered if she'd be upset if she knew that he'd spent the last year and a bit keeping very tight tabs on her. She'd probably be shocked at how much he knew about her coming and goings, and then again, he decided it was best kept a private secret.

Brushing off his thoughts he slipped his arm under hers, tapping her hand with his and ushering her into the restaurant. It was one of Stew's favorite places because it was a quaint quiet little place that was owned by a European family of fabulous cooks. It had been an old farm house that had some how survived the city growth around it and after being lovingly restored, was now Stew's home away from home for dinner.

The place was dimly lit, softly romantic with sun streaming through some windows highlighting all the dark, wood on the walls and the European type, heavy ceiling beams. Each table had soft cream colored material table cloths and a red rose in a single vase in the center. The whole setting was simply old fashioned with all the important homey details.

They were ushered to a lovely smallish round table in the corner where it faced a corner window and was just off to the side of a carefully positioned stone fire place that had obviously been burning for most of the day, even though the air conditioning was on.

Caity sat in a chair opposite to Stew, looking all around in complete appreciation of the atmosphere of her surroundings.

Without a word, a young waiter came over, opened a bottle of Stew's favorite Red wine and after the official tasting and agreement, he poured them each a glass and was gone.

"I hope you like red wine lady "Stew said smiling, while Caity nodded in agreement warmly looking at him and smiling back. "Uh huh" she responded while she sipped from her oversized delicate crystal glass. Putting it down and enjoying the flavor she said, "Good choice, it's a soft bouquet, fruity with no hint of citrus and best of all no oak type flavor." Proud of herself for the surprised look on Stew's face. "What's wrong Stew, surprised that I know my wine?" Caity half smiled and half giggled as his facial expression unknowing that Stew wasn't even thinking about wine. He was fascinated with her face, her smile and her eyes and as she spoke about the wine, and all he could think about was how much he was dying to kiss those inviting lips. Stew cleared his throat, worried that his thoughts might be read if he didn't catch himself. "Not at all lady, but it's nice to know that someone else can taste wine for flavor and not just drink it for the sake of it," Stew replied lifting his glass and toasting her while he went to take another sip. Actually Caity, it's one of my absolute favorite reds. There is just something about it, I could sit and sip it all day." Caity caressed the glass lip with the tip of her fingers as Stew was talking and then she mentioned that she remembered drinking the same one the night that Maggy and her, were waiting with her parents for him to get home from the crime scene.

"Oh yes, I remember that! From what I remember Caity, you were all passed out cold when I got home that night." Stew half giggled as he spoke, trying to make light at what may have been a very negative memory for her.

In order to change the subject, Stew reached down into his briefcase which he'd nonchalantly brought in with him and was now sitting beside his chair on the floor. He'd pulled out one of those university composition type books that were about nine and a half inches by seven inches or so. It was the hard covered, leather bound type that Caity had often seen law students' use. Curiously enough, it had a white address label stuck on to the middle of it, which was noticeably put on quite crooked. At that there appeared to be some handwriting in pencil scribbled across the middle, which read; "The Catholic Cult". It seemed like the words were screaming out to her but she just couldn't say a word. Caity sat there just staring at the book as if it contained some mystical key to the past.

"What's this Stew? Have you written a book?" she asked picking it up to look at it more closely, but hesitant to open it and see what was inside. Just then, the waiter came by quietly placing their appetizers in front of them and was gone again. "Actually, not really, but I guess you can say, sort of." Stew said as he watched every move and expression Caity made. "You know Caity, the first time I ever heard you use that expression, "The Catholic Cult" I kind of thought Maggy had introduced me to some crazy nut case that was two steps short of reality. I just have to say, that you, or I, for that matter; could never have known at the time, just how perfect a description it was for what I found out. This book is really just a compilation of all my notes and all the things I found out about the murders, the church and everything in between. Over the past year of all my digging up of information is in there."

Stew paused taking another sip of his wine, and then continued as he watched Caity sip hers. "I actually even looked up a description in the Webster's II New Riverside dictionary for the word "CULT" and it described it as, obsessive and faddish devotion to a principle or person; a group of persons sharing such devotion: sect i.e. Cult.

Although it wasn't exactly the description I would have given it, I actually liked your definition of a cult better because it made more sense to tell you the truth." Stew sighed as Caity looked up and added. "You mean the part about that if something and or someone is controlling your life in a manner that is against how you feel inside or it is a lot of work to try be a part of that group or person, that it is more like a cult that controls you rather than a religion?" she asked knowing full well that it was exactly the quote Stew was talking about. "You couldn't have been more accurate if you tried.

Caity knew exactly what had been wrong with Jack. In his heart he wanted to be with her and start a new life, but for some reason he'd been tied to this cult that controlled him. It was what had prevented him from being true to himself and his heart. With that thought pressing on her mind, the waiter returned and asked if they were ready to order their meal. They talked about how hungry they both were and with some coaxing, Caity let Stew order a whole bunch of stuff for the both of them to try.

"Trust me Caity; you'll love all of it. I've never eaten anything here that disappointed me. In fact, I get frustrated sometimes because they don't have take out!" Stew's comment made Caity laugh softly. "Stew don't you ever cook? I mean you've got that beautifully equipped kitchen, why not make homemade sometimes?" She had to admit she was awfully curious as to who used all those fabulous appliances. "You know what I think it really is; the fact that eating alone every night is lonely enough as it is. I find that if I have to cook it for myself it just makes me feel lonelier." Stew was talking to her matter of fact like, but gazing warmly and deeply into her eyes as he spoke, daydreaming of what it would be like to come home to someone every night, not just someone; but Caity.

Feeling a big uncomfortable from the energy that occurred between them, Caity looked down at the book again hoping to find out everything that Stew knew. She also used it as a way to keep herself occupied and hide the fact that he not only made her nervous, but that she was suddenly started realizing how deeply attracted to him she really was!

"Caity, this whole story turned out to be a lot more complicated than anyone could have guessed." Stew paused, trying to find just the right words to use to tell her the whole story. As Stew spoke, Caity could picture all the characters. They actually sat at the restaurant for hours eating, drinking and talking.

Actually, Stew did most of the talking with Caity sat totally absorbed in every word. When he'd finished, she didn't know what to say except to tell him how overwhelming it all was. The food had been excellent …just as Stew had promised, but now in reflection of all the news Caity wasn't sure she'd digest any of it. It was just past four when they headed out of the restaurant. Looking at Stew she asked if he minded that they take a small drive to some place with a view that they could just sit and relax while she wrapped her brain around it all before having to go home.

Chapter 33

The drive to the lake only took a few minutes from the restaurant. They parked down near the Mississauga Boat Club on Lake Ontario. The water glistened in the afternoon sunlight and made the world look better than it had over lunch. They parked in a fabulous spot to the far end of the parking lot, facing the lake and the sky, Caity asked if they could just sit there for a while and hoped that he understood. Stew just nodded and leaned his head back to look up at the sky through his sun roof while Caity sat there watching the waves and the sea gulls dance amongst themselves. How peaceful life could be for some and not for others, Caity thought as she sat there mulling over everything. How that Bishop McDuff had been a dirty cop and brought that style with him into the church. That he had indeed created his own cult which worked with his dedicated and sometimes forced followers. That when families were to be paid off by the church for the wrong doings of a priest or even himself with young alter boys….the creep had seen to it that forty percent of the money from the church fund for the cause went into a Swiss bank account where he was building a retirement nest courtesy of the parishioners and the hard working souls who gave generously each week.

Unbelievable as it all seemed, the bank account in Switzerland, the properties he bought and sold under the guise of a company that he owned, and all the rest of the worldly positions that the police had uncovered were no where near as bad as the fact that the cops had finally tied him to the two murders and he was finally awaiting trial. Caity remembered how Stew had described in detail the search of the Bishop's residence. That the cops had details on two Swiss accounts both containing over a million dollars each. Apparently not all coming from the collection box, but that some of it came from other illegal dealings which were still in the process of being investigated. According to Stew, Father O'Malley had been in the process of accumulating information on the Bishop's activities so that he could turn him into the police and the church. Unfortunately he was killed before he could get it all together. Stew's theory is that Father O'Malley was collecting all the information so that he could use it to stop the Bishop from revealing his own very dark secrets. Who knows, but with his death, the secret and the truth died with him as to what his real motive was.

Bishop McDuff had been a crooked cop and an even more crooked member of the Catholic church, and no one would have ever found out about all of this stuff if things hadn't started coming to a head by not only Stew investigating everything but also the fact that Jane of all people had hired a private detective as well . Jane was an evil woman who was trying desperately to find dirt on Jack's life in order to screw it up even more than she had. Who knows, if the detectives hadn't been out digging for dirt, then the Bishop may have gone on indefinitely without ever being discovered and the dirty secrets that went along with him.

As far as the cops knew, Father O'Grady was just an innocent victim, sent to the wrong place at the wrong time, and he ended up paying for it with his life. His record turned up to be spotless. There was nothing negative in the guy's past. With all the digging they did they couldn't find any deep dark secrets to help justify the murder. It turned out that everyone they had interviewed; mostly described him as a hard working good soul that was a true Christian and dedicated member of the church and community.

The strangest and ugliest twist of the whole story was the fact that Jane had actually been inadvertently responsible for all the deaths. Had she not hired a private detective to try find some dirt on Jack, and who had been hoping to find out that he and Father O'Malley were somehow having an affair? Were it not for her dirty digging, maybe the Bishop's dirt would have remained hidden and the deaths would never have occurred. What a nightmare, Caity thought. What a horrible woman and to think she was a mother!

Stew looked over at Caity, who was consumed in her thoughts making her eye brows twitch and move covering her entire face with a tense scowl. He knew that she was probably thinking about Jane since the last time he'd seen that look on Caity's face was at Jack's funeral. Stew sat there in silence watching Caity mull over her thoughts. He thought it was best that he just sit there until she was ready to say something.

Caity hadn't even noticed Stew watching her. She was staring out over Lake Ontario. Looking out at the white cap waves, the diving Sea Gulls, and the puffy white clouds which were each traveling singularly through the richly deep blue sky. Sitting there she was desperately trying to digest the worst part of all of the information that Stew had told her at lunch. Caity was thinking that if it hadn't been for Jane and all her greed to try take Jack for everything he had; the deaths may not have occurred. Maybe Jack would even be alive today if he had not kept it all inside him. What had Jack known that he took to his grave? Caity really believed the truth was what really killed Jack because he must have carried it all inside him. The more she thought about it the more she realized that all this had been way too much for his heart, and was the only reason he was dead today. The whole harsh reality of the lies in his life had been what had caused his heart attach. It was the only explanation.

As she sat there thinking, she couldn't believe how truly twisted Jane really was. All of this was started by Jane who wanted to find dirt on Jack and force him into a position to give her even more money, and complete and total custody of the girls. Caity shivered as she sat there thinking, and was so deep in her thoughts she didn't notice that Stew had placed a car blanket around her shoulders for all the shivering she was doing.

Caity's eyes welled up with tears with the thoughts of how Jane's detective had somehow discovered all about Jack's Mom and Father O'Malley. Jane knew all about Jack being the illegitimate child of Father O'Malley and she also knew and told Jack that their two daughters were really not Jack's at all, but instead they were the product of her affair.

Caity now wondered just how much of all this was in fact what made Jack treat her the way that he had. Caity sat there wishing that Jack had shared all of his fears and facts with her so that she could have helped him deal with it all. She wondered how long he had known the truth about everything, before he died. She knew that Jack had never been a strong man. In fact, Caity had often seen him as spineless when it came to Jane and other members of his family. It was the one characteristic that Caity had admired the least about him, but as with anyone you love; Caity had accepted his faults as easily as his strengths.

She sat there thinking how she'd had spent the last year feeling so grateful that she'd thought he'd died without knowing all of the details of his life, but sadly this afternoon; she'd found out the exact opposite. That he'd died with the full knowledge of all the ugly details of his life, and it all had probably been what really killed him in the end.

She was sitting there gripping her hands in her lap, playing with her fingers while she remembered how she'd lovingly kissed the tips of her right hand and had touched the top of his gravestone. It had been her way of kissing him when she'd leave, but as if a twist of fate had occurred, she suddenly realized that would be the very last visit she'd ever make. It was important for her, and for her very existence, that she leave all this darkness and deep sadness behind. She needed to start over. To continue going there would only keep the darkness of the devil alive in her and all around her.

Caity knew it was time to open the doors and let the sunshine in. With that she looked over at Stew, whose eyes were half shut, while he day dreamed, and without saying a word, place her left hand into the palm of his right hand that was just sitting open on his knee. Without opening his eyes, he smiled and closed his fingers around hers to let her know she was safe and cared for.

"So what are you thinking about Caity?" Stew said, while his eyes were half closed but while softly caressing her hand with both of his.

"I don't know Stew; all of this is almost too much for me to be able to take in. I can't see the bishop hiring a hit man and maintaining a little cult of crazy business for himself. It's almost too crazy to picture. I was thinking that you finally got Stephen Fraser out of prison before they were able to try him for the murders, and that there really was a "Catholic Cult" controlling Jack's entire life and all his actions. More than that, I was really thinking about how very sad all of this horrible stuff really was! You know what though? The worst part is how it all affected my life!" Caity paused with her eyes full of tears.

Speaking with a lump stuck in her throat she continued. "All of this heartache for everyone was all caused by selfish people, for greed and money. Thank God they finally let Stephen Fraser out of prison for being wrongfully accused! You know Stew, when I used to use the term "Catholic Cult" I used it because it always felt that Jack was being controlled by the whole Catholic guilt thing that seemed more like a cult than a religion, but the truth is all the other stuff I found out about him actually makes me sick! You know Stew, Jack was an obsessed Catholic, who let his religion control who he really was and wanted to be, but I can honestly say that all this other stuff is too sick for me to really grasp today! You know what I mean?"

The tears were streaming down her face, and Stew just watched and listened somehow knowing she wasn't quite yet finished. "I just can't help feeling so sorry for myself, in a way, all this stuff has taken such a toll on my life. The deaths, the secrets, and the money corruption were all taking place under the guise of the church and religion. It's all too much for me to come to terms with. You know Stew, just because I'm not Catholic, doesn't mean I'm not a good Christian at heart and I'll never forget when I told Jack that I wasn't Catholic I thought he'd choke on his breakfast. In fact, I've never been able to wipe that picture from my memory. We were having breakfast at Mc Donald's of all places, right after the first and only time we ever went to church together. He was saying I had crossed myself wrong, but it was the way I had been taught. I guess he'd always just assumed I was Catholic, and he never asked me so I never brought it up. It happened on our first weekend we spent together. If you had been there you would have sworn that it was if I'd told him I was an atheist of all things. To Jack, the only people that counted in life were Catholics. I should never have spent one more minute with him after I saw the way he reacted. I should have ended it early on and never stayed in that horrible mess of a relationship! I don't know what I was thinking! The truth is Stew that I don't judge people on their beliefs and couldn't really believe that he would either. I guess in my heart I always knew that he never saw me as good enough because of it."

She was heaving and crying while she spoke and Stew had somehow managed to get his arm wrapped around her trying to sooth her. " Stew; I really believe that the reason Jack treated me so badly, was simply because I wasn't Catholic. Looking back now, I can tell you that everyone in his life that was Catholic, no matter what type of a person they were, good or bad; he treated with respect and like gold. I just never really got that till now. I know now that it was just me he treated this way!!" Caity buried her head in Stew's shoulder crying so hard he was worried that she'd bring on a bad asthma attack. "Hey Caity." He said as he patted her hair trying so hard to sooth the pain out of her. "Caity, how about you take a pump of your asthma medicine and we head out to my house and sit in the sun room for a while. We can listen to music and watch the sun set, and the best part, I have a ton of tissue you can go to town with. How about it? What do you think? I can order a pizza? Hummm?" Stew said desperately trying to cheer her up. Caity just nodded her head in a yes, wiped her drenched eyes with her already soaked tissue, moved back into her seat and put her seat belt on. Stew looked over at her brushing her bangs out of her face with his fingers, softly caressed her cheek and put the car in reverse and headed home.

As they drove in silence, Stew held Caity's left hand in his right one, resting it on his leg as he softly caressed it to let her know that he cared and was there for her. What he didn't know was while holding Caity's hand sent shivers down his spine, and all he could do was think about kissing her; she was having the exact same reaction.

As he pulled into his driveway and parked his car on the curve right in front of his door, Stew squeezed her hand and said, "You know Caity, there is one happy note to all this. You may not see it that way, but I sure do!!!" Stew's voice sounded choppy, almost nervous when Caity looked over at him and asked, "And just what is that?" She was curious as to what he could find happy about all this stuff.

"Well," Stew stared and twisted sideways in his chair, having turned the engine off he was better able to give her his full attention. "Truth is Caity, if it wasn't for all this craziness, I would never have met you." He put his fingers on her lips to silence her from saying anything, but it sent her pulses racing in a way she'd hadn't felt in a long time. "Don't say a word and let me finish. I know you have been deeply hurt, and I know it may take you an even longer time to get on with your life than you think, but I spent the last year hoping and waiting for you to get past this because I can't stop thinking about you! Something happened to me that had never happened before, and Maggy spotted it the same day we met. You sent my pulse into a frenzy. This last year I haven't been able to think properly and I day dream about you so much that I have to punish myself by working like a dog just to keep some sense of normal around me."

Stew leaned just a little closer, looking right into her deep eyes. "Lady, in all my years I've never met a woman I wanted around me for any length of time till now, and I'm damn well willing to wait as long as it takes for you to give me a chance and date me!" There, he'd said it. His heart was racing, he couldn't catch his breath and all he could think about was kissing her. She wasn't saying a word, her breathing was choppy but he didn't know if it was because of her asthma or because of him. He was so desperate for her to say something that he felt like he would die waiting. Stew hadn't realized that he'd still held his finger tips on her lips until she lightly kissed them in response.

Just as Stew leaned forward to kiss her, his lips lightly touching hers at first so as not to scare her, his cell phone went off. Startled by their moment being somehow broken, he gave her a light peck on the lips and leaned back into his chair and answered his phone watching Caity as she sat there stunned.

" Hey Charlie, what do you want?" he said as he caressed the back of Caity's neck as she sat there silently watching him, wanting him to hang up the phone and kiss her again, only this time for a lot longer. Caity wasn't paying attention to their conversation because all she could think about was how her heart was beating and how very alive she suddenly felt at that moment; and she didn't want anything to interrupt how great it was to be alive again.

Stew hung up looked at her, leaned back over softly caressing her lips with his and gently whispered, how about coming in and we can continue our conversation inside over dinner. There is lots of food in the fridge and we can always order out. He smiled while she softly touched his hair with her fingers and said, "Sounds great!" As he leaned back into his chair, and then out of his door before she could even unbuckle her belt, he made it round to her door, opened it, and helped her out. As he lifted her out he pulled her close to him for a great big hug.

Stew had never known anything like this before but he knew it would be addictive. He wanted to hold her, touch her, kiss her and find out everything there was to know about her. Her past, her dreams, and her thoughts. He wanted to know it all! He hugged her for a few more seconds then not wanting to scare her off, he softly placed her hand in his and led her inside.

Chapter 34

Hours had passed since they'd gotten back to Stew's house. Caity and Stew lay on the big old comfy couch with throw covers keeping them warm. They'd gotten carried away hours ago, and after having made love sat cuddling and touching and talking for hours. It was just past eight and Caity could hear Stew's stomach gurgling. Guess it's time we made something to eat. Huh? He said kissing her gently all over her face. "Did I tell you how beautiful you are, Caity?" He asked as she nodded, smiling and snuggling closer. "As a matter of fact, you have, at least a dozen times, but you can keep on saying it as much as you like, because I love hearing it." Kissing him on the nose as she spoke in an affectionate, adoring way she said, "Stew, I feel so lucky right now, I can't seem to put it into words. You make my heart beat and you are treating me so special I don't know how to handle it because I'm just not used to it". Stew picked her up wrapping her in the blanket and grabbed his pants telling her to relax till he assessed the food situation.

Just as he was about to head off to the kitchen, the door bell rang. Looking at each other in a panic, Stew grabbed his shirt and while heading to the door with Emma on his heels told her to stay in the family room and get dressed. He closed the main doors to the large room behind him and headed off to see who could be calling.

"Guess you forgot I was coming, eh Stew." Charlie said as he came in. I was kind of surprised to see your front gates open; usually you got to buzz me from down there. Was I disturbing something?" He said as he tapped Stew on the shoulder implying he had a woman in his midst. "As a matter of fact Charlie, I did forget. Guess you could say I was pre-occupied. Why not come with me into the kitchen and you can tell me what it is that you couldn't tell me on the phone this afternoon."

Caity was relieved to hear the two men head off into the kitchen and she slowly dressed herself putting a comb through her hair, not wanting to look like some ravaged female in front of one of Stew's friend.

Charlie and Stew were deep in a conversation and had no idea that Caity was listening. They didn't even remember that Caity was even in the house. They were deep into the gory facts while she'd gotten dressed, and while she had originally intended to join them in the kitchen, when what she was over hearing left her stopped stiff in her tracks. She paused just a few feet before the kitchen doorway. She was able to hear everything with out being seen because of where she stood in the darker shadows of the hallway. It hadn't been her intent to eves drop she just couldn't seem to move from where she was standing. Almost paralyzed and totally glued to every word.

"Stew, can you even believe all of this shit? After a whole year of almost searching the globe, it turns out the killer was here all the time. Right under our very noses all along and the damn feds knew all about it. It took them long enough to get the proof don't you think?" Charlie was more frustrated than Stew had seen in years, partly from not having figured it out himself; and partly because he wanted one more big case under his belt before he retired. Stew knew that Charlie had worked night and day on this case because he had so desperately wanted to be the cop that solved this case. His last big case before he retired some time this or next year, and the Feds scooped him.

Stew shook his head for a lot of reasons but mostly disbelief of how this all turned out. Stew looked at his friend and handed him a tall cold glass of beer. "Who would have guessed Charlie, I mean really, Scott Fraser….successful business man, Jack's brother…or should I say half brother…..and of all things…a trained marksman. How did we miss it? How Charlie? I thought we'd covered all the bases a thousand times and back? There was no record anywhere of his abilities! How is that possible? How Charlie?" Stew stood leaning on his kitchen counter in front of Charlie who had made himself comfy in one of the bar type chairs. While they each took a drink of their beer and wine, there was a slight pause of silence between them, which Caity took as her cue to walk in.

As she came up to Charlie leaning on the counter nursing his cold beer in one of Stew's crystal pilsner glasses, Caity smiled at him as he looked over and said. "Hi, haven't we met? I'm Charlie. Putting out his hand to greet her and sitting him self up a little straighter in the chair. "Hi Charlie, I'm Caity Anderson, it's nice to meet you!" She responded as she took his calloused swollen older hands in her delicate and soft hand to shake it. "Oh, thee Caity Anderson? The owner of a beige Hyundai Elantra plate number KPL2743? That Caity Anderson?" Charlie asked really curiously. "Why Charlie?" Stew jumped in. "Well because, I had to tow her car out of the cemetery today. God, the grounds keeper was like a pit-bull trying to stop us and saying we couldn't do it, but we had to have the area cleared. Sorry Stew, I didn't know why the name really rang such a bell with me at the time." Charlie added as he looked embarrassed for having had the car towed. "Wait a minute, what were you doing at the cemetery Charlie?" Stew's curiosity was peaked and he wanted to know that second as to why Charlie had been there and why on earth he'd had to have Caity's car towed.

"Oh you're that Charlie." Caity said. "The one and only!" Stew answered, smiling and walking around the counter to her and placed a soft kiss on her lips while he put an arm around the back of her waste. "Don't worry about the car honey; I'll pay to have it out first thing in the morning." Stew said as he placed another little affectionate kiss on the tip of her nose and speaking to her in an almost whispering tone.

"Hey do you guys want to be alone? Cause I can get lost faster than, what's that thing?, oh ya, faster than a speeding bullet, if I need to." Charlie was half laughing while he spoke and his smile went from ear to ear as he looked at the loving couple. All he could think of was…thank God that Stew finally found a keeper!

"Don't be silly Charlie, Caity and I were just talking about ordering dinner when you stopped in so how about I order Chinese for the three of us and you can finish telling us all the gory details of the rest of this case, huh?" He half asked and half stated; and without waiting for any answer from either of them, headed over to the phone and speed dialed his favorite Chinese delivery place. He hadn't even noticed that Charlie and Caity had just nodded in acceptance, while Charlie added that he was so hungry he could eat a house.

While Stew ordered Chinese food for eight, Caity giggled thinking it was just like him to order in and not cook. Not only was he ordering in but it seemed like he was hoping to have leftovers for breakfast. And while Stew ordered the mountains of yummy food, Caity watched Charlie sitting in his chair, shaking his head and tapping his fingers softly on the table as if he had the weight of the whole world on his shoulders. By the time Stew was done ordering, Caity had helped herself to a glass of the red wine, gotten another cold beer out of the fridge for Charlie and had hopped up on one of the comfy bar stool chairs beside Charlie. She was leaning forward on the counter playing with her glass when Stew leaned over the counter and kissed her nose. As he sat back down, he heard Charlie complaining that if he kept that up he was going to lose his appetite. They all shared in a light laughter and then got deadly silent as if waiting for a bomb to drop.

Stew started. "O.K. Charlie, I can't wait any more! Give me the whole story and don't leave out one gory detail!" "Hmmmm, you guys sure you want to know it all? Caity? Are you sure you can handle it?" Charlie asked before continuing. After Caity assured him that she could, she positioned herself across from Stew at the opposite side of the counter; facing Charlie as he spoke.

Charlie spoke softly and hesitated when it came to some of the details but by the time he had told them the whole story their jaws may have well been on the floor because both Caity and Stew were shocked and stunned.

He started with the fact that when the feds had jointly arrested Scott Fraser with some of his boys and taken him down to the station to be interrogated. How one of the first things out of his mouth was that Jack's death was no accident and that Jane had actually snuck into the hospital and poisoned him in his sleep. We thought that was a strange thing for him to start out with and that it didn't make sense, but Scott bargained on the fact that they'd check it out. It turned out that there was no autopsy filed on Jack. That it had been taken for granted that he'd died from a second and fatal heart attack. They also couldn't understand how Jane could be tied to it and they all more than believed Scott was trying to put blame on someone else for a crime he committed. Legally, they ordered the body to be exhumed from the grave and that was why he'd been at the cemetery that afternoon. Fact was, he'd probably gotten there not long after Stew and Caity had left.

They'd dug up the body but when the casket had been opened there was no body. Nothing inside but two small cards. One, a hockey card for the Boston Bruins team, and a holy card, the kind that you'd get from the priest. It had been a holy picture of a guardian angel with the inscription, Bless the Lord. All ye His Angels, and on the back was Bishop Mcduff's name and home number. As Charlie told the story he handed Stew photo copies of the two cards which hadn't made sense to anyone all day.

Caity sat there rather shocked by there not being any body in the coffin and hadn't uttered a word throughout the whole story except to tell them that the Boston Bruins were Jack's favorite team. He'd even owned bright yellow team shirt. She' remembered him wearing it on the first weekend they went away and of how happy and joking around he'd been in it, teasing his friends because they were all Toronto Maple Leafs fans. Caity shivered, deep in her thoughts and darkly shadowed by the news and wondered what really had happened to Jack and if he was still alive somewhere. Stew was worrying what impact this would all have on Caity; when the door bell rang and suddenly caught him off guard. In a split second, Emma and Stew were off to greet the Chinese Food delivery guy.

Unable to really say much, she played with her wine glass and sipped some of it. She was thinking that it was already her second glass and if she didn't eat something soon she'd probably fall right out of the chair. At that exact moment, Charlie jumped out of his chair heading toward the cupboards to get plates and the lot. "Better get down from there and head to the table Caity." Stew said as he brought his mounds of bags into the kitchen and plopped it all in the center of the kitchen table.

"Just bring tons of spoons and stuff and we can all dig in as we go, Charlie." Stew was ordering as he massaged Caity's shoulders in a feeble attempt to take some of the tension out of her. As Charlie was fussing with all the stuff, Stew leaned forward and whispered in Caity's ear. "Are you alright honey? If it's any consolation, this stuff is just as shocking to me too!" He added as he headed over to help Charlie and get them all settled around the table and start digging into the aromas that engulfed them.

Despite where they had left off in the story, Caity was starving and didn't hesitate to dig in and eat while Charlie continued telling him the rest of the story. Truth was, all she could think about was where was Jack's body and why didn't it seem to bother her like she thought it should. No wonder Jane wouldn't pay for a grave stone…maybe she knew there was no body there. Was Jack still alive or had someone just stolen his body so that they couldn't prove the murder?

Charlie told them how the second replacement priest was just some guy that was working for the Bishop. There was no trace of that guy and without the Bishop or Scott Fraser's help; they'd probably never locate him. It was like looking for a needle in the haystack. Even the cops that briefly met him couldn't give an accurate description because of the chaos that surrounded Father O'Malley's death that day. The impact of that scene far erased a lot of other memories. It didn't look like they could get Scott to go against the Bishop either. All Charlie thought was that between them they must have one hell of a Swiss Bank account for all their corrupt actions.

It turned out that Scott Fraser and Bishop McDuff, had been working together for years. Actually, Charlie said that if Jane's detective and Stew hadn't been snooping around and digging for information, the way he saw it; Father O'Malley and Father O'Grady the real replacement priest that they found dead in the shed; would probably both be still alive. The murders only happened to keep the deep secrets of the clergy members quiet; but the weird thing was…. that the same murders they used to try keep things secret, actually were the reason so many of the secrets came out.

How ironic! Charlie even said that if it hadn't been for Jack and Caity's relationship, the truth about all the affairs and hidden happenings may have stayed hidden for eternity. Charlie felt bad about saying it; but it was true. Caity sat at the table eating and glued to every word. She looked from Charlie to Stew and back to Stew again watching and listening to every minute detail while she weighed the truth of Charlie's matter of fact comment, about the relationship she'd had with Jack. Had it been a relationship or had it be just some sick game he played with her. Maybe it had all been some strange nightmare!

Stew asked questions for details and dug deep into everything Charlie was talking about, but all the while he worried about how Caity was really handling all of it. She appeared to be o.k. but Stew was no fool, people often looked like they were handling things just before they went of the deep end or something. Maybe it was the man in him, but all he could think about was the fact that he was so glad they had made love this afternoon. Maybe this new start was going to be exactly the cure that Caity needed to be able to deal with all this.

Charlie didn't miss a beat and probably felt like after the last tidbits he'd better keep on talking, so he did; as he kept his mouth full of the tasty treats in front of him. It turned out that Jane had an alibi for the day Jack died; but Scott didn't. Strangely enough the Bishop did, because Stephen Fraser had placed him at the scene of Father O'Malley's murder. The fact was; the cops never really believed that Jane was ever a suspect because Scott Fraser said that she was the one that murdered Jack through a lethal injection into his intervenes. Even though they didn't believe it, they certainly had to consider it. Truth was the cops really believed that Scott killed his half brother by doing that simply out of the pure jealousy he'd harbored for his brother, his entire life.

The body was exhumed earlier that afternoon because there were too many questions as to what really happened. It was too bad that the hospital hadn't really done an autopsy at the time of Jack's death. To the hospital staff, Jack had been brought in with a heart attack and his death appeared typical of a second heart attach. They had made an assumption based on circumstances that now had to be rectified. It was the hospital's lapse that now created the problem, even though they tried to justify that it was probably a result of the fact of under staffing. With no body they'd never find out the truth.

As for the morning of Father O'Malley's death, that morning; Scott got the call on his cell phone. He knew that Father O'Malley was headed home, and he waited across the street from the church, deep in the bushes; just waiting for his pray. It was simply an unfortunate coincidence that his father was actually acting on doctor's advice and began his new jogging routine on that day. He'd been in shock and chased Scott after what he witnessed which explained the grass stains; but didn't explain why he returned to the scene of the crime where everyone assumed he'd been the marksman. Charlie also believed that for some reason, Stephen Fraser must have suspected something about his son for a long time. After all, Scott still lived with him and he must have seen him leave that morning, and may have even seen the weapon case. No one could really be sure about that fact, or about the fact that Stephen Fraser had gone a little loony and was in doctor's care since he'd gotten out of jail for being wrongly held. All Charlie could talk about was what an absolute mess it all was.

Charlie went on about how after witnessing the murder, that Stephen Fraser was probably in some kind of weird shock. The guy had learnt the truth about his wife and eldest son, and then just a week later witnessed his real son kill his dead wife's lover. If that wasn't what soap opera's were made of, Charlie didn't know what was.

The way Charlie put it together was that Stephen Fraser probably assumed Scott killed the old priest out of jealousy or hate for what the old man did. As a father, Stephen probably felt that this was his only way to make up for the past. Sadly, they found out during interrogation, that Scott knew that he was the product of his father raping his mother, and that he'd lived with that horrible truth since his mother had told him at age ten. But when he found out that she'd really never loved his father Stephen and that she had been totally in love with the priest, he went off the deep end and completely blamed Father O'Malley for everything bad that had happened in his life. Scott told the cops that if it hadn't been for his mother's affair, his life may have turned out to be completely different. He wouldn't tell them how he and the Bishop had come to be corrupt business partners; but he admitted with prided that he committed the murder of Father O'Malley.

Scott Fraser also claimed that the Bishop himself had murdered the innocent Father O'Grady and stuck him in the shed because he had no way to prevent him from coming to work at the church. Stew was sipping his wine, they were on their second bottle, and he was totally glued to the story. Caity was working on her fourth glass of wine but at least she was eating, actually he thought; she was probably eating more than normal just because of the wine and the story. For some reason, he took her appetite as a good sign.

Charlie continued to tell them about how Bishop McDuff still had the nerve to deny all charges and the Church's lawyers were all over the story like bees to honey. That the court case was not only going to be interesting, but quite the media fiasco; for sure! Unfortunately, the press was all over this story and they ended finding out about the body being exhumed this afternoon and it turned out to be a real circus.

Actually that was an understatement, especially when some idiot opened the coffin at the scene. The reporters were all over it like paparazzi would be to their favorite star. Charlie paused for a moment worried about telling both Caity and Stew the last part. He had thought he'd bring it to Stew and they could handle it together, but realized since the way things were going he may just as well get it over with. "Actually Caity, I found something in the front seat of your car. I kept it from the Feds for now since I didn't think it had anything to do with the case but I found it odd that you left your car doors unlocked. I know you were at a cemetery but God girl, leaving your car doors unlocked is dangerous for any woman to do. In other words never leave your doors unlocked!" Charlie said in a raised deep voice. It was partly because he was passionate about Caity's safety and partially because the detective in him was thinking she may know something but didn't want to come right out and say it especially in front of Stew. "I'll need you to tell me as much as you can about this once I give it to you." Charlie said as he got up and announced he was going out to his car for a minute and he'd be right back.

With that Stew looked at Caity and asked, "Do you have a clue about what he's talking about? Did you leave something weird on your front seat of your car?" Stew asked Caity feeling quite puzzled and realized she was just as puzzled as he was.

"There was nothing on my front seat, Stew. I don't know what he's talking about! Usually my car is a bit of a mess, you know; things kind of all over the place, but I just had it professionally cleaned yesterday. I emptied everything into my storage closet at the condo, I can't imagine what it is he's talking about." Caity said, confused and anxious to find out what it was that Charlie had found. Just as she picked up her glass to drink more wine, Charlie walked back into the kitchen carrying a good size white gift box. It had a gold ribbon on it and a card addressed to Caity.

The minute he looked at Caity's expression he knew that she'd never seen it before. Shocked and curious, Caity took the box from Charlie and placed it at the clean end of the table, standing over it, and looking very afraid to open it.

"What is it Caity?" Stew asked curiously now standing by the end of the table next to her and across from Charlie, who eyes were glued to the envelope and the box. "I really don't know Stew, I didn't put this in my car. I never saw it before just now, and oh my God; the hand writing of my name, Stew, its Jack's writing!" Caity said in a nervous high pitched voice. She was shivering and Stew knew better than to touch her. He was just as anxious as the rest of them to learn the contents and was a bit pissed off with Charlie for not having opened it and read it before now.

Why in the hell had he not? Stew thought. Or maybe he had and he wanted to see her reaction to it. Stew would have to confront him later when Caity wasn't around. Unable to stand the suspense any longer, Stew announced. "Caity if you don't open it, I will!" And with that, Caity grabbed the card from the top of the box and read it.

It was a birthday card. Dated for her birthday almost two years ago, and a good ten months or so before Jack died. It was his writing, she knew that much, but she was frozen in her spot by the card. It said, "Happy 29th Birthday," that would have been for her 40th or no, her 41st birthday. It was obvious that the card meant more than anyone could really know. Stew looked at it puzzled so before opening to read the contents Caity explained to them that Jack and her always joked about how she was twenty nine and he was just thirty one or something. It was an on going thing with them when they first started dating, because the truth was that they had met almost 15 years before they dated. Back then they had both wanted to date each other but something had blocked it from ever happening and then of course a few years later Jack met Jane and the rest was history. When they did finally get together, they talked about it being their second chance and how his girls could have been theirs. Jack had told her how he had wished that his girls were theirs and they had had a life together. Caity was crying soft tears down her cheeks as she spoke and neither of the men interrupted her. It was either out of fear that they felt if they interrupted her she'd stop telling them the rest of the story; or the fact that they just knew it was better to stand there and listen.

When she opened the card, it had the standard Hallmark greeting about a birthday, but there was a lengthy hand written note on the left hand side of the card, that read:

Caity, I love you! I've never loved anyone the way I love you! But Caity, all that appears to be, is not how it is! Sometimes being totally in love with someone just isn't enough to create the courage I would need to make the changes in my life for us to be together. Sometimes the fear of changing my life for you is far greater than choosing to live my life as I want to. My life with you would be filled with love and happiness, but for me it seems so much easier to leave things just as they are. Even though I've told you many, many, times that my life is "crap", and I truly feel that, it is far easier for me to be a coward and walk away from the best thing that ever happened to me than to make the changes I need to make. I would also be forced to live with the fear that one day someone will come along and steal you from me. I know that through all of the heartache I have caused, I know in my heart that you have always been faithful to me. I guess the truth is that I'd rather live with the pain of losing you now, than to trust myself and believe in us and our love enough to take a chance. I guess I'm really scared of being happy, because it makes me vulnerable and if something were to ever happen I would never be able to go on. It is far easier and simpler for me to travel through time simply living a numb existence than to risk everything for the love of my life and the one that holds my heart forever....YOU! Sadly, because of my religious following, I am still waiting and praying for Jane to take me back and build a life with our girls. It is a prison I have built for myself and it is my religious beliefs that hold me to it. As I have said to you before, "what God has put together, let no man," well you know the rest. I'm giving you my most treasured possession, the shirt my Mom bought me for my birthday and the one I wore on the best weekend of my life. Our first moments together are my most treasured. Know that by giving this to you, I am trying to prove to you that you will have my heart forever and this shirt is a symbol of that. With all my heart, always! With all my love, Happy Birthday! Love, Kisses and Hugs ..... Jack X O X O

Caity was choking as she read the letter out loud, and the tears streamed down her face from welling eyes. Charlie and Stew were speechless and helpless as to what to do next, except to pass her some tissue. Stew wasn't even sure he should try hugging her at that moment either. Intuitively sensing that Caity needed to be the one that controlled the room right now, both he and Charlie sat silently waiting to hear what she had to say about it all.

They sat there watching Caity heave and cry, blowing her nose and what seemed to be an endless stream of moisture. Her eyes were puffy and she sipped another bit of her wine, and after inhaling as deeply inward as she often sighed outward, Caity looked up at Charlie and asked. "Charlie, is Jack still alive?" She said in a quivering voice and with tears still silently streaming out of her eyes.

"I don't think so Caity, but after today, I can't honestly say. I'm sure if he was he would have been in touch with you and his girls. Everything that I know about the case, the guy would never go over a year without seeing his girls. You know that Caity. I mean in my entire search, I read all the court documents about his separation and the fight he put up for custody of those girls and there would be no way that he could go this long." Charlie paused and then added. "I don't know who put this on your seat but I'm willing to bet that it was Jane. She probably found it amongst his stuff ages ago and wanted to get a kick out of play a cruel prank on you. I know it couldn't be Scott, because he's in jail. I'm willing to bet Jack's ex wife isn't through trying to make peoples' lives miserable especially since her new husband dumped her and filed for divorce last week."

Stew jumped in and couldn't believe it. "So there is a God, huh? Finally that bitch is getting her share of heartache!" Stew was semi angry because if Jane gave this to Caity now after over a year of Jack being dead, her whole goal would be to cause heart ache and grief. What an absolutely horrible woman. "Maybe she did kill the guy Charlie. What kind of proof did they have at the hospital, if any, of the last few minutes of his life? They must have the print outs of his machines or something. Hopefully they keep that stuff." Stew was talking so quickly and he was so into the case that for a brief moment he had forgotten all about Caity and her grief.

"Sorry Caity, I'm just brain storming." Stew added as he patted her hand to try to comfort her. It's O.K. Stew; I just can't help but wonder where Jack's body is if in fact he is really dead. Caity sounded confused and aching. "Look, I don't for a minute doubt that he's dead, but I think someone stole the body to hide the evidence of the real cause of his death. The thing is....when did they steal the body? Caity asked with her eyes full of tears. Then Stew jumped in and asked. "Do you think the Feds will be able to find that out Charlie?" Sighing heavily and looking at Caity with his heart breaking for her.

"Who knows? The best we can expect is finding the damn thing to begin with in order to find out what really happened and that being said; you know that forensics may not find anything but a heart attach after all this time since some drugs may be hard enough to detect." Charlie signed, heavy hearted as he spoke while watching the depth of Caity's grief that was written all over her face. His daughter was about Caity's age, maybe a bit younger but just as vulnerable. Suddenly Charlie felt like an instant father and that Caity was kind of like his daughter. His heart was breaking for her, and he couldn't help how curious he was to see what was in the box. In order to distract the grief, he looked at Caity and said. "Aren't you gonna open the box, girl?"

Caity was just as curious but pretty sure she knew what was in there. As she took the gold ribbon and the beautiful oversized matching bow off the box, she was sad by the fact that this had been the only gift that Jack had ever given her. The saddest part was that he wasn't even here to share it with her. Before she lifted the lid off the beautifully wrapped box, Caity looked up at Charlie and Stew and shook her head sideways as she said; "Do you know that in all the years we spent together, Jack never bought me anything. Not a flower, not a little something that said, Hey I was thinking of you! Not a thing for my birthday, or Christmas. Not even a dollar store trinket. Jack gave me absolutely nothing! I don't understand how he had this for my birthday and he never gave it to me. Does that even make sense to you guys? The sad truth is if he had this and never gave it to me, it would mean that the only gift he ever gave me was a birthday gift and a good bye gift. How awful is that?" Caity said as she kept shaking her head.

Her hands were shaking, and once she lifted the lid that was professionally draped in matching wrapping paper from top to bottom, Caity saw it. It was Jack's favorite sweater. Actually it was his prized possession. His Boston Bruins hockey team jersey that his mom had bought him not long before she died. How ironic! Caity picked it up and she could still smell his cologne as if he had just put it on. Polo never smelt like that in the bottle, it meant he wore it just before he put it in the box. As she cradled the sweater sniffing it, Stew and Charlie watched. For Charlie, he was just unsure about what would happen next, but Stew was feeling really jealous suddenly and he knew if anything, he'd better hide it from both of them.

"Oh God guys, it smells just like he took it off a few minutes ago. It smells just like him. He wore it because it smells just like him." Caity said as she sniffed the shirt not looking at either Charlie or Stew, not realizing the impact it was having.

Stew looked at Charlie and in a rare moment that wasn't usual for him, he spoke without thinking of the impact of his words. "How long would a smell like that last in a box Charlie? I mean, how long you would expect that type of smell to last before it expired. Could it really last two or more years? Could it really be that vibrant after all that time?" And without thinking of the impact of his questions on Caity, Stew waited for Charlie to respond.

Charlie was shocked at how Stew had lost his professional edge and he could tell by Caity's facial expression, what the full impact of Stew's questions had on her. "I don't know Stew, but common sense tells me if the box had been sealed all this time and it hadn't been opened, I would think it would stay for years and years." Then he added, "And there is no doubt in my mind that Jack is dead and it's only a matter of time before the feds find the body." With that Charlie threw a disappointed questioning view at his friend and realized that jealousy was getting the best of him. And at that very moment Caity got up clutching the jersey and ran off to the closest bathroom just around the corner from the kitchen.

As Stew was getting up to follow her, Charlie jumped up and grabbed his arm and said, "Don't. Let her have a few moments. It's not a reflection on you Stew; she just doesn't have closure on the past. You know that right?" He said and asked, at the same time.

"Ya, I guess so Charlie, how'd you become so smart and sensitive anyway?" Stew sat back down as he spoke looking directly at Charlie. "Don't know Stew, but it also helps that I'm not emotionally involved like you are. She's a great girl, and if you let her come to her own terms, you won't lose her. If you don't give her the space she needs Stew, you'll risk losing her." Stew nodded listening to the wisdom of his best friend and then Charlie continued leaning forward and whispering. "I'm gonna check with a buddy in forensics to see how long a scent can last and let you know, but in my gut; I think it's been sealed and the smell will last for years. If not, the bastard is alive and hiding somewhere and we have a whole new case on our hands. You know he had a hell of a big life insurance policy and Jane and the girls were the recipients. I can't imagine where this would lead if he was still alive. How about for now we just think about it as possible that the smell managed to survive at least a year or more, and go with the fact that the guy has to be dead." Charlie could see that it was all getting too much for Stew and he himself was exhausted.

Charlie got Stew to call him a cab and said he'd be back for his car tomorrow since he'd had too much wine to drive. By the time the cab had arrived; Caity was still locked in the main floor bathroom and they could hear her crying noises right through the door. She was obviously sobbing into the jersey trying to drown her heartache and memories. Charlie left when the cab arrived and Stew closed the door behind him, setting up the gate alarms and the rest of the house security with just a touch of a few buttons on the panel just off to the side of the front door, Stew paused to listen to Caity.

For some reason Stew felt very unsettled and a little unsafe. He wasn't used to feeling uneasy and vulnerable and he chalked it up to the fact that Caity owned his heart and she may never be his. The fact that there was a body missing, and a murder out running on the loose made him feel a sudden chill run down his spine as he instantly felt very protective over Caity.

Stew shook himself and knelt down and grabbed Emma's face in his hands and softly caressed the soft sides of her jowls and then her ears. He buried his face in the top of her head and kissed her. You know Emma, you taught me how to love and now you have to teach me how to keep Caity. He leaned backward looking right into Emma face, and as if she understood she licked him on the nose and trotted off to the bathroom door. When she got there, she sat outside scratching at it and wining for Caity to let her in.

Stew just stood frozen in his spot a little shocked wondering if in fact Emma really was a whole lot smarter than he could ever imagine. Thank God for Emma, he thought just as the bathroom door opened enough to let Emma in, and then it closed again.

Stew wasn't sure what he should do so he headed off to clean up the mess in the kitchen, hoping with all his heart that Caity would follow when she was ready.

Chapter 35

Weeks passed as if they were years. Stew was stressed to a point that he had never known in his lifetime. He and Caity were still spending time together, but it was always in a public place, a restaurant, a movie, a park. Rarely at his place and absolutely never at hers. He'd found out from Maggy, maybe a little unethically because she isn't supposed to give out information about her patients, something that he found really odd. Apparently until the last night that Caity and Jack had spent together, Jack had never been to Caity's home and that he had always made a point of not going there. That night was actually the very first time he had ever been there. According to Maggy, he had always used the excuse that if she went to his house the priest would give him absolution for his sins because she had pursued him and seduced him in his home. He claimed that if he went to Caity's house however, he would not be able to get forgiveness at confession because he had in fact gone looking for it.

Stew was shaking his head as he thought about all the sick things that Jack had said and done. In reality he wasn't really sure if in fact the guy had been an all out nut case or if he was some obsessed religious cult like freak. Stew had been raised Catholic, been to church every week for most of his young life, and then rarely till his parents had died. The church had never had this kind of effect on him or his life. He was pretty sure he was kind of normal and his brain wasn't that screwed up. As he sat there in his office thinking, he realized that Jack had probably really been mentally screwed up ever since he'd been the priests' sexual toy as a boy. Stew shivered at the thought and knew if something like that had ever happened to a son of his, he more than take care of the bastard forever, even if it meant jail! He threw his head back causing his chair to rock backwards and giving him a better view of the ceiling.

The rocking motion made him think back to Father O'Malley's death and it sent a cold shiver through him. Stew had definitely been too involved in this case. Leaning forward with his elbows on his desk, he looked around the room thoroughly, finding a type of peace in his surroundings. The sixteen by twenty office space was a decadent size for a house, but it housed a wall to wall, floor to ceiling library, with shelves that were made out of the perfect shade of oak. Not too dark and not too light, but all masculine in design. His desk placed off to the side with an angled view of the panoramic windows looking out the back of the house to the park, allowing him to enjoy the view while he worked.

Caity had told him that she found this room really inviting to read in. The camel colored puffy soft suede arm chairs that were positioned in front of the big windows, facing inward; allowed you to read with natural light and get lost in a book.

Thinking of Caity brought Stew back to reality. She'd been seeing Maggy professionally at least twice a week since the night of the Jersey and Chinese food, and Stew felt left out since she refused to share any of it with him. Something about needing closure and having nothing to do with him, but to Stew; it was all about him. He knew that he was helplessly in love with her and that he may never have her heart, or maybe; never have her full heart....just a part of it. Could he handle sharing her with a dead memory or should he just let her go? What was that stupid expression he thought as he doodled Caity's name all over his blotter? Oh ya, if you love someone let them go, if they come back to you they're yours; if not, they never were! Stew didn't know who wrote that expression, but he really didn't like them very much right now.

What if he'd let her go and she'd take that as a sign of rejection and he'd lose her for the wrong reasons? What if he didn't let her go and she stayed with him for the wrong reasons? As he sat there staring out the window, he knew it was time for him to get his act together.

Ever since the first night that he'd met Caity, his life and career seemed to be on hold. He'd worked like a dog for the whole year just after Jack died, but ever since that night of Chinese food and the first time they'd made love that afternoon, Stew wasn't the same. He was like a love sick puppy, working day and night to find answers, but most of all; Jack's body. He thought if he could prove that much to Caity she could finally let go. There was no trace of the body and each passing day seemed to be more of a torment for him than her.

Lost in his thoughts, the ringing phone was a pleasant relief from his deep and draining thoughts. It was Charlie; telling Stew that his friend down at forensics wasn't sure about the smell thing. It would depend on how it was packaged, where it was stored. The probability was that it could still hold a smell for years, but only under the right circumstances. If not, then the guy was still alive somewhere. They'd managed to do a full search on Jane's life and background, and now that it was complete they didn't think she was in any way tied to any of it. Strangely though, she wasn't trying to take her new husband for anything in the divorce. There had been no money demands; and not even a claim on property either. Charlie found that very strange especially after what people had told him about her. All that he had heard about the woman through interviewing people that knew her, and everything that Caity had told him of what she knew in the last few weeks all pointed to it being strange. The Feds had even managed to unofficially get an undercover detective in the girls' school as substitute teacher who carefully asked the right questions and determined if they hadn't seen their father since his funeral. That part Charlie told Stew to keep confidential and not share with anyone because his friend at the feds would get into trouble for sharing things with him.

Stew agreed knowing that at this point he wanted to share as little of the information with Caity as possible. The only thing he ever wanted to tell her was that they found Jack's body and he couldn't wait till they did. He was half day dreaming while Charlie spoke about all the little details, but one thing caught him and he asked Charlie to repeat it.

"Say that again Charlie." He said as he sat up straight in his oversized high back leather desk chair, slamming his feet into the floor as if he'd discovered something. "I said, strange thing is, Jane knows a lot about Scott. Almost too much, you know, more like a lover and not an ex-sister-in law. Makes me think she knew that Scott had a ton of money somewhere and she had her sights on it while landing her new husband. I just think it all sounds too sick, but when I interviewed her I would have bet she was Scott's ex-wife and lover and not Jacks. Charlie sighed. Then he said, "You know Stew, this whole damn thing has been way too much for me to wrap my brain around. If in fact it was all true, not only is it the sickest thing I've ever come across; but Jane could have been in on hiding Jack's body. If she did, just where do you think the bitch would hide it? Huh Stew?" Charlie asked knowing from the way Stew was breathing, he was thinking hard and trying desperately to come up with some real ideas.

"Charlie, she was in on it. She had to be. That's why she refused to spend the money on the gravestone and let Caity pay for it. She wouldn't spend money on a body that wasn't there. So where is it?" Stew asked, and then added, "Think Charlie, with all the things you've found out about this woman over the last year or so. Where do you think a broad like her would hide a body if she was in on it? Where? Huh Charlie? Where?" Stew said almost panicked with hope. If they found a body, he and Caity could get on with their lives; there'd be closure.

Charlie and Stew stayed on the phone just breathing and not saying a word searching deep into their thoughts of where it could be. Charlie coughed and suddenly said, you know Stew, Jane sold off all of Jack's stuff and the house in an awful hurry. She even took less than market value for the house. From everything we know about this woman none of it make sense because she's so money hungry. What if the body is buried under the house or in the back yard or something? What if there are clues we missed because we weren't looking for it. Jack's death wasn't tied to any murders, the guy was buried privately and the feds and the cops weren't looking for any tie-ins at the time. What if the house had clues and we missed it?" Charlie sounded frustrated with himself for not having thought in that direction till now. "What if there are clues we've totally missed out on? What if the house was the key to everything?" Stew excitedly asked Charlie.

"Stew, don't get too excited. You know how hard it is to get a search warrant. We have to have a strong case and especially strong evidence. All we got is you and I going on some kind of gut feeling that we can't sell to any judge that I know of. I tell you what; I'll call

all my contacts and call you back as soon as I know something, till then, sit tight and Stew." Charlie paused. "If you were ever a religious man, now's the time to pray for a miracle break through." With that, Charlie hung up and left Stew to his millions of thoughts and worries running through his mind.

It could be hours or days before Charlie got back to him and Stew thought he'd lose his mind and his patience. He felt panicked and knew that the only peace that Caity would ever have would be if she found out the whole truth. All the way through her relationship with Jack she endured a lifetime of lies and secrets. If she never found out if he was really dead of alive, it would probably drive her nuts and never set her free to go on with her life. As Stew sat there, he was almost sure that the only reason Scott would have encouraged them digging up a body, would have to have been a win in it for him somewhere. But where? Stew leaned back in his chair, running his mind through every detail he'd discovered throughout the investigation. Somewhere, hiding in all the details was a hint as to why Scott would want to disturb all this now, more than a year after Jack's death. What was in it for him? What?

Stew racked his brain thinking and almost missed the phone ringing. It turned out to be Caity, she was canceling their dinner tonight, wanted to stay home and have a hot bath and such. Stew knew it was an excuse and he was o.k. with it for now. At least this way he could focus on the case all night. In the time they chatted and hung up, Stew had managed to convince Caity to see him tomorrow night instead and told her he loved her just before they hung up.

Staring at the phone, Stew knew that he wasn't as bad off as he thought because Caity had closed it by saying she adored him and kissed the phone as she was hanging up. Maybe all those sessions with Maggy were helping, but the one thing he didn't want her to know about was the latest stuff. It would set her back months if not years, and Stew couldn't bear to go through much more.

Chapter 36

Three days went by before they got the definite "No" for a search warrant of Jack's old house. It was a defeating moment that both Charlie and Stew mulled over at a local pub and a cold beer at the end of another really long day.

There wasn't enough evidence for anyone to buy their theory, and the best they could hope for was a break in the case through Jane or Scott. But which one and how? They couldn't harass Jane; she'd file a complaint with the cops even though Charlie was a cop. Scott was being held in jail for his trial and the number of times they tried to get anything out of him, they found him to be a smug laughing bastard. He had made it very clear that he knew everything and they knew nothing. All they ever came away with was anger and frustration.

Leaning on the bar, staring at Charlie through the big old mirror on the back wall of the bar, Stew wondered what he'd missed. Charlie sat there wondering the same thing. Why was Scott so smug? What did he know? Could they negotiate a lesser sentence for information? Was Jack's murder tied to religion or a greedy ex-wife and brother? Was it a real heart attach that conveniently killed him or was he murdered in his hospital bed? What did he mean when he told Caity in that letter that all was not as it seemed? What did that mean? The questions hung over them like dead weight and a dark tunnel with no light at the end in sight.

"What do you think it is Charlie? Stew asked. What do you think the answer is Charlie? Pausing, and deep in thought going through the repeated questions, Charlie paused and said, "You know Stew, I think we really missed a small detail, but I just don't know what it is and where we can look to find it."

"Charlie, do you think that Jack knew about Father O'Malley and the Bishop McDuff and Scott and his Mom and all that stuff; way sooner than we gave him credit for? Do you think that maybe the weight of all that knowledge was the reason he couldn't commit to Caity, because he didn't want to ruin her life with the mess he was somehow surrounded by? Do you even think that those girls are even his? Maybe they were Jane's ex-lovers'. Do you think he knew something and was trying to come to terms with it? What do you think Charlie? Huh?" Stew had never been more stumped, and it frustrated him. He was too close to the case to see anything clearly. Maybe he needed to take a few steps back in order to see ahead.

With out noticing any movement behind them, Charlie and Stew just sat there leaning over the bar and drowning their frustration in their beers. Startling them, a very young, talk dark haired women came up between the two of them and asked if one of them was Stewart Banks. Not sure what she wanted and noticing the long dark hair went halfway down her back along the lines of her extremely fit young figure, Stew asked. "Who wants to know?" Thinking that she was probably some ex-mistress of some cheating husband he'd turned in sometime in the past.

"My name is Carla; I used to work with Jack Fraser. I heard you were looking for as much and any information you could find on him." She answered so matter of fact like that Stew's attention was now held and he turned completely toward her on his bar stool in order to get a better look on what he was dealing with. "Really, huh? Just worked with the guy or do I detect an ex-lover here?" Stew asked, half hoping to prove that Jack was the louse he mentally painted him as. "Ex-lover, and ex-co-worker too. I worked with Jack for years. We'd had a thing before he met Jane and then we got back together when Jane cheated on him. He kept me a secret from that girl Caity Anderson because he said she was some nut that was chasing him. I knew about her but Jack never had anything to do with her other than some old family ties or something." Carla answered so sure of herself that Stew smugly smiled knowing the girl was one of Jack's secrets in the big game.

"So tell me Carla, what do you think happened to Jack?" He asked noticing Charlie was glued to his seat and his lips were shut tight with curiosity.

She paused and looked at Stew then at Charlie, then back at Stew. "How about the fact that I know where Scott hid Jack. And the reason I know that is because Scott came to Jack's office a few weeks before Jack had his heart attack. I don't know everything they talked about but Scott threatened him that if he did anything to stop him, he bury him in a particular spot, next to their mother, in an unmarked grave so no one would ever know where he was." Carla stopped and asked if they would buy her a drink and sit somewhere.

After they positioned themselves at a pub table and Carla was sufficiently looked after with her cosmopolitan in hand, she sipped it and sat silent as if waiting for something to happen. "So how is it you never told the police this story? And how is it you waited more than a year to come forward with all this? Huh?" Stew asked, "Yet better still, how did you know that you should come and talk to us today? How do I know that you're not just some flunky working for Scott and the Bishop? Huh?" Stew asked and spoke quickly trying not to give her any time to think.

"You don't, but the fact is, you don't have any useful information either and I'm all you got. According to the news stories covering all this, the cops are at a dead end. They had a missing body and no where to look. I didn't think about any of this till I saw the story on the news a few days ago and I over heard some people talking at work today about you guys. I didn't know about the empty coffin till the story broke on the news with all that trial stuff. Apparently you were in asking a lot of questions when I was off sick one day, so I thought I'd take a chance and meet with you. It's worth finding out, isn't it"? Carla asked.

"So what's in it for you Carla?" Charlie asked, too impatient for Stew to keep playing his word games. "Let's get to the chase. Something is in it for you and we need to know what it is if we are going to check out your story. Not that we will, because we've heard so much unbelievable crap the last year that you better have something good for me to follow up on!". Charlie made it clear that he hadn't quite bought into the story yet but was anxious to hear her response.

Carla paused, nervously sipping her drink, and looked like she was carefully thinking about the words she'd use next. "Charlie is it?" Charlie nodded. "Well Charlie, there is a lot in it for me. You see, I used to work for Scott until he fired me when I wouldn't sleep with him, that's when I met Jack in his office and the guy hired me without even an interview. It was the best move I ever made. I got a great boss and a lover all in one great package. I personally want to see Scott spend as much time in jail as possible, and if you can prove that he murdered him as well as stolen his body, then wouldn't you have more to hold him on?" Carla asked, looking at the two men for answers.

"To tell you the truth Carla, Scott is going to be in jail forever based on the proof we have for Father O'Malley's murder. This info isn't going to really make much of a difference to him but it will sell papers though, but that's only if it's true." Stew said with Charlie nodding in agreement.

Stew and Charlie didn't know what to make of the whole conversation. They sat and chatted with Carla for about an hour. After saying goodbye to the girl and sticking her in her car, they took their prospective cars and headed straight for Stew's house.

Stew drove quickly and quietly. He couldn't even listen to the radio, wondering what game this Carla girl was playing. What was she hiding that she didn't share. Was she a bitter ex-lover of Scott's? Was she really Jack's ex-lover? Had Jack cheated on Caity? Did Caity know? She said she always suspected that she couldn't trust Jack, but she was never sure. Stew was sure that it was better the way she knew it now than to find something like this out now. This could really mess with Caity's head. It was just as bad as the rest of the evidence they kept finding on a daily basis, and Stew knew he had better think about what he would and wouldn't let Caity find out about.

Chapter 37

Less than twenty four hours after their meeting with Carla, Stew, Charlie and a group of other people required to do the gruesome task, were at the cemetery. The last thing Carla told them was that Scott had said an unmarked grave beside where Jack's mom was buried. After just hours of investigating, it was discovered that the same day of Jack's funeral at a cemetery across town, an unknown man paid for a funeral of an apparent street person who would be buried in a humble unmarked grave. As luck would have it, strangely enough; the funeral home remembered Jane insisting that Jack be buried as far from his mother as possible.

The bill had been paid in cash and the man had stayed to make sure that the grave was completely buried and marked before he left. All that was said on a little plaque that was buried in the ground at the top was "here lays a man that was lost in life". It was a grave site that was two down from Mary Fraser's grave. Was "two" a significant number standing for the number of years between the two brothers? Stew didn't know but he certainly thought about it as he watched the site being excavated. He wondered if it even meant anything more than the fact that it was as close to Mary Fraser as was available at the time.

The coroner's office was on site and when it appeared that things would start to be gruesome, both Stew and Charlie took a step back thinking they could wait for the official news when forensics was finished.

Charlie knew that Stew hadn't said a word about any of this to Caity or Maggy, and though he'd better talk some sense into the guy before he screwed up what Charlie thought was the best thing that ever happened to him. "So when you going to tell the girls about this Stew?" Charlie asked as he watched all the action from a far.

"I don't know Charlie. I mean think about it. I can't very well tell Caity that Jack was cheating on her; can I? Stew paused just long enough to take a breath. "And you know if I tell Maggy, she'll feel obligated to tell Caity…and what effect is all this going to have on me and Caity? Shit Charlie, I've never been so unglued in my life. If it turns out that this body isn't Jack's, I'll lose my edge. I've had it with all of this shit. Religion my ass! This is like the worst form of a cult than anyone could imagine. For all me know, Jack was part of something too! Charlie, what the hell am I going to tell them about all this?"

Stew was clearly tired and fed up, and Charlie tapped him on the back, and then gave him his two cents. "Tell you what Stew, how about you head home and take a break. I'll call you as soon as I know something, and then you can figure out how and what to tell the girls. You don't have to tell them about Carla if you don't want to, but if I were you I'd tell them about this cemetery thing before they hear about it on the news. Do you know what I mean, buddy?" Charlie asked as he started walking along side Stew to his car.

"Ya, I got it Charlie, thanks, I owe you one!" And with that Stew got in and drove home for a few hours of peace. Watching him leave Charlie hoped that today would put an end to this for all of them and they could put this all behind them and finally get on with their lives. Just as he turned to go back to the excavation, he noticed Carla standing off in the distant crowd and somehow knew they just couldn't be that lucky, just yet!

Walking right to her, Charlie had thoughts pounding in his brain. What was in it for Carla? What? He went straight to her and without saying a word paused and stared her down before asking. "So, what's really in it for you honey? Money? How much did they offer you? What's the game Carla? He said in a deep matter of fact voice that made it more than clear he expected the truth. Charlie waited and watched Carla. "So, let's see; first off, is the hair real or is it just a wig? Did you dye it Cathy or is it just for this gig? Carla didn't answer him but stood extra still while he talked. She was breathing heavy and was really nervous trying to figure out what his next move would be.

Charlie took her quietness as an admittance of the truth, and that she really was Cathy, a local small time criminal that had crossed paths with him before. Back then she was a blond with short cut straight hair and hardly any make up, and now she was a long haired brunette with a case of the goop on face. He shook his head thinking that she had almost pulled it off. If he hadn't seen her standing in the crowd watching in the same way she had so many years ago on another case, he would never have put the two together. He stood there hoping she'd say something. Hoping she'd admit to something; anything. Or at least say something that could give him another clue.

Carla couldn't take it any longer. The silence was killing her and she had to admit to herself she was a little scared. She wondered if she could she actually do time for posing as someone? Could doing this small time job for those two murderers get her in real trouble? She couldn't stop thinking about how much they'd paid her for this. When she accepted the job from one of their outside contacts she was overwhelmed at how handsomely the job paid. All she had to do was lead the cops to the grave site and her job was done. It hadn't even seemed illegal at the time, and standing there next to Charlie she began to think it wasn't, otherwise he probably would have arrested her by now, or would he have? Getting up her courage she paused and then half looking at Charlie while watching the scene ahead of them she said. "So what's in it for you Charlie? Huh?" As she tried hard to show that she wasn't intimidated by him.

Charlie looked straight ahead, paused and then turned and looked right at her in order to answer her, but the quiet pause made her continue. "I just wanted to find out the truth about Jack, like everyone else. I really just need the peace that comes with knowledge". She spoke softly trying to act sincere and sound like the ex-lover she was being paid to be.

Charlie was no fool, he could tell she was just playing the role and knew that she really was Cathy. He'd have to smoke her out some how, and without even thinking, out of the blue Charlie spouted out. "So, how much did Scott promise you for coming to us with this?" Charlie watched her reaction as he spoke. He was a great cop and an even better detective and often his timing was bang on. Her body language and her facial expression all confirmed his suspicions. She was a hired actress. A bad one at that, but the only thing he didn't know just yet, was why? He'd have to find out quick, right now while the iron was hot. But how?

They stood there side by side for a few minutes with out exchanging another word. The silence between them clearly unnerved Carla. She knew that Charlie wasn't going anywhere especially since he'd figured out that she was really Cathy Taylor. He'd booked her years ago, on a misdemeanor. How in the world did he recognize her? Cops; it figured! Some of them, like Charlie were like blood hounds. They'd meet you once and remember you for life. It figured. What was her luck? Twice she'd tried the criminal life and twice she got caught. But was this really something he could book her for? She wasn't sure. But she was going to find out.

Leaning forward to whisper softly in his ear, she said; "How about I pay you $50,000 to forget you ever met me here, huh?" She asked in as sensual deep a voice as she could muster, hoping to have some effect on the guy, mostly with the money; but partly with the sensual approach too!

Slowly leaning back to her original position, Carla waited for some kind of reaction. Meanwhile Charlie was standing there completely dumb founded. He couldn't remember a time in his career when he'd been so speechless. If she was offering him fifty thousand dollars to keep his mouth shut, he couldn't imagine how much she'd been paid for the job. Fifty thousand? It rang in his ears like buck shot. As for her whispering sensual attempt, Charlie smiled at how it didn't even get a response out of him. She was garbage and he knew it and if there wasn't anything that gave him a cold shower faster was a cheap scheming woman trying to play him. He'd been faithful to his wife for forty five years now and not even money could convince him to screw up the best thing that ever happened to him.

Somehow he'd have to get more out of this broad than a money offer to be able to get the pieces of this case together, so an hour later, Charlie found himself sitting across a table from her. He met her at his favorite local cop bar and made sure they sat at a little table off a quiet corner. He chose this one because he knew he'd always have back up hanging around if he needed it, and that Carla was too much of an amateur to know it was a cop hang out.

Sitting there in silence, waiting for their drinks to come, Charlie couldn't help but notice how Carla and Jane were such similar women. They could be sisters especially the way they both obsessed about money. Jane had left a definite imprint in Charlie's mind, even thought they'd only met two or three times and spoke very briefly; at that.

"Got a sister?" Charlie suddenly blurted out without thinking. "No" was Carla's short answer as the waiter arrived with their drinks and a plate of finger food Charlie had requested.

"So....Charlie. What do you think about my more than generous offer? But for that kind of money, I need your help with a few other things before I pay you." Carla was sure she'd hooked him. Inside he was smiling at what an amateur she was, but on the outside he played like he was in for the catch.

"Come on Charlie, you look like a guy that's about to retire soon and could probably use the extra cash. Who couldn't use it huh? Bet your pension is not all that great and it could help pay for the little extras, huh?" Carla was hoping to hear something come out of his mouth soon. He was unnerving her with his deep silence and dark thinking eyes. All Charlie could come up with was the thought of booking her for trying to bribe a cop. He so desperately wanted to be the one to solve this case and retire with one last big one solved. Carla could be the one crucial source he needed!

By the look on his face, Carla thought she had him in tight, so she continued. "You guys are all obsessed with the murders and stuff but you missed out on the biggest piece of pie. The big picture, you know? Behind all the darkness of death are huge secrets and unbelievable large sums of money for the take." She sat there spouting out so convinced that they were a team now, she was excited in her speech and her actions. Leaning forward into the table, holding her drink close to her lips, she continued.

"Charlie, Scott needs someone to help him on the outside until he gets out. Think about it." Carla said with the gleam of greed radiating from her eyes. "Those two jail birds will both be put away for a long time, maybe even life and they'll never be able to spend a dime of it or enjoy all the money they made. I'm out here with the right plan. I can access it once I get the final details from Scott and then I can enjoy the rest of my life." Carla spewed hoping that this old cop with all his connections would not only help her but would team up with her to get everything in place. She needed to brag to someone and who better than this old, and from his clothes, obviously poor cop!

Charlie put his glass down on the table, thinking hard and slowly before leaning back in his chair. He had to play this just the right way if he was going to achieve his goal. He paused, letting out a deep sigh and said, "And just how are you planning to get Scott and the Bishop to give you access to all their money?"

"Oh they'll never give it to me. Even though Scott and I are lovers, he cheated on me you know, with Jane. All I want is to burn him for cheating on me and to give me a fair share of what he earned while we were together. Here I thought he was this failing business man and all the time while I was pinching my pennies living with him, he was a multi millionaire with multiple other lovers. Go figure huh?" Carla felt better talking out the story that had been given to her to play out and she thought it sounded just right.

"So, let me guess. Your are a scorned lover on the verge of revenge. Is that what all this is about?" Charlie asked. "Not at all, just let's say I'm an entrepreneur that just got smart." Carla said as she was smiling at her new found friend and felt relieved that she was finally going to have someone help her. She then added. "You see Scott always thought I was stupid or something, and he used to call me a dumb blonde all the time because I don't speak so polished. You know something, the truth is Charlie, I'm not as dumb as I look. I know he doesn't trust Jane, and he thinks I'm too dumb to screw with him and his thugs. But they will never find me once I got the money. I'll be down south on a nice sandy beach somewhere before he ever knows what hit him." She said as she was sitting there, proud of herself for what she'd thought she'd achieved so far.

Charlie was glued. Scott was right about Carla, she was a bit dumb but she had drive and imagination and that could get her into some real hot water. He thought it might even get her dead if she wasn't careful and he told her as much. Looking worried Carla just added, "That's why I need you Charlie, if we find Jack's body, Scott and the Bishop will be so focused on that, we'll be able to side swipe them."

Carla took another sip of her drink and went on. "You see Charlie, Scott needs me to run around and do his dirty work, pay the guys, do the banking and all that stuff. So when I finally get the bank accounts from him, you and I'll be off. So what do you say? Are you in?" Carla wanted a confirmation as much as she needed help.

"I don't get it Carla. What can an old copper like me do for you anyway? Seems to me you've got the whole plan laid out and everything. Huh?" Charlie said leaning forward on the table to get closer to use the power of body language to make her continue.

"I need you for protection Charlie, and the inside track on things like Jack. Is he still alive or is that his body in that grave? You see, Scott can't afford to have Jack still alive, but he doesn't know for sure if he's dead. Until he is, Jack is a big problem for Scott because Jack knows everything! Jack came across all the stuff a few years ago and I'm surprised he wasn't knocked off instead of the priest. Who knows, maybe that wasn't a real heart attach he had. Maybe his brother actually poisoned him to look like he was dying from a heart attack. You cops wouldn't be thinking to look for poison would you? The thing is; that it really doesn't matter. Scott is going through a lot of trouble to make sure his brother is dead and gone for sure! If we don't work for him, someone else will and they'll get all the money instead of us." Carla was trying desperately to convince Charlie that they had it in the bag and was sure he was completely hooked.

Charlie was trying to put the pieces together. "Carla, I'm confused. Just what makes you think that Scott is going to give you the number of his Swiss bank account and then give you access? And besides that, why is it so important to find Jack! What does he really have on these guys?" Charlie asked and watched Carla carefully to try and determine if she was telling the truth.

"Well for starters Charlie, I actually thought the money might be in the grave, instead of a Swiss account. Funny thing is though, now I'm pretty sure there has to be a Swiss bank account because Scott's phone bill came in after he was arrested and he'd made a lot of calls to Switzerland. I mean, come on, why else would he be calling there if not for his money?" Carla half asked Charlie and half told him.

"Carla, I hate to burst your bubble, but how do you know the money isn't stashed somewhere in a safe or something. Maybe it's even buried in a church basement or something. It's the cops and the Feds biggest mystery as to where the money is. Don't you think the Feds will find it before you? Or what if they find it before Scott tells you where it is? Then What?" Charlie looked at her and she had a very deeply puzzled look on her face." Then he added. "The other thing Carla, is this. You could land yourself in Jail and there goes your life. Haven't you even thought about what you are doing and how you could get caught? I mean, I'm a cop for Christ sake and you're sitting here telling me about how you're helping these criminals, and that if by helping them you find out Jack is still alive, you're going to help kill him. Carla, don't you even realize that you could be an accessory to his murder if he's killed? Don't you even realize that if you help Scott pay the guy you're as guilty as he is? Don't you even get it girl?" Charlie asked; trying desperately to put the pieces together before he officially hauling her in for questioning.

Taking another swig of his already warming beer, Charlie shook his head puzzled as to what the missing pieces of all this were; when Carla flagged down the waiter and ordered them another round of drinks. Then she leaned forward whispering right at him. "Charlie, I've done a few small jobs for Scott over the years and one of them was that he sent me to the hospital to spy on everything. While I was there, I over heard Jack having a conversation on the phone with Scott. He was threatening him that he would turn him, the bishop and the money in. I think that was why he was meeting with that detective guy the morning he had his heart attach. All of that stuff was too much for Jack to be able to really handle. I mean, according to Scott he was a real bible pusher you know".

The more Carla spoke the more she revealed her lack of intelligence and education, Charlie thought as he sat and listened to her intensely. "Anyway" Carla went on. "Jack was telling Scott that he needed something like inner peace or something and that he couldn't take it anymore. Scott thinks he faked his own death or something. You know what I mean? To escape or something, but Scott had some friend of his check all the hospital records and even though they said that Jack died from a fatal heart attach, he doesn't believe it for some reason. Scott told me that he was sure that one of his guys saw Jack a week after the funeral. He didn't say where, and of course the guy who saw it is one of the ones Scott doesn't really trust but now he's all messed up because he needs Jack dead so he keeps his mouth shut." Carla talked without taking in breaths. "You know Charlie, I don't get it. They were brothers and Scott hated his brother Jack. I mean, like he really hated him! I never saw anyone hate their brother like that, it wasn't normal or something, you know what I mean? I don't know what the whole story is but I bet it had to do with a woman. It had to be." Carla was shaking her head and waving her hand about like she couldn't figure out any of it before she added, "That was before my time anyway, but she must have been some real piece of work, if you know what I mean." Carla added and then finally stopped to take a breath and sip her fresh drink when she saw Charlie stand up without even touching his second beer.

"I've heard more than enough Carla, you're coming with me down to the precinct and you can give your statement there." With that, Charlie slapped the hand cuffs on her and dragged her screaming out of the bar.

Two hours later the department was holding her on charges and Charlie still didn't have answers to get to the bottom of the case. Frustrated, tired and ready to put his fist through a wall, he finally reached Stew and told him all the details, hoping he could put it all into perspective.

Chapter 38

Stew leaned back into his old high back leather chair, tilting back just enough to put his feet up on his desk to get comfy and think. Like all of the furniture in his house, he had hand picked this chair for its softness and comfort.

In this position, sitting here with his desk facing the huge picture window in his office he could watch people in the park. It was how he did a lot of his deep thinking and it was something he really enjoyed. The view was phenomenal and it looked over his back yard and because his office was actually almost two whole stories off the ground it had a full view of the entire west side of the park. His house was beautifully situated from back to front and Stew always took the time to appreciate it.

Today was different though. He was impatiently waiting for someone and they were almost an hour late. He could hear his nephews giggling and splashing in the hot tub on the raised deck just to the left of his window and he knew Caity and Maggy were sitting out there watching the kids and sipping ice cold coolers while they waited for the BBQ to get hot. Lunch was going to be burgers and dry chips as the kids requested.

It was a beautiful sunny warm afternoon and life should have been perfect, except for the huge dark cloud that loomed over them.

Stew sat there feeling the guilt eat him up inside. Were it not in her best interest he would never have been able to lie to Caity. He had just signed a special confidentiality agreement with the Feds, knowing in his heart that he was doing the right thing and that it could go no other way. Emma had been sitting at his feet to keep him company and was restless and uneasy, because he was. She got up and nudged him to rub her but when he was too occupied to respond she walked out of the room and went to sleep on her big round pillow in the kitchen by the air conditioning vent. It had been two whole days since he'd lied to Caity and told her the body in the unmarked grave had been Jack's. Of course the press release that the cops had issued had said as much and it had been front page news on every local paper and newscast.

Truth was, they weren't able to identify the body but they needed closure for the case and it all fit into the tight plan that had been in motion for over a year. Stew counted himself lucky to be in so tight with the Feds, but then again he'd often done a lot of work with them, and for them in the past, and there was a strong professional bond that was to the advantage of both sides.

Suddenly he caught a glimpse of a flash, and in that second he leapt forward in his chair landing both feet flat on the floor and leaning on his desk to get a better look. Yep, it was Fred; he had the LED flashlight blinking at Stew from behind his back so no one else would notice. Stew didn't know his real name nor did he want to, just that Fred would flash him from the park as his cue to go out and be on the deck outside with he girls.

Jack stood next to Fred, they were both in track pants and t-shirts looking like they were two joggers winding down from a run. Of course, Jack's hair was died blondish red, army cut short and a small matching mustache had been added along with a large prosthetic nose so he didn't look like himself

Amongst the hundreds of people spread out jugging, running, rollerblading and walking a long the paths, the two men blended in completely. Fred flashed Stew a second time to cue him to go out on the deck.

Rushing out of his chair, he walked quickly through the kitchen and out the patio doors. He was a bit short of breath mostly from the tension that raced through his entire body, but partly from racing around and not having caught his breath because of his nerves.

The two women looked up a little surprised by his instant hurried arrival and Maggy was the first to ask "What's up Stew? You look like a deer caught in the head lights". She said while she was still stretched out in one of the big lounge chairs.

Caity quietly looked at both of them and sipping her strawberry margarita, but with her eyes curiously transfixed on Stew.

Pausing Stew came back with, "Nothing, I just heard a huge bang and thought one of the kids may have slipped in the hot tub or something", thinking quickly he added, "Besides that, I'm starving are those burgers ready yet?"

Caity giggled, "Should we tell him?" She asked Maggy smiling and then looked dead on at Stew and said, "We haven't even put them on yet. I guess we kind of forgot. Sitting here sipping drinks and snacking has been so relaxing I guess we lost track of the time" She answered him smiling and slowly standing up to put down her drink and hug him as she softly kissed him at the same time.

Stew tried to act natural while he scanned the park to see where the two men were. He let out a heavy sigh when he spotted them off to the side sitting on the grass pretending to stretch and drink their water from their water bottles. Caity thought he was sighing because he liked her greeting and cuddled him a little longer before leaving him and walking over to open the BBQ and put the burgers on the grill.

Stew's eyes were transfixed on the two men in the park. Fred acting like the RCMP agent that he was, spent his time constantly looking around for anything that might indicate trouble; while Jack's eyes were glued only on Caity. Stew joked around with the boys trying to act normal, while the whole time thinking of how hard this had to be on Jack. If he had had to watch Caity with another man he knew he'd be dying inside. The only difference was that Jack had had a lot of practice at watching Caity. He'd done it the whole time they'd dated. Even this whole last year he'd watched her from a far in the cemetery, and God knows where else. Stew shivered internally thinking at how that was like Jack had been some weird stocker and Caity his victim. He didn't like that thought one bit and trying hard not to let his emotions show on his face or in his body language tried to push those thoughts from his mind and focus on what was taking place right now.

Stew had only found out about all of this mess a few short days ago because it had been to the Fed's advantage to use him. He was on the inside, and could control the situation and especially Caity. It had placed him in a very weird spot, but he felt that because his intentions were in the right place, what he was doing was for the best for everyone involved.

Even his good old friend Charlie, had a win in it. After all was said and done, it looked like he closed his last big case and was going to retire happy and the way he always dreamed about. As he stood thinking about it all, Stew remembered being furious at how Caity had been duped into believing Jack was dead, and it frustrated him to know about all the energy she had wasted in heartache at the cemetery for a whole year. It ate at Stew's heart to even think about it. Life was so short and fragile and Caity had just wasted a year of hers'. At least now she had a chance at a life that would be good for her in the long term. He knew that she would finally have the peace and love she longed for. Maybe she didn't love Stew now the way she had loved Jack, but as he stood there in the midst of the whole scene he silently prayed that she eventually would. Looking at her, Stew knew in his heart that she was the love of his life, and she owned his heart to the very core of his being.

Stew watched Caity dance around with the burger tongs and joke with the boys to get out of the hot tub if they planned on eating. He saw her dance to the tune on the CD player as she asked him to join her while they waited for the food to finish. She was joyous, happy and it showed. She had regained her long lost spirit and now Jack had to sit helpless off in the distance and just watch.

Stew glanced over periodically thinking how tough this had to be, but Jack knew his life was in danger if he ever surfaced and this was the closest he would ever get to Caity again. In fact it would be the very last time he would ever see her.

Jack had known all of Scott's and the Bishop's important secrets and where to get the evidence for both of their trials. Through Jack's help, they'd both been charged for their real crimes. The down side was that Jack had to be placed in protective custody and be presented as dead. He'd be given a new identity and a new life in order to stay alive. Both his half brother Scott and the Bishop had the contacts to have him wiped out if he ever surfaced by mistake. By thinking he was dead; the two had nothing to go after.

In the end, Jack lost everything, Caity and his girls would never see him again, and life would go on as if he had died. He knew there were others besides Scott and the Bishop who would want him dead so this was the only solution.

The Feds had gone to great lengths to give the press a lot of details on the body in the unmarked grave, along with a lot of fake details of other things to throw everyone off. They needed the press to believe that Jack was dead, in order to sell it to the public. . More importantly, Jane, and Scott had to buy into it in order for the Feds to achieve their goal. Stew knew that it was only a matter of time before Jane was arrested and charged. Even with all the complications and intricate details, the local cops and the federal agents were working night and day to tie it all together.

The biggest problem the agents had was in meeting one of Jack's demands. Somehow they had to let him see Caity one last time before he went into witness protection. They used Stew to help them which was the reason he'd set up this intricate BBQ get together on his patio by the park. As Jack sat there in torment watching the love of his life go on with hers, he could have never realized the impact of how difficult it was going to be until that very moment.

As Jack sat on the grass pretending to be a jogger taking a break and drinking water, he watched Caity dance around the BBQ and affectionately hug Stew. He could see her joking around with Maggy and the boys as she giggled and lifted up one of the kids up and hugged them. All the while wondering what their life could have been like had things been so very different.

Tears streamed down his face as he sat beside a total stranger who was just doing his job. Wiping his face in the belly of his shirt Jack realized he'd seen all he could handle and turned to Fred to leave.

Stew hadn't missed a beat. His heart hurt for the guy, while at the same time he thanked God for the blessing of Caity in his life. Jack was gone for good and Caity and him could live their lives and go on. Stew watched Jack and Fred walk out of the park, and when Stew could no longer see them he let out a huge sigh of relief.

Caity turned around from her post at the BBQ and leaned over and kissed him on the forehead. She had a big old red checkered BBQ mitt on one hand and the flipper in the other. "Stew, if I had known you were that hungry I would have paid more attention and put the burgers on sooner." She said looking right at him waiting to see if he'd let out another giant sigh of impatience. "Sorry sweetie" Stew said, "I guess I didn't have any breakfast and I'm starved, I'll run in and get the buns and stuff; Maggy ...why don't you get fresh drinks for us while I do that." With that said; Stew got up and went through the patio doors and into the kitchen.

Maggy was making the drinks and the boys were sitting expectantly at the table and Stew was standing at the kitchen sink looking out the window that had the same view as the deck and his office. He stared trying to see as far as he could, but couldn't see Jack or Fred. They really were gone.

Reaching down under the sink, he pulled out a bottle of his favorite old cognac and took a double shot. He'd always kept a bottle there for emergencies and this was definitely what he'd call an emergency. His stomach kept leaping into his throat and doing wheelies from all the lies he'd told and kept secret.

This was one of those horrible secrets that he'd have to take to the grave with him. He'd seen this stuff in the movies and in the old book, where the characters had deep incredible secrets that they kept for life. They were always life changing secrets that were always dark, deep and huge! Secrets that would either tear the characters apart or be the reason for someone getting hurt, but it was different now. The life changing secrets weren't in a story in a movie or a book. They were a deep part of Stew's life and he wished he'd never been told most of it. Instead he'd have to carry these to his grave, along with the heartfelt guilt that gripped him to the bone.

He wondered what would happen if Caity ever found out. She'd probably hate him for keeping the secret. Somehow blame him for not finding a way out for Jack, or maybe she'd be grateful for by sticking Jack in a witness protection program they'd actually been able to save his life and rescue him from the prison he'd inadvertently ended up in. Jack would finally have a normal life but with out his three loves, his daughters and Caity......and Stew wondered what normal really was. Of course if Jane was convicted of her crimes Stew was sure the feds would find a way to get the girls back to their only living relative.... their father. No one had proved that they weren't his, so that meant that things could work out for Jack in the end. At least he hoped so.... in his heart.

Stew was sick to his stomach so he poured a second jigger of a two ounce shot glass of cognac and downed it faster than the first. He caught his breath, closed his eyes and made a wish for life to finally return to normal. At least what he used to think normal was.

When Stew heard Caity walk into the kitchen looking for him, he opened his eyes and looked right at her, waved the cognac bottle that was still in his hand and asked, "Want some?"

"Are you all right Stew? I'm not stupid you know.....I know something is really wrong. What is it?" Caity asked as she stepped behind the counter and wrapped her arms around his waist while placing her ear on his chest as she cuddled him.

"You're right something is really wrong." Stew said trying to think fast and come up with something believable, and then it came to him. Right from his heart he had the excuse he needed and it would be the honest truth.

Stew grabbed Caity's shoulders and pulled her back far enough to be able to look into her eyes. "Caity, today I realized how lucky I am to have met you, and how lucky I am to have you in my life. I have to tell you that I've never been more scared of losing anyone or anything in my whole life. I'm so scared to ask you this but I just have to do it. I've been trying to get the courage together all day but I have to tell you that I'm really scared about what you'll say." Without really even taking a breath Stew looked deep in her eyes and continued. "O.K. Miss Anderson, uh, here goes. I have to know something; Will you marry me Miss Caity Anderson? Do you love me enough with the kind of love that makes people grow old together? DO YOU? WILL YOU? Huh? Or am I just a substitute for Jack? Stew spoke so fast that Caity had to put her hand on his mouth to shut him up.

She looked up at him and smiled, "Yes, yes, yes, yes and no to the last one. How's that for an answer? Huh? She teased as she kissed him on the lips and standing on her tip toes so she could reach him she leaned back just far enough so he could hear and see her at the same time.

"I love you Stewart Banks and you are not a substitute for anyone. You are my here, my now and my always. Got that!" Caity sighed and planted another soft kiss on his lips and added. "And I'm not only in love with you but thank God every day for having sent you into my life and rescue me. You took me away from all that dark sadness that surrounded me with Jack. I may have loved him but he never loved me back. I know that now. The worst part is that I lived with such deep sorrow for such a long time, just waiting and hoping for him to make me a part of his life. I don't even know why I even believed anything he said after a while." She held Stew's face in the palms of her hands and after gently caressing his lips with hers, she said. "You, however, opened these big teddy bear arms from the very first day I ever met you. I've been a part of your life with no strings attached or any rules of when I could or couldn't call you. You're honest and loving and you make me happy inside. Stew when you invited me into your heart with no conditions and then you kissed me and made my knees go weak, I knew I had found kind of love everyone needs!"

With that Stew scooped her up and sat her on the counter and wrapped his arms around her and kissed her senseless. He kept telling her he loved her and he'd protect her forever.

It was quite a while before they realized Maggy was yelling at them from the deck. Hearing that the burgers were ready brought them back to reality. Caity tapped Stew's bum and told him to lift her off the counter so they could hurry out with the buns and stuff before Maggy and the boys starved to death. Giggling, Caity ran out ahead of Stew, holding buns in one hand and condiments in the other.

Stew took one last glance out the kitchen window to the park to make sure the two men had really gone, and then he opened the fridge and grabbed a bottle of champagne and headed out to the deck to join his family and start the rest of his life.

As they sat on the deck laughing and eating Stew knew his life was finally complete. He could picture having kids together maybe even having grand children and while he sat there enjoying life's celebration of their future, he realized his life was finally on the right path.

Caity was eating and looking around at her life and she could actually picture their future. This house would hold quite the family if they wanted and Stew would make a great dad. She'd finally found the life she had spent years longing for, the hope for peace, love and happiness and the dream of fulfillment was all around her. Caity looked around the table absorbing all the laughter and joy over hamburgers and Champaign and she realized that for the first time in her life she could feel that she had a future and was building a life of her own. How wonderful to have a home of her own with a man to help build it. It was something that she had longed for, for so very long! Something that she had dreamed of sharing with Jack and now was sharing with Stew.

She loved Stew, she knew that and she had joy in her heart for their future. Caity knew that there would always be love in this house. As she sat there at the table sipping her champagne she could feel something strange, like a pulling to look out to the sun that was setting at the edge of the park. As she gazed to watch the sun set Caity felt a strong cold shiver as she watched a red headed jogger go by, glancing at them as he passed. For a second she thought she knew him but he didn't even look familiar, he just felt that way. She sighed and could feel tears welling up for her loss of Jack and how she had wanted this with him, and suddenly looking over at Stew she realized she was his now and that life would go on............but her heart.......well the sad truth was........she knew that her heart.......... would never be the same!

Author C. D. Nolan

C.D. Nolan was born the middle of three girls in suburban Montreal. With parents that taught her that no dream is off limits, she got her degree in Communications at Concordia University, studying journalism, audio and video recording. Looking to move to Ontario, she took a job in transportation sales that was supposed to be for one year while she worked to get into media; but it lasted twenty. In a job that challenged her serenity; writing brought her the relaxation she needed. She's now calls Brampton Ontario, her home with her beloved 10 year old Bichon Frise – Maggy, and all her boxes of books that she transported around the country with every move.

Although she is an accomplished oil painter and musician, her passion is writing. She believes that books are a window into another world for an adventure that you never have to leave home for. The greatest gift about writing is that it lets the writer create the characters' past, present and future and their world can be anything you make of it. You can escape your own personal heart aches and challenges and be totally in control in a world you create on paper, or for that matter;

read about one that takes you away from yours.   For C.D. Nolan, writing is an amazing tool that with each word, you create and change the direction the characters travel in.

Once told that to write well, you have to have experienced great love, great loss and truly understand how events affect our lives. Today having gone through many life altering and challenging hardships. She's realizes just how true that is.

Stories that challenge the mind; initiate great conversations! C.D.Nolan.